Archangel

Archangel

GARRY D. KILWORTH

VICTOR GOLLANCZ

LONDON

First published in Great Britain 1994
by Victor Gollancz
A Division of the Cassell group
Villiers House, 41/47 Strand, London WC2N 5JE

A catalogue record for this book is
available from the British Library

ISBN 0 575 05762 9

Photoset by Rowland Phototypesetting Ltd
Bury St Edmunds, Suffolk and printed in Great Britain by
St Edmundsbury Press Ltd, Bury St Edmunds, Suffolk

To Faith, for her assistance
and additions

WEST GRID STAMP					
NN		RR		WW	
NT		RT		WO	
NC		RC	11/94	WL	
NH		RB		WM	
NL		RP		WT	
NV		RS		WA	
NM		RW		WR	
NB		RV		WS	
NE					
NP					

Because he knows a frightful fiend
Doth close behind him tread.

(Coleridge, *Rime of the Ancient Mariner*)

Prologue

Nine a.m., Quinquagesima Sunday, 2002 A.D., New York.

Bishop Cates had a human failing: he was afraid of dying. It was not being dead that concerned him, because he felt fairly confident of going to the right place, but *dying* usually involved pain and stress, and he'd had a sufficiency of both of those in his life. As a chaplain in Vietnam in the 1960s he'd seen pain in plenty and enough stress to warp a nation.

On his way to Kennedy Airport, the Bishop was nervous. He kept staring out of the back window, to see if the cab was being followed. This fidgeting in turn made the driver wary, wondering if he had a member of the *Cosa Nostra* in his taxi: maybe the guy who had handed John Gotti to the feds? The driver was a Jamaican ex-street gang member who had left his home island in search of a less perilous and more lucrative life and found himself in one of the most dangerous jobs in one of the most dangerous cities in the world.

'Hey, man, what's the grif?' said the driver, pulling over. 'You steal somebody's socks, eh?'

The accent bewildered the Bishop for the moment, but he caught a couple of the words and understood the driver was concerned that the car might be hit by hoodlums.

'No – I – er, I'm a member of the Church, my son . . .'

'I in't your son, white rum.'

'No, of course not, that's just an expression,' laughed the Bishop, nervously. 'It's true that someone might be following me, perhaps to kill me, but it isn't anything to do with gangsters. It's terrorists . . .'

The Jamaican's eyes opened wide. 'You mean like them Middle East terrorists, man? Hey, hoist your luggage out of my taxi, man – you got problems I don't want.'

'Not Muslims, necessarily. They're more likely to be from

7

our own Southern states – Christian fundamentalists. I'm on my way to an important conference in London. There are people that might want to stop me getting there. It's very important – worldly matters.'

A police car drew up alongside them and a cop yelled, 'Hey, cabbie, get that vehicle moving. You're stopped in a no-parking zone. Move it.'

The taxi driver did not want trouble with the police. Trouble with terrorists was bad, but trouble with the police meant deportation. His visa had expired and he had no work permit. Smiling a big smile, he waved and pulled out into the traffic again, looking in the rear-view mirror every so often at the Bishop. When they arrived at the airport he flew round to the back of the cab and dumped the luggage on the ground, snatched the proffered fare, jumped in his taxi and drove away quickly.

The Bishop sighed. He wheeled his suitcase through the automatic doors and found himself being accosted by a colleague, on his way back from somewhere.

'Bishop? Where are you off to?'

'Oh, Cardinal Jefferson.' The Bishop laughed nervously. 'Hello. I'm – I'm on my way to London. I've been invited by the Archbishop of York – the *old* one, you know – to a seminar on, er, Catholic-Anglican Views on Sexual Promiscuity in the Young. Can't stop . . .'

He hurried off, leaving the Cardinal looking puzzled. The fact was, Bishop Cates was not allowed to tell anyone, *anyone*, about the conference. He had told the taxi driver because he couldn't think of something else quickly enough, but a New York cabbie would not question the significance of his remarks. So a bishop was on his way to London to a conference? So what? The Cardinal, however, would be intensely curious about such a conference and would undoubtedly take it further.

At the Pynchon Conference Rooms in London, there would be representatives from all the world's major religions and sects, and the Bishop was proud to be one of them.

But he was still scared. There were many who would kill

to stop such a conference from going ahead, from reaching an agreement such as the one proposed – the *only* item on the agenda. The Bishop did not want to be martyred. He was happy being a bishop. He did not aspire to sainthood, not if it meant a bullet through the brain to achieve it.

He found the flight desk, checked in his luggage, and went immediately to the departure lounge where he was able to relax a little. There he chatted amiably with a family bound for a European holiday until he boarded his aircraft.

It was only when the flight neared its destination and was on the approach to Heathrow on the other side of the Atlantic that he again felt apprehensive. But this time it was not a physical threat that worried him. A sense of spiritual unease crawled all over him, like a skin allergy, until he began to sweat feverishly in the same way as he had once on eating a bad curry. Only this was not food poisoning.

The Bishop was an imaginative man, whose mental images of the horrors of evil were as vivid as the paintings of Hieronymus Bosch. He could visualize the tortures, the rape of his soul, the agony of an impaled and flagellated spirit. This kind of suffering was very real to him, and he sensed in the situation below a potential threat of this kind, to himself personally, and to the public in general. He was so scared he thought he might vomit.

'Are you all right, sir?' said the first-class stewardess, stopping by his seat and looking into his eyes. 'The sick bags are in front of you.'

'I'm OK,' he lied, sinking deeper into his seat.

But he wasn't all right. He sensed something in the city beneath the aircraft. A strong, malevolent presence. It made him recoil within, as if from the stink of evil.

Something was rotten in the City of London.

Chapter One

South of the Thames the clergyman's wife was out for the evening, visiting her mother, and he was putting the children to bed. The eldest child was Samantha, who slept in her own room on the ground floor of the large semi-detached house. David and Noel shared a room with a dormer window.

'Shall I read you a story?' said their father, on tucking them in. 'How about *Flat Stanley*? You both like that one.'

'Pull the curtains more,' ordered Noel, going under his sheets. 'I can see the black.'

The priest did as he was asked, closing the gap in the curtains, knowing from experience that if he did not, or tried to persuade Noel otherwise, there would be broken sleep and wails caused by distressing nightmares.

'Right, now, the story . . .'

The story was read, the boys kissed goodnight, and the night-light left on.

The priest went downstairs and found his daughter watching television, instead of doing her homework.

'Have you done your work?' he asked.

'In a minute. I just want to see this.'

It was a soap. All the children seemed to watch the soap operas. The priest sighed. 'Well, the minute it's finished, I want that off and you doing your homework, Sam – do you hear?'

'Yes, Dad.' The eyes did not leave the screen.

Skip, the family's dog, a golden retriever, lay at the girl's feet, allowing its ear to be absently played with, occasionally getting a stroke or two and rolling liquid brown eyes in Samantha's direction whenever this treat was forthcoming.

However, once the programme was over, Samantha dutifully switched off the set and did as she was asked. Her father gave assistance, in between writing his own papers, when requested. Finally, the last line was ruled, the last word was scribbled, and Samantha announced she was going to bed.

'Can I phone Jacky before I go up?'

'No, you can talk to her tomorrow, at school.'

'But I just want to check something about homework.'

The priest sighed again. 'Are you sure she's still up?'

'Course. She's allowed to stay up much later than me,' came back the retort.

'All right, then, but make it quick.'

The phone call, as he had guessed, was not really about homework, but about the programme she had seen earlier.

Finally Samantha came into the room, kissed him on the cheek, and said, 'Goodnight, Pops.'

'Father to you.'

'Goodnight, *Dad*.' She smiled.

Skip padded after her hopefully, but was ordered back into the living room by the priest.

'No dog hairs on the beds, thank you,' he said severely to the animal.

Skip padded dutifully back to his warm spot on the mat by the chair as if he understood the problem exactly.

Once he believed the children were settled, the priest went to wash the dinner dishes.

After the washing-up was done, he discovered that the stainless steel sink was rather greasy. He took out some cleanser from the cupboard beneath and began to clean it. Half-way through he thought he heard a noise from outside and went to the kitchen window to stare out into the back garden.

The house was in a particularly quiet spot and while the odd drunk or two might occasionally stroll by causing a disturbance, little else unsettled the neighbourhood. There was always the chance of burglars, of course, and this was what was troubling the priest as he peered out into the darkness. Recently he had been considering getting security lights, but was concerned that cats and foxes might set them off all the time and worry his wife.

Seeing nothing outside, the priest went back to finish cleaning the sink. He wondered, as he was doing it, about serial killers. Did they ever wash up the dishes and clean the sink? Did it worry terrorists, for instance, whether their ties were straight, or their shoes shined? All those small, mundane tasks that ordinary people, people who had never committed an offence against humankind, carried out automatically: did the murderers and the rapists of this world worry about them, too? Did they concern themselves about wearing clashing colours, or whether their lawns were cut at the weekend, or their cars washed properly, or that the corners of the pages were turned down on a favourite book, or that they had committed a *faux pas* in front of the Bishop? Did they ever think about *anything*, except food, drink and killing?

It was beyond the priest's ken, but he couldn't see how someone could worry about getting a haircut *and* be planning their next murder at the same time. Just as he was thinking about whether he had a clean surplice for the Sunday service *and* planning what to say in his sermon. He felt that killers had one thing and one thing only on their minds: the killings they had done and the killings they would do.

There was a scratching sound outside, as if someone were climbing on the roof.

His heart beating fast, the priest opened the back door and went out into the garden. He always told his wife to call the police if she was in the least suspicious of anything, but he failed to follow his own preaching, afraid of making himself look a fool. He crept to the back of the garden and looked up.

He could see the boys' bedroom night-light, glowing through a chink in their curtains. His eyes scoured the V-shaped valleys in the roof, looking to see if a cat was up there. It was quite a dark night, however, and though there were stars out, there was no moon. He wondered about going inside and getting a torch and shining it up there, so that he could put his mind at rest, but in the end decided he was being silly. It might have been a pigeon, or some other bird, since flown.

13

Going indoors, the priest decided to let the dog out into the garden. He was not a bad watchdog, as dogs went, though he tended to bark at cats and other dogs, which nullified his use outside.

Skip barked a little on first being let out, but after a while fell into the occasional growling and whining in the back of his throat, as if complaining about his treatment.

The priest locked the back door and went to his desk in his study to finish the piece of writing he had started earlier in the evening. It concerned Sunday prayers for the successful outcome of the Meeting that was taking place below the City of London. The priest was excited about the Meeting, as were most of the clergy, and eagerly awaited the outcome. He was sick of the violence in the world perpetrated in the name of his God, in many countries including his own. It served only one purpose: to feed the corrupt with human blood. There was no excuse for such carnage and he hoped that the condemnation of united world religions would be enough to stamp out the fanatics and extremists for good and all.

At about ten o'clock he heard a terrible yell from the boys' room. He left the study quickly, to find that his daughter had woken up and was wandering through the hallway.

'What was that?' she said.

'Go back to bed, dear,' said the priest. 'I think Noel's having a nightmare.'

Samantha did as she was told and the priest continued up the stairs to the boys' room. On going into their bedroom he found Noel bolt upright in bed, covered in sweat, crying. His brother was still fast asleep in the adjacent bed.

'What's the matter, son?' said the priest, gently. 'Bad dreams?'

Noel didn't answer at first, he just sobbed while he was being cuddled.

Finally the little boy stared fearfully towards the window and said, 'Daddy, someone tried to get in.'

The priest glanced at the window, then said, 'I'm sure it was just a dream, Noel. Just a silly dream.'

The priest got a towel and wiped his son down, stroked his

14

brow for a while, and fairly soon the little boy lay back on the pillow and fell asleep again. The priest sat there for a while, looking at him. Then he stared at the dormer window. He got up and pulled the curtain aside, looking out into the blackness. Although he could see nothing, he sensed something.

This troubled him: his psychic hackles were standing on end. He was sensitive to things that troubled his spirit. Of course, he told himself, there was a lot of evil in the world, it wasn't surprising that occasionally one's spirit was troubled. Such a man as himself, who dealt with the metaphysical side of life every day, and was sensitive to changes in the psychic atmosphere, was bound to receive twinges occasionally, especially so close to an inner city with its night hawks.

But even as he sat there, persuading himself that all was well inside the house, his concern deepened. He had the distinct feeling that something was above him, lying in the crevice between the two roofs, resting. Whatever that something was, it was not a real man.

The priest had never been one of those clergymen who believed in the Devil as a corporeal being, a person of flesh and blood, walking the streets and carrying out evil deeds. He was a man who believed that evil was an inherent part of human nature, that the evil was within humankind, and that men and women had to be wary of themselves, rather than some supernatural creature abroad, creating nefarious acts.

Yet, as he sat there on the edge of his youngest son's bed, he felt this proximity of something dire, something frightful, above the place where his family slept. Mental images flitted through the priest's mind, first seen as illustrations in old holy books, kept in the library of the college where he had taken his theology degree. He could not get over the idea that between his two sons and an iniquitous entity were a few roof tiles and some loft rafters.

He had the feeling that only one force was keeping the *thing* outside the house and that force was his own presence. He was a priest, a man of God, and therefore repulsive to any diabolic creature with heinous intent.

The feeling was so strong, he might have tried to carry out an exorcism there and then, on his own household, had he known exactly what was required. As it was, he was a fairly unexceptional rector, with three churches in the district, and his mystical side had never been pandered to beyond ordinary prayers and administering the sacrament.

He did think about performing the Eucharist in his study below, but found it difficult to move from his sons' bedroom.

He might have stayed where he was indefinitely, had not the front door slammed.

Getting up and going downstairs quickly, he found his wife had come home. She was taking off her coat and scarf in the hallway and hanging them up on the hooks beneath the stairs.

'Everything all right?' she asked, not looking at him, and expecting his usual answer.

'I don't know,' he replied.

She turned to stare at him. 'Whatever's the matter?'

'Oh,' he muttered, then decided not to frighten her, 'Noel's had a dream.'

She looked relieved. 'Well, poor love, he's a bit coldy at the moment. He gets feverish when he's got a cold. I'll go up and have a look at him.'

She went up the stairs and the priest watched her go, wondering if he should accompany her. Then he decided he was being over-imaginative. There was much of Noel in him – or rather, much of him in Noel. They were both fairly sensitive, close-to-the-edge people, when it came to atmospheres.

The priest sighed and went into the living room to tidy up some magazines his daughter had scattered on the floor.

Then he went to the back door to let Skip back in for the night.

'Skip?' he called. 'Come on, boy.'

There was no answer.

'Skip?'

It was then that the priest felt an unmistakable wave of nausea strike him like a soft blow. He shut the door quickly and gulped down several breaths. The *stink*! It had robbed

16

him of air. It made him gag with fear. Something *was* out there: some creature from another plane. The priest leaned back against the door, wondering what to do about it. What did it want from him and his family in the first place?

It was then that he remembered a passage he had read recently in an old religious work written by a monk in the eleventh century, on the island of Lindisfarne.

He ran to his desk, took the book from the bookcase, and found the relevant passage: '. . . *if a demon is sent to earth by Satan, the first act of that demon is to eat the bloodfilled heart of some innocent creature, such as a child, in order to satiate its hunger and thirst after its journey from the regions of Hell*'.

The priest stared at the passage for a long second, his stomach turning over. He felt the bile rise to his throat, threatening to choke him. Panic and shock held him there until he suddenly ran out of the room and along the hall, straight to his daughter's bedroom. Wrenching open the door he yelled, 'Samantha?'

'Daddy?' cried the girl, sitting bolt upright in bed.

She looked terrified, her eyes round and wide – but she looked whole and well.

'It's all right, dear,' he said. 'Don't worry.' He stared at her for a moment more then ran frantically upstairs to the boys' bedroom. He rushed into their room to find his wife picking up a few scattered toys in the gloom of the night-light. She looked up, startled.

'Thank God!' sobbed the priest, seeing his two sons still fast asleep.

The priest returned downstairs, grabbing a cross from a window niche on his descent. With no thought now for his own safety, he went out into the back garden. Half-way across the lawn he tripped over something. He looked down and in the half-light from the kitchen window he saw Skip. The dog's golden form was stretched out, cold and stiff, on the grass.

Skip's chest was like a grisly cavern, empty, the heart missing. It was as if someone had grabbed his front legs, pulled

17

them apart, splitting him down the middle, then reached in and scooped out the main organ.

The priest stepped back, his mind swimming, and then he was sick on the grass.

Recovering from the giddiness which had overcome him, he went back inside and bolted and locked the back door. He picked up the telephone in the kitchen, dialling 999.

'The police,' he said to the operator. 'There's a . . . there's been a . . . my dog's been . . . please, I need someone here, immediately.'

The priest sat by the telephone and waited for the police to arrive. They came about ten minutes later. He let them in and thanked them for responding so quickly. 'It's my dog,' he said, 'outside the back door.'

He led the way and showed them the mutilated carcass on the lawn and they told him they would have a look round.

They used the priest's ladder to check the tiles on the roof by torchlight and they found bloodstains and bits of gristle scattered in and around the gutter. One of the policemen remarked that it looked as if something had been having a picnic up there: a wild beast or a bird of prey.

His friend below, thinking he was joking, told him not to be so sick.

'I'm not,' the first policeman told him, 'I'm serious.'

More disturbingly, there were deep scratches like claw marks in the corner of the dormer window, as if something had been trying to get in at the children and had abandoned the task.

When they told the priest, he waited until they had left and immediately performed the Eucharist, after which he sprinkled holy water around the house and prayed throughout the night to drive the evil away from his home.

The next day he piled his family into their car and drove them up to Derbyshire.

Chapter Two

Archdeacon Lloyd Smith suddenly sat up in bed. He was one of the few residents who lived within the Square Mile: a district consisting mainly of banks, finance houses, churches and other institutions. Lloyd had been disturbed by something: a sense of unease had infiltrated his sleep. He felt alert, but wary.

The bedroom curtains were slightly open and the deep, black shadow of a medieval church steeple fell across the floor. The shape of the iron filigree cross on the spire flowed over the white sheets of the bed, stark, and warped by the folds of the bedclothes. It seemed to be trying to swallow him, like some winged snake sent by Manasa Devi. A dark gargoyle was struggling to get into the room through the gap in the curtains, rippling its ugly head and narrow flanks when the breeze blew, falling still and sinister when the breeze dropped.

Lloyd was not normally concerned by night fears, but he shuddered and clutched the covers.

The room was murky-light. Lloyd stared at the picture on the wall opposite his bed – a print of Botticelli's *The Birth of Venus*, which he was finding increasingly erotic since his wife had died. Venus seemed to be telling him to rise up, out of his wrinkled bedclothes, as she was rising out of her corrugated clam shell.

Why was he so apprehensive? Why did he feel he had to get up and go out? Why did he feel this *dread*?

It hadn't been a dream, of that he was sure.

A noise? At sixty-three, not as strong as he used to be, he was just beginning to fear such possibilities as struggles with burglars. There had been a number of male rapes in London recently and Lloyd was terrified, not so much of the rape

19

itself, though that would be bad enough, but of catching something ugly from the rapist. Admittedly most of these crimes had been committed on the tube, it was said by people who were not actually gay. Like female rape, he thought, such violations had little to do with sex and more to do with the exercise of power.

As he listened intently for any sounds, Lloyd slid from his bed and began dressing. However, when he had on only his vest and pants, socks and shoes, and spectacles, he went to the front door of his flat and opened it, stepping into the hallway. Other residents of the block, also in various states of undress, were going out into the street.

Lloyd stared out through the landing window, which looked over the Thames, and saw that the surface water of the river was jumping about, dancing, as it were, with strange little wavelets. The gleaming river was also abnormally high up its banks, threatening to wash over into the roads. It struck the Archdeacon as peculiar, since he knew that at this time, on this date, the river should have been at low tide.

Lloyd joined the people out in the streets.

It was very, very cold.

Even as he walked along, shivering and self-conscious in his underwear, Lloyd kept thinking, *What am I doing? Where am I going?* – but there was no thought of *not* going, of turning back. He was compelled to leave.

The streets of the City were flowing with people, not all going in the same direction, but vacating the area. It was as if a siren had gone off – an air-raid or a flood warning – and their response had been automatic. The City of London was about to be devastated by something and everyone had to get clear, to some safe area outside.

They passed by alleys, under arches, and through narrow streets, without speaking. It was an exodus, but no one knew from what they were fleeing.

Perhaps, thought Lloyd, Salvation Day is here at last, and in the London churchyards the dead are dancing.

When he was about six hundred yards from his block of flats, he turned like many others, to observe.

'Look,' cried someone, pointing up at the sky.

Lloyd stared.

It appeared to be a shooting star, a meteor, hurtling towards the City. Lloyd instinctively took a step backwards and stepped on someone's slippered foot. He turned quickly to say 'sorry' to a young man in a tweed dressing-gown. He need not have worried. The man was too intent on the sky to worry about a little pain. Lloyd returned his attention to what he believed was a meteor about to destroy his home.

The light in the sky grew brighter and fiercer the closer it came to Earth. Most people had to turn their eyes away, but Lloyd was wearing reactorlight glasses which darkened with the onrush of the light. He was able to observe the meteor almost until it struck.

As he watched he could have sworn that the heart of the ball of light had form, not just the nebulous shape of a lump of rock and minerals but a definite set of features, possibly arms and legs, torso and head, though he could not be sure. Then the *thing* hit the earth, there was an explosive *whumph*, and the centre of the City burst into flame. Finally, the light was so white and intense that even Lloyd had to turn away and stare outwards, towards a Holborn of sparkling windows. He was no longer cold. The heat of the fire on his back was intense.

'Did you see that?' cried the man next to him unnecessarily. 'Did you see that?'

A woman, next to the young man in the dressing-gown, whispered softly, 'Wonderful.'

Lloyd swivelled to stare at her. In the light from the fallen star Lloyd could see that the woman was incredibly lovely, and Lloyd considered himself an unbiased judge when it came to female beauty. She was exquisite: a figure of black opal. His photographer nephew, Holden, would give his eye teeth for such a model. A rare thing. Unlike the rest of them, this woman was fully dressed, though without a coat. She had on a simple white dress that emphasized the soft black texture of her skin. Her hair fell like a black waterfall around her bared shoulders. Surely an Ethiopian princess or Nubian temple virgin?

21

'I beg your pardon?' said Lloyd.

'Isn't it wonderful?' she cried, turning her shining brown eyes on to his face. 'Isn't it magnificent?'

'Well, spectacular or awesome would be more *my* choice of adjective – something a little less suggestive of enthusiasm. That's my home it's landed on. All my precious bits and pieces are in my flat. They're probably ashes now.'

'Oh, you mustn't concern yourself over mundane things. They're easily replaced. You've just witnessed something that will be the envy of all those who *didn't* see it.'

'"*And gentlemen in Knightsbridge, now a-bed, shall think themselves accursed they were not here,*"' paraphrased Lloyd.

'Yes, I think so,' the woman said, seriously, missing the irony.

'It's just a meteor.' The Archdeacon snorted dismissively.

The fire was raging now and the sound of the wind rushing in to fill the vacuum was frightening.

Oh, God, he thought suddenly, the Meeting!

Behind Lloyd, from the heart of the conflagration, came explosions, cracking noises, rumbles and the crashing of falling buildings. Dogs, cats, mice and rats were passing the people, running from the flames. Ignoring humans and each other, eerily silent, the animals were intent only on reaching safety. It was a wild, surrealistic scene out of some horrible nursery rhyme. Lloyd, along with many others, began running again, instinctively ducking now and then, as a fresh explosion rent the early morning. The older children, athletic and excited by the event, were well out in front. The slowest were parents carrying toddlers or people assisting sick neighbours. In the middle were those like Lloyd, whose age and indulgent lifestyle was a hindrance to escape.

He could hear the clamour of fire engines now, hurtling to the fringes of the pillar of flame. They swept between the fleeing refugees like magnificent battle wagons, rushing to defeat the enemy. Some of the children cheered. Lloyd knew that this was no ordinary fire, which could easily be brought under control by the forces of London's magnificent fire fighters, trained on terrorist incendiary bombs.

In his mind, like an insistent chant that would not go away, were the facts of the Great Fire of 1666. As a schoolboy he had memorized those facts and figures for a history exam and they came tumbling back into his head.

The 1666 fire had started in a baker's shop in Pudding Lane and, as legend would have it, was extinguished at Pie Corner. Four-fifths of the City had been destroyed: 13,000 buildings, including old St Paul's and 87 parish churches.

Lloyd realized that Pudding Lane was, by remarkable coincidence, only a few hundred yards from the place where the meteor had landed, and had been engulfed by the fire. He began to wonder whether it was true that there were fire spots, like ley-lines, which were weaker and more vulnerable to fire than other areas of the Earth. He was not fond of paranormal suppositions, but it did seem strange that two great fires had sprung up in this area – perhaps more, if one were to have a complete historical record of the area at one's fingertips.

The young woman, hurrying next to him, broke into his thoughts with a question. 'If it's just a meteor, why are you running along in your underpants? Why did you leave your flat? Why did any of these people leave their homes? You believe a meteor would send prior warning of its descent?'

'No, of course not,' he said, uncomfortably, aware of his exposed flabby body, wishing he could pull on a pair of trousers and a shirt right at that moment. 'However, it might have caused some sort of radiation in its projected path, set up vibrations or something . . .' Even as he was speaking he knew it was drivel.

It was still very difficult to look directly at the conflagration. Ambulances and police were beginning to arrive now. Blankets were being handed out to the poorly dressed elderly and children. Lloyd decided he would be an elderly person for an hour or two, until he could get to some decent clothes, though he would normally have resented the epithet.

When he turned to speak to the beautiful woman again, she had moved away. He followed her, his curiosity aroused.

Feeling like a North American Indian in his blanket, Lloyd

finally caught up with the woman. 'Where are you going?' he asked.

'To a hotel. Where else is there to go? I haven't got relations in the area.'

'You have money on you?'

'Yes,' she said. 'Would you like to have some?'

Have some. Not *borrow some.* She really was a most peculiar woman.

'Thank you. I'd rather go to a hotel than spend the rest of the night in some makeshift hostel. I suspect that's where they'll take people. I still think it's a ghastly thing to happen, despite your . . . your ideas.'

'That's because you don't understand yet. You will.'

'And you do, I suppose? You realize that there must still be some people in that conflagration behind us? Not everyone will have got out. There'll be one or two drunks and street people, unable to heed the call.'

She nodded cheerfully. 'They'll be all right.'

'You seem very sure of that.'

She regarded him with those dark eyes again. 'I'm *absolutely* certain of it. Now, this looks a likely hotel. It's probably used by all sorts of dubious people, but they're bound to have rooms. Would you like me to get you one?'

Lloyd looked at the sleazy-looking backstreet hotel with disfavour. It was called the Majestic and half the neon sign was unlit. The other half fizzed as if it were going to explode at any second. The entrance was a narrow hallway, not a lobby or foyer, behind an ordinary street door. No doubt the place had once been a private house, when the street had been properly residential. He wondered whether the sheets would be unaired, or even worse, whether there would be fleas.

However, what choice did he have? In the morning he could call in on friends or look for something better. Just at that moment, though, he began to feel desperately tired.

'Thank you, yes. I shall repay the money tomorrow.'

She smiled. 'If you really want to.'

They went into the hotel, Lloyd feeling very self-conscious

in his blanket. He turned at the doorway to take one last look at the devastated City.

'Nothing left in there,' he murmured.

'Oh, yes, there is,' said the woman. 'The Pynchon Conference Rooms. Underneath and within that dome of light are the world's religious leaders, still working for a common goal.'

'Yes,' said Lloyd, angrily. 'This has cost us dear – it's destroyed the possibility of unification and world peace.'

'You don't understand,' she smiled. 'It's come to *protect* the Meeting. It isn't a meteor, it's an archangel.'

He could not remember his own name.

At first the young man was afraid he was going mad, but eventually the deterioration reached the point where he no longer cared about madness or any other state of mind. He felt his spirit, his very psyche, was being eroded, eaten away by some foreign entity that had invaded his body. This *thing* inside him, spoke to him, tried to engage him in debate.

He had been taking photographs in Highgate Cemetery of the grave of Karl Marx, one of which would possibly be included in an article about the Father of Communism. The sun had been slanting a particular way on to the marble, giving off a sheen which he had to combat with his skill as a photographer.

He liked these difficulties. It gave him some satisfaction to know that he had come a long way since he had begun his career taking photos of the civil war in former Yugoslavia. The romantic Tim Page who had found his way to Vietnam in the 1960s as a young man and had emerged scarred but skilful, was his idol in those days. He liked to think that his experiences had been similar to Page's, that they had had a common beginning.

It was while he was taking an angled shot from the southwest that a shadow seemed to pass rapidly over the gravestone and he felt a sudden shock of cold. It appeared to come directly out of a nearby ash tree. Normally such an occurrence would have annoyed him, while in the process of taking a shot, but this one frightened him.

He made his way back to his studio immediately, by taxi, and even as he travelled he felt an insidious presence creeping through him like some canker.

Don't try to fight me, a voice seemed to say, *you have no chance of winning*.

But he did try to fight, and experienced great pain while so doing.

'You all right, mate?' asked the taxi driver, as he paid the fare with a shaking hand.

'Yes – yes, I think so. Something I've eaten.'

'You ought to lie down. You look like death.'

He felt like death. He felt as if death had entered him in that graveyard.

'God,' he whispered, as he turned the key to his studio, 'what's happening to me?'

Everything was crumbling now: his thoughts, his memories, his *soul*. Outside he was normal. Inside he was falling to pieces, like a piece of charred paper. Bits were flaking off, disappearing, being swallowed up by the alien entity within.

The cat attacked him as he came through the doorway, claws extended, fangs bared, fur bristling. He strangled it, then broke its back, throwing the carcass across the room. It lay in the corner, twisted and still. Fond of animals, he had loved that cat almost like his own child.

He shrieked as his spirit was crushed within him, staggering around the room, crashing into photographic equipment, breaking tripods and scattering lenses. From the first entry into the body, to the last fragment of himself being obliterated, took a little under thirty minutes.

Then he was indeed, dead, and the new creature relaxed, looked around him. Superficially he looked the same, but keen observers would notice different gestures, different movements, different stances. Those familiar with the young man would have noticed that now he smiled a very different smile.

Chapter Three

Aboard the jumbo 767-500, in the process of landing at Heathrow International Airport were two policemen from the USA. Dave Peters and Danny Spitz were detectives, seconded from the San Francisco to the London Metropolitan Police Force. Lieutenant Dave Peters was tall, lean and angular in contrast to his shorter, rounder partner, a detective sergeant.

Back in the locker rooms of San Francisco they were known as Mother Teresa and Friar Tuck, but not to their faces. Dave didn't like being called Mother Teresa because he felt it was disrespectful to that magnificent woman. He had earned the epithet, it was said, because he was holier-than-thou – or at least, holier than the rest of his contemporaries.

Danny, dumpy-looking and balding, was especially resentful of his nickname. He argued that he didn't over-indulge in food and drink, and that he wasn't celibate, which made him nothing like a friar, especially the legendary Tuck. Naturally, these arguments had made both nicknames stick like glue.

'Jeez, look at that,' said Danny, leaning over to look out of the window, down on to London.

Dave stared at the distant white dome of light in wonder. It was like nothing he had ever seen before, even during the angel's reign of terror in 1996, when all the arsonists of San Francisco came out of their holes and torched the city to its financial knees. In the centre of the blinding hemisphere was supposed to be an archangel.

An *archangel*! Because of their former experience Mother Teresa and Friar Tuck had been requested by the Socialist Government of Great Britain to help find a solution to their problem.

Neither of them, nor their advisor on matters of theology, Professor Vanessa Vangellan – Dave's lover back in San

27

Francisco – had any idea how to get rid of the unwelcome and destructive visitor from heaven. Vanessa, who had done the most reading on the subject, had spoken with the two men before they had boarded their aircraft in the USA. She had informed them that the archangel, if it was indeed such, had established itself in the most revered building of the City of London.

'Yeah?' Dave had replied. 'You mean St Paul's Cathedral?'

'Never,' said Danny quickly. 'An archangel would *never* come down to St Paul's.'

Dave raised an eyebrow and stared at Vanessa, who shrugged at the unspoken question.

'Okay, hot shot,' sighed Dave at last, while Danny continued to look grimly out of the window, 'why not St Paul's?'

'It's a Protestant church,' said Danny, a firm Roman Catholic. 'An archangel would never come down to a Protestant church.'

Dave had nodded. 'Fine, yeah, OK. I'm not going to argue with you, because that's what you want, but—'

Vanessa, who knew that despite Dave's words he was building himself up to battle pitch, had interrupted. 'Before you two get into one of your fights, it was the Bank of England, not St Paul's or any other church. The archangel came down in the centre of the financial district.'

The two men stared at her for a moment, then Danny said, 'It's trying to tell us something about money being the root of all evil.'

'The *love* of money is the root of all evil,' said Dave, eager to grasp another argument to replace the one taken away from them by Vanessa. 'That's an entirely different thing. You should get your quotes right. I thought you knew your stuff, but obviously you don't know as much as I do, and hell, I'm no intellectual . . .'

They were met in the airport lounge by a man who gave his name as Lloyd Smith. He told them he was an archdeacon belonging to the Anglican Church.

'No dog collar?' queried Dave.

'No, my work is more secretarial than ministerial or pastoral. I handle money matters, investments and such for the Church, and I also take care of overseas visitors from time to time. You're aware that there's a conference going on in London at this time?'

'You mean the religious leaders?' said Danny. 'Yeah, damn good thing too. About time they all got together.'

'My sentiments exactly,' smiled Lloyd, silkily. 'Let me apprise you of developments to date and you'll probably soon grasp the reason why you were sent for. Several days ago it is believed that someone – some creature – arrived here. I asked for you two because of your past experience in these matters. I understand you were both responsible for vanquishing an angel in San Francisco some five years ago.'

'Six,' said Danny, 'and by the time we busted his butt he was a fallen angel – a demon if you like. No one can take out an angel, let alone an archangel, we learned that much. So we're wondering what the hell we're doing here.'

'That's what I want to speak to you about. You're not here to – er – *take out* the archangel. We believe the archangel is protecting the conference going on underneath its wing. There's an evil element here, too, intent on breaking up the Meeting. It's with regard to that element we need your assistance.'

Dave asked, 'How do you know this *is* an archangel? I mean, I've seen the dome of light, *white* light, the kind I've seen before, so I'm inclined to agree that it's a divine presence of some kind, but what made you settle on an archangel?'

Lloyd Smith looked a little sheepish and seemed about to hedge when he obviously changed his mind.

'There is a, a woman who claims to be in direct contact with the archangel – telepathic contact, that is. She says she has been chosen as its spokesman – sorry – spokes*woman*. There's a car waiting outside to take us to her. We've put her up in the Bedford Arms Hotel, in Holborn, which is as close as we can get to the archangel without being influenced by the glare. Are you too tired to meet her immediately? I shall understand if you want to get a shower and some sleep.'

'Hell, let's get to it,' said Danny.

'Lieutenant Peters?' queried Smith. He pronounced it *Lef*tenant, which threw Dave for a moment.

'I'm OK. Let's get to Hoe-bun.'

Lloyd Smith led them to the doors, flanked by police in civilian clothes, but at the last moment he turned and said, 'I take it you have no firearms?'

'Couldn't bring them on the flight,' confirmed Dave.

'Some of our police now carry handguns. If you wish I can arrange for weapons. I know you people get proper training in the handling of such things.'

Dave shook his head, much to the annoyance of Danny, who always felt safer with a heavy piece of iron about his person.

'No need,' said Dave, 'we're not here hunting criminals. A handgun is no protection against angels – or demons for that matter.'

'Well, we have a rather special weapon,' said Lloyd Smith. 'I'll tell you about it later. And London's not as safe as it once was. Only the other day my sister had a huge chunk of concrete miss her head by a fraction, as she was getting into a car. Came out of a window in the Royal Festival Hall.'

On the way to London, Dave asked Lloyd Smith how much damage and loss of life the archangel had caused.

Lloyd Smith was sitting facing him in the limousine; his small dark eyes looked troubled behind the lenses of his glasses. In the short time since their meeting Dave had decided there was something about Smith which he found disconcerting. He had met a few Englishmen in his time – and Scots, Welsh and Irish for that matter for San Francisco was a cosmopolitan city – but it wasn't Smith's cultural reserve that made Dave uneasy. It was something deeper than that. Smith was armed against something, seemed ready at the drop of a hat to protect himself against the world, and that disturbed Dave. He decided that either some personal tragedy had befallen the man recently – or that he was trying to hide something important from them.

Both Dave and Danny liked to know everything about

everyone connected with an assignment, if it were possible, so Dave set about discovering Smith's secret.

'The archangel has caused no loss of life,' Smith was saying, 'but the financial cost of the destruction has been enormous. Billions. This archangel is straight out of the Revelation of St John.'

Dave looked at Lloyd for an explanation.

'The angels in Revelations,' he said, 'are very destructive creatures. They devastate the world in thirds – and the sun, moon and stars. Wormwood and blood poisoning the waters, fire and hail mingled with blood to destroy a third of the forests and all the green grass, the rivers, and also a third of the firmament. Pretty gruesome stuff.'

'But no loss of life in this case.'

Smith shook his head in confirmation. 'No, not in this instance. In Revelations the wicked are slaughtered by the angels, I believe, but this archangel gave prior warning of his descent – subliminally – and even the wicked were permitted to escape. I myself live in the district which is now at the heart of that ball of white fire. I was aroused from my bed by a – well, a *feeling*, nothing more. But it was a feeling impossible to ignore, you understand. So I went. Others living around me did likewise. Once everyone was clear of the area, the descent took place. A few animals died – must have done – but they have instincts of their own, which they probably pick up from fleeing people, and most of them got out too. Very strange experience, I can tell you.'

'You live alone?' said Dave, picking up on something in Smith's tone.

The elderly man's dark eyes misted over a little behind his spectacles. 'Yes – I – er, yes, alone.'

'You're not married then?' said Danny, slipping easily into interrogating mode.

'Are you?' Smith suddenly snapped back.

'No,' said Danny, nervously. He looked around him. 'Neither of us are – now.'

Smith took off his glasses and wiped them on a tissue he found in his pocket.

31

'I'm sorry,' he said, 'I didn't mean to jump down your throat like that.'

Dave said, 'I guess you must be thinking that we're pretty nosy, but we're cops, and when we sense something's wrong we come right out and ask. You strike me as having something on your mind. Something that's concerning you. Is it anything to do with your experience with the archangel? I mean, if you've got any ideas about it, let us in on them. We need to know everything.'

Smith smiled a sad smile. 'You're very sensitive for a—' He stopped what he was saying, suddenly, and Dave finished it for him.

'For a cop?'

The Archdeacon laughed. 'I was going to say "for an American" which is even more insulting, isn't it? You must forgive me my prejudices – they're not very deep, I assure you. Somehow I've picked them up on my travels. You see, you're right, there was someone of whom I was extremely fond. We lived together for twenty-three years. Now, I'm alone.'

'She left you?' Dave asked.

Smith hesitated for only a moment before replying, 'She left me, then she died, not long afterwards. Cancer. I think she wanted to spare me the pain of having to watch her die, so she told me she no longer loved me and wanted to leave . . .' The tears were running down his cheeks now and, realizing that he was embarrassing his visitors, he tried to smile through them. 'I say I was extremely fond of her, but that's an understatement. The British use the understatement as a protective shield, you know, to ward off any tacky emotional responses. We're not very emotional – not like you.'

'No,' said Danny, 'we can see that.'

'Actually,' Smith added, seemingly eager to change the subject, 'I do have American connections. My youngest brother became an American citizen when he married a woman from California. His son, my nephew, works over here, a photographer. Calls himself Holden Xavier, would you believe? Not his real name, of course, but Smith doesn't look so good on a letterhead.'

32

'My brother Samuel rejected any contact once he left England. He began writing articles in a magazine, calling me a British colonialist. *Me*. He's the one who went out to the colonies, so why am I the colonialist? Anyway, you can see where I get my prejudices. It still makes me a little angry . . . and now you know what's bothering me, and it has nothing to do with the archangel.'

Dave had found out what he needed to know and was satisfied that it wasn't going to affect their working relationship. What had been worrying him was that if the archangel could control people subliminally, then how were he and Danny to know they weren't being manipulated through this man Smith? The creature at the centre of the white light could be out to avenge the destruction of the fallen angel back in '96. It could have been manoeuvring the trio into place before destroying them. Lucifer had been the Angel of Light. Maybe this ball of whiteness was not an archangel at all. Maybe it was the Biggest, Baddest Fellah in Hell, come to avenge the death of his newest recruit, six years afterwards, or a nanosecond in Hell's time. All Dave had to go on was feelings, and his hunch had told him to be concerned about Smith's inner problems. Now he knew what they were it was OK.

Smith said after a few minutes, 'I hope my little outburst didn't embarrass you?'

Danny replied with a laugh, 'Hell, we're from San Francisco, man.'

'Yes,' Smith smiled at them. 'I visited it once. It's a nice city, isn't it?'

'Nice? I hope that's one of your British understatements,' cried Danny. 'It's the best goddamn city in the world!'

'Oh, I wouldn't say that,' said Lloyd Smith, entering into the spirit of the thing. 'Personally I think Florence has a little more to offer than San Francisco.'

'Go wash your mouth out,' said Danny.

With that they let the subject drop. Dave stared through the heavily tinted glass of the vehicle at the oncoming dome of white light, wondering what was going on inside it. If there was a living archangel inside it, what was it thinking about, why had it decided to remain stationary? Why not hunt out the evil itself, instead of relying on mortals?

Dave felt extremely privileged to be one of the investigating officers on this case, even though he had not been chosen because of his police work, but rather because of an accident that had happened to him and his companions some six years previously. It didn't matter. He was here, on an important assignment, and he was pleased about it.

Had he known what was stalking the streets of South London, Dave might have changed his mind.

Chapter Four

He intended to establish his base camp in and around Richmond Park, where he rested from his labours. On arrival he had been very weak, but since then he had built up his strength with the food and drink necessary to revitalize him. A few nights after he had taken over the body of the young man, he stood in Richmond Park and began addressing passers-by. His message was not that of the usual soapbox preacher, urging people to renounce their sins and follow the ways of the Bible. In fact, he seemed to be insisting that they do quite the opposite.

At first he was ignored, but then a crowd of drunken louts stopped to heckle him. He dealt with them in a rather spectacular fashion for a lay preacher: he threatened them with mayhem and violence. They jeered louder. One of the youths took him at his word and the gentle-looking preacher felled the yob with a single blow of his lean-fingered fist.

His blue eyes flashed and his mouth curved into a red crescent as he cried, 'If thy brother offend thee, then strike him down. If he offend thee further, then stamp his face into the earth, shatter bone with boot, destroy him utterly, for he is not worthy to be called *brother* any longer, and must atone for his transgressions with his very life.'

This sounded very biblical, like a quotation from the Old Testament. People who heard it thought they recognized it. Though it seemed somewhat distorted, they felt sure they had read or heard it sometime, perhaps at church, or at school. It sounded just the sort of thing that was needed to sort out the gangs of yobs, the car thieves, the burglars, the muggers and rapists, the murderers in society.

The other youths went to the assistance of the gang member lying on the ground, now being stamped on the head by the preacher. They pulled out iron bars and hammers, knives and bike chains, intending to teach the preacher a lesson. Instead, the lesson went the other way, as one youth had his arm broken and another suffered a fractured jaw. The preacher was lightning fast at unarmed combat. His slim frame belied the strength in him and he fought like a wildcat. The youths ran away, dragging their wounded, screaming blue murder.

By that time a crowd had gathered.

'You don't have to stand for that kind of intimidation,' said the handsome young preacher. 'If someone threatens you, then give them as good as they deserve. We've been frightened for too long by bullies and cowards. If a stranger enters your house at night, are you allowed to attack him?'

A voice from the crowd, cried, 'It's against the law to use more force than necessary.'

'But how do you know how much force is necessary? How do you know he hasn't come to kill *you*? My advice is take the first opportunity to stick him with a knife, or if you own a shotgun, use it. Explanations can be given later.'

Despite themselves, the crowd were mesmerized by this right-wing rhetoric. Ordinarily such talk might worry them, but when they looked into the young man's eyes, they felt they were hearing the truth at last. He didn't look strong enough to defend himself, yet they had witnessed him defeating seven strong youths with weapons. He was surely some kind of avenging puritan, out to cleanse the world of its dross.

He had such a soft tone, such a hypnotic voice. Surely a young man like that, with those angelic looks, couldn't be bad? And if he wasn't bad, why then, he must be good, and the words he spoke, right and proper.

They fell under his spell, drinking in his words, nodding to each other, saying, Yes, he's right, why should we have to put up with it? Why have we got this barricade mentality? We should take the law into our own hands and deal with things in our own way. The next time we see someone stealing a handbag, or shoplifting, or spraying paint on a wall, we should lynch them, by God, hang them from the nearest lamp-post or tree. We should tie them to a car and drag them through the neighbourhood. They won't do it again after that.

The preaching became more and more outrageous, fuelling the brute in them, but the crowd, which began to number in hundreds, only heard that which seemed to them to be common sense. For too long, they were told, they had suffered and turned the other cheek, now, *now* was the time to make a stand, to strike back. The young man's words reached down into that base part of themselves, the Mr Hyde, which stirred and awoke, and *listened*. The beast in each of them grew, filling their souls and spirits. The clean part of their minds became unhinged and flew away, leaving the rotten cankerous part to creep through them, overrun them.

A political candidate's van was commandeered with its loudspeaker system, and the young firebrand was then able to speak comfortably to the several thousand or so who had swelled the crowd before him. He told them he had come to save them, not from sin, but from oppression. He had come to lead them forth from the wilderness of persecution to a future which was free of fear. But first the streets would have to flow with the blood of the guilty and the blameworthy.

'You have to rise up now, fight for what is yours, and let no man stand between you and justice.'

They cheered him wildly. Anyone who seemed to have a dissenting voice was shouted down by members of the mob, silenced by some sleek-looking men and women who seemed somehow to be part of the preacher's team. They had come as individuals, but they recognized one another instantly, and they saw in the preacher a fellow like themselves. It was as if they had been waiting for him, a messiah of sorts, to lead them.

A police van arrived and several officers got out and forced their way to the front of the crowd.

'It's time to go home,' called a senior officer. 'Let's go, everyone, break it up.'

The preacher seemed to swell in stature, his face becoming like some terrible mask. His voice was no longer gentle. He roared through the microphone. 'These police have been corrupted. They take graft from the local Mafia. The criminals use them while we go in fear in our own streets, in our houses, in our own beds. The guilty go free, while the innocent are thrown in cells and beaten, sometimes to death, by the very people who should be protecting us. They deserve to be stoned—'

It was not the words he spoke, but the tone of his voice which drove the mob into fury. The men in uniform were dragged to the ground, kicked and punched as they tried to force their way through the crowd. One of them, a young constable not more than twenty, panicked, took out his truncheon and began laying about him. He was taken, struggling, by the sleek-looking bodyguards of the preacher. Two females hoisted him up into a park tree and hanged him with his own belt before a suddenly silent crowd. His face was a mask of terror as he clawed at the leather around his throat until his legs stopped kicking, his eyes glazed, and he slumped.

Some of the crowd began to drift away, running off down the side-streets, obviously horrified by what they had seen. Others, still hypnotized, remained. The preacher then began to whip the rabble to a fury with his calm voice, reminding them of the atrocities that had been perpetrated against them by street gangs and thugs – and the police. Petrol was taken from the police van, and other cars around the park, and used to set things alight. They stripped the battered policemen and burned their uniforms. They stopped motorists and dragged them out of their cars, overturning and burning the empty vehicles.

'Thus shall the iniquitous be punished,' cried the young preacher. 'Thus shall our enemies perish.'

The crowd screamed in delight.

'Now go,' cried the speaker. 'Go and drag the complacent from their homes, tell them that the meek will *never* inherit the earth, that only the strong will survive. And if they tell you they have no wish to assist us, then burn their cars, burn their houses, *make* them pay for their complacency—'

Thus began the riot that spilled out into the streets of Richmond and beyond. There was insanity in the air, a lust for blood, which was satisfied in every way known to man. There was murder and rape, old scores were settled instantly, feuds revived and carried to their terrible conclusion.

For eight hours carnage reigned. The buildings and parks of Richmond reeked with gore. Evil had established itself in the vicinity and even armed police and the army would be unable to root it out.

A ragged ring was drawn around Richmond on the map and everywhere within that wavering circle declared an unsafe area: a woman would be sure to be attacked if she went in unprotected, a man would be sure to be mugged and beaten, often killed, if he did not drive through the streets quickly, the doors of his car locked.

'Have you been sent to fetch us back?' the sleek young bodyguards asked the preacher.

'No, but you would be wise to assist me while I'm here,' he replied. 'Once we have won, we shall be returning for those who deserted us. It will go better for you if I can report you were of use.'

The young men nodded to each other. 'Tell us what we must do,' they said.

Thus the preacher's base was established and his corruption spread outwards, reaching almost to Hounslow in the west and Wandsworth in the east. Barnes and Surbiton formed northern and southern limits. Within that ring his influence was incredibly powerful, corrupting not only the ordinarily honest, decent citizens, but the police, magistrates, politicians and every corner of officialdom.

There were murders and rapes in broad daylight, in the streets, with onlookers watching and jeering. Law and order broke down, the police accepting bribes and forming their own lawless groups. There was fornication in public places, drunkenness, kidnapping of children, assassinations, beatings and every kind of vice and crime. Wild excesses were encouraged: the meek soon fell under the boots of the bullies.

Clean police were drafted in from other parts of London, only to be contaminated almost as soon as they arrived. Those who could not be corrupted were run down by fast cars, were forced by their superiors to do despicable acts, or were simply found dead in the gutter. Drug abuse flourished, churches were closed down, burned, or used for nefarious purposes.

Those people who wanted no part of the scene within the dark ring either fled from the area or were subject to intimidation. There was a rottenness at the core of Richmond, a cancer impossible to dig out. It got so that no outsider, unless he was evil himself, would venture into the ghetto. Those who were in trouble with the law on the north side of the river, or from clean areas in the south, fled to the sanctuary of this foul region.

In Richmond normal crime-fighting had ceased and the criminal could do much as he pleased. The drug trade became an unhindered business, and pushers were to be found everywhere, openly selling coke, crack, heroin, whatever was required by the drug shopper.

'Why are you here?' the preacher's new followers asked him, as he performed a black mass in Richmond Park, his associates acting as his bodyguard.

'By being here,' laughed the preacher, 'my presence shall be the cause of despair, terror, riots, violence and death. Before I'm through with them the people will be driving out all those religious fools. The *people* will do this. All I have to do is visit the horrors upon them.'

Chapter Five

Lloyd handed dark glasses to the two Americans as they travelled along in the limousine. When the car eventually stopped outside their hotel, they alighted and stared in the direction of the City. Had they not been wearing shades, they would have been blinded by the huge dome of light that covered over a square mile of the London financial district. It had its equivalent in the light released from a nuclear weapon on the point of detonation, except that it was frozen, permanent. Dave had seen it on TV, of course, but the cameras naturally had to have darkened lenses, and the whole show, though it made spectacular viewing, was always muted on the screen.

'What's inside the dome, apart from an archangel?' asked Dave.

Lloyd said, 'The Bank of England, the Stock Exchange, St Paul's, St Olave's, a very fine medieval church, the Royal Exchange, the temple of Mithras, more banks, more churches, more insurance companies – even the Old Bailey was singed. The Tower of London just escaped the fire circle. All these establishments were there before the archangel came, but they're probably ashes now.'

Dave was awestruck as he stared into the white dome, the light so intense he was unable to see anything within. It seemed to be almost a physical presence, solid, impenetrable, as if it were made out of small hemi-sun. He had the feeling that, were he to wander inside, he would be engulfed by the whiteness, dissolved by its density. This was no light the world had ever seen before now. This was an archangel's textured light, the light around which ordinary angels clustered like moths, a marvellous light which had been woven first by Lucifer, before that ambitious angel had grown in

41

pride and had been sent crashing from his birthplace to the loathsome pits he now inhabited.

And yet, Dave had the feeling that this magnificent light was but a candle flame beside that of the Creator's own.

'Has anyone ever been inside?' he asked Lloyd.

Lloyd smiled. 'There's an *archangel* in there. The police have put up barriers and posted guards, but still there are some who slip through the cordon. No one has come out again, not to my knowledge.'

'I mean, officially.'

'Yes, of course, but no contact was made. No one can approach such a creature. It was felt best to keep the area off limits to everyone, even politicians and the military.'

'Let's have the full story,' said Dave, staring at Lloyd.

'Frankly,' replied Lloyd, 'we try to frighten people to keep them out of the dome. There's an important meeting going on in there. We don't want to make an unstable situation worse by some bumbling idiot upsetting the archangel, so we tell the general public that the light is harmful. Actually, it's not. We've sent a couple of teams in, but they can make no contact with the creature inside and quite honestly they get spooked. They come out shaking. There's little to be gained by approaching this creature directly. We know what it wants, and I'll come to that later.'

'That light', said Danny distantly, almost as if he were alone, 'is *pure* light. Imagine being bathed in it. Imagine it washing through your body, purging you, cleansing the sin from your spirit. That's it. You wash your body with water, but you wash your soul clean with light – *that* light.'

Lloyd turned slowly and stared at the small, inspired man beside him.

'I beg your pardon?' he murmured.

'Don't mind him,' said Dave, 'he's a religious nut.'

'The hell I am,' snarled Danny. 'I just – well, you know how I sin, Dave.'

'You figure you could do it with a whore every night, then go back to your apartment, have a shower in holy light, and everything would be fine, eh? You could have your curry and

42

still come out the other end without a stain on your under-shirt? Is that it?'

'Yeah,' said Danny, softly.

Dave shook his head. 'Danny, you'll never change. What about the women, don't they deserve to be purified, too?'

'They could take a shower with me,' said Danny. 'I like taking showers with them.'

Lloyd witnessed this exchange between the two men with a feeling that the Government had made some kind of a mistake in bringing them to London. They were surely a comedy double act from a night-club, not two serious policemen on whom he could depend for assistance.

Dave caught him staring.

'Don't let this fool you,' he said, 'we know our job. It's our way of relieving stress.'

'Yes, I see,' said Lloyd, unconvinced. 'Well, shall we go in?'

They entered the hotel lobby and took off their dark glasses. Once they had booked in they all went to the bar. Lloyd ordered drinks for them and ushered them to a table at which a woman was sitting.

The woman was the most stunning beauty any of them had ever seen. Danny stopped dead in his tracks and stared openly. Dave growled in an undertone, 'Close your mouth, Danny boy, you're drooling.'

Danny managed to get his legs working and he stumbled to the table and took a chair, still unable to take his eyes off the lady sitting opposite him. Lloyd made the introductions and Danny caught the name Petra. He held a soft, silky hand for an instant and then had to let it go.

The drinks arrived: he took his mechanically and held it until Lloyd said, 'Cheers everyone.' He had ordered Haig Dimple Scotch whisky, which was a treat for him, but he drank it without tasting a drop. It was only when he felt a burning sensation in his stomach that he realized he had swallowed the lot in one gulp. Petra, it appeared, was drinking mineral water.

'I've seen the two most beautiful sights in the world this

43

evening,' said Danny throatily, 'and I'm looking at one of them right now.'

Petra spoke directly to him for the first time. Her voice was as soft and smooth as her hand. It made Danny's gut tingle. It gave him the same sensation he got when he was standing on the edge of a high cliff, looking down at a drop which was inviting him to jump.

'Beauty is superficial,' she said. 'You mustn't be impressed by it.'

'Mustn't I?' said Danny, the words awkward in his mouth. 'Say, where are you from? The Caribbean?'

'I'm from here.' She smiled, sipping her mineral water and staring at him with wide brown eyes. 'Britain. I'm British you know, despite the colour of my skin, born and bred.'

'Yeah, sorry, I guess you must get tired of people asking that question. Pretty dumb, huh?'

'It's a natural thing to ask, but it does annoy a lot of second-generation West Indians.'

'I bet it does,' said Danny, trying to drink from his empty glass.

'Hey, Danny, we're all here, too,' cried Dave, from the other side of the table. 'Don't drown, my bucko. I need you.'

'Yeah, sure,' said Danny, reluctantly dragging his gaze away from Petra. 'I'm listening.'

'Like hell you are,' growled Dave. 'Now, Miss . . .'

'Just call me Petra.'

'OK, fine – Petra. We understand you're in contact with that creature out there inside the dome.'

'Creature?'

'The archangel. Do you mind if I ask you a few questions?'

She shook her head in assent.

'OK, firstly, how do you communicate with it? Is it telepathy?'

'That's what Mr Smith calls it.'

'What do *you* call it?'

She said, 'I don't call it anything. I simply have dreams.'

Dave nodded. 'Ahh, good, you dream things. What do you

dream? That the archangel is talking to you? Or are these exchanges visual, or what? Does it use symbols?'

There was an edge of sarcasm to his voice.

Petra stood up suddenly, as if to leave. 'I can see you don't believe in my contact, so we might as well stop here.' She looked annoyed and upset.

'*I* believe you,' cried Danny, jumping up too.

'Danny,' said Dave, 'let's keep this professional. If this woman is on the level, then we'll find out soon enough, but the only way to find out is to ask questions.' He turned on Petra again. 'Look, what's the objection to answering a few questions, even ones you might consider sassy? I need to be satisfied that you're not some nut taking us for a ride. Now, you want to leave, go ahead, but if you're being straight with us, you'll be back anyway. You can't keep an archangel's thoughts to yourself – I don't believe it's possible. If he's using you to communicate with us, lady, then you'll do it. You won't be able to help yourself.'

Petra stayed standing, staring up at Dave.

Danny said, 'Look, why don't you tell Dave what he wants to know? What does it matter?'

'He's humiliating me,' said Petra.

'He's a cop,' said Danny, 'he tries to humiliate *everyone* – even me sometimes – because he thinks it's his right to get to the truth no matter what means he uses. Why don't you humour him?'

Dave looked sharply at Danny and frowned, but Petra sat down again.

She cleared her throat and said steadily, 'He tells me there's a dead soul here in London, a dead soul from hell.'

'What's a *dead soul*?' asked Danny.

The Archdeacon interrupted here. 'The soul of a dead mortal, which might go to heaven or to hell, of course, depending upon the judgement. We know something has happened south of the river – it's an area which has become one of our worst crime spots, things are out of control there. We think this dead soul has established a base there for its evil activities.'

45

'What's it here *for*?' asked Dave.

'You must be aware of the Meeting?' said Petra. 'We believe it's been sent to prevent a successful outcome. The archangel is here to protect the Meeting. A direct confrontation between them would devastate the whole city, millions would die, and we must do everything in our power to prevent such conflict.'

'So what does it call itself,' Dave asked, 'this dead soul? Who was the live one?'

Petra murmured, 'It calls itself Manovitch.'

No one said anything for a few moments, then finally Dave broke the silence.

'If I didn't believe your story before,' he said unsteadily, 'I think I believe it now.'

The man was quite tall, with an angular face. He had on a long raincoat. His hands were slim but strong-looking. His name was John Fields.

The woman at his side was also tall, reaching past the man's shoulder. She had on a woollen coat. Her right arm was hooked through his left. Her name was Susan Fields.

It was two o'clock in the morning and the couple were on their way home from visiting friends in another part of the neighbourhood. The district was not especially dangerous, though nowhere in London these days was completely safe, so when a young man stepped out of the shadows in front of Fields, he evinced surprise mingled with caution.

'You startled me,' said Fields, becoming a little angry. In the few seconds during which they stood regarding each other under the lamplight, he assessed the other man, and felt himself to be the physically stronger and more able of the two.

'Peters?' said the man.

'What's he talking about, John?' asked the woman in a shrill voice. 'Come on, let's go home.' She tried pulling her husband out into the road, so that they could bypass the man who was accosting them.

'You're not Peters,' said the man.

'No, I'm not,' replied Fields, now aware that this was no mugging, but more likely a feud. He was actually a little relieved. He was not Peters. The young man in front of him had business with Peters, not with him. The young man had something *bestial* about him, which frightened Fields, and made him want to get away quickly.

Strange eyes stared into his with a malevolence Fields had not seen in any man before this night.

Fields allowed himself to be pulled off the kerb into the road by his wife, intending to go round the man, when the other stepped forward suddenly and gripped him by the throat. Fields let go of his wife's arm immediately and tried to prise the fingers open. They were immensely strong. He felt not only that his windpipe might be crushed, but also his spine.

He heard his wife scream. She kicked at the figure that was now dimming before Fields's eyes. A hand lashed out, sent her spinning across the road and in front of an oncoming car. There was a squeal of brakes and then a thudding sound.

Fields felt his eyes bulging, his tongue lolled out. He kicked out savagely at his attacker's genitals, missed, struck a thigh. Someone came to assist him, the car driver, and he felt the pressure relax. He staggered back against the wall, choking, white lights dancing before his eyes.

When he looked up, he saw the driver being picked up bodily, a wriggling figure, all arms and legs, and being slammed down against the kerbstones. There was a sharp *crack* from somewhere on the driver's body. Fields began running.

Susan was lying in the road. She was moaning. John wanted to go to her, but he couldn't. Instead, he continued to run away, sobbing with humiliation, fear and pain. He had almost made it to the bottom of the street when a piece of kerbstone struck him in the back, and passed through him.

Chapter Six

'Manovitch,' repeated Danny, softly. 'That son-of-a-bitch. That's all we need.'

Manovitch had died in 1996, during the great wave of arson that swept through the major cities of the world, in the time of the angel. His body, identified only by the teeth, was found in the burned and gutted apartment belonging at the time to Detective Sergeant Dave Peters. Manovitch had been attempting to booby-trap the building and had fallen victim to his own incendiary bomb.

The locker-room boys said Mother Teresa had gone back to his apartment after defeating a fallen angel in a mighty battle at the cathedral to find himself homeless and all his possessions destroyed. Mother Teresa hadn't minded that so much, since his wife and child had recently died in an apartment store fire, and it enabled him to make a clean break from his former life.

'There couldn't be two Manovitches,' muttered Dave. 'Not like that one.'

'You knew him, then?' Lloyd asked.

Once more Dave had the feeling that Lloyd Smith was already aware of the relationship between himself and Manovitch, but he patiently explained that he and Danny had had their run-ins with Manovitch at one time.

Lloyd leaned forward and stared at Dave. 'OK, well, you're here to help us get Manovitch before he destroys our Meeting – or before the archangel decides it has to confront Manovitch itself. Petra tells me that the archangel is here essentially to protect the Meeting with its presence on this side of the river, but Manovitch is apparently one of Satan's most successful and favoured generals on the battlefields of Armageddon and the archangel wants him badly.'

Dave stared hard at Lloyd and decided it was time for a showdown. 'Are we being set up?' he asked, leaning forward. 'Are we being used to draw Manovitch out of hiding?'

'Yeah,' said Danny. 'Sounds like we're the bait.'

'That's a rather crude way of putting it,' said the Archdeacon, knitting his fingers and apparently not fazed in the least. 'It's a very complicated scenario and I think you're oversimplifying things by talking about "bait" and "set-ups". It's – it's part of the reason why you're here.'

Dave asked, 'Has there been an increase in arson in London?'

Lloyd nodded. 'We're trying to keep it quiet, to stop the copycats from crawling out of their holes. The big fire – the one caused by the archangel – has them all awestruck at the moment, but if they learned that there had been an increase in smaller fires, we would have another wave of arson on our hands, just like we had in 'ninety-six. The media are screaming, but the Government has warned them not to publicize these fires.

'Murders have also increased dramatically – we think that's probably Manovitch himself, practising his art. They're mostly stranglings, often after rape, men *and* women. I understand from Petra that his sexual appetites, now he's taken on his earthly form again, will be extremely strong. If you were to see some of the victims, it would turn your stomach.' Lloyd gave an involuntary shudder.

Dave nodded. 'You were saying we're not just here as bait.'

'Well, you are, but as I said, it's not simply that. Petra tells me that Manovitch will be able to sense you're in the city, so he'll be out and about more, and thus more vulnerable to those hunting him, be they angels or men. We have literally hundreds of people out there ourselves, waiting for Manovitch to make his move. When he does, we'll destroy him.'

'Before he gets us, I hope,' growled Danny. 'What are you planning to destroy him *with*? How do you destroy a dead soul?'

Petra, eyes now wide open, answered this one. 'The same

way you destroy an angel or demon when it comes to earth, with holy fire, if possible.'

Lloyd said, 'We've developed a new handgun, one that shoots incendiary projectiles. When they strike an object they vaporize on impact and the latent heat produced on changing so rapidly from solid to liquid to gas is enough to ignite them. You'll each be supplied with one of these weapons later.'

'Glad to hear it,' grunted Danny. 'But what about the "holy" side of things?'

Here Lloyd looked acutely embarrassed, and he murmured, 'We've had the whole batch of ammunition blessed by no less than an archbishop, in the same way one would produce holy water, so you see . . .' His slim, waxen hands fluttered in his lap.

'An archbishop *blessed* a weapon of destruction?' cried Dave.

Lloyd squirmed in his chair. 'Well, it seemed like a good idea. We're not sure it will work – Petra can't even tell us that. Now,' he continued a little more briskly, 'as I said, the reasons we need you here are manifold – or, at least,' he smiled, 'more than one-fold. One, Manovitch will be hunting you more intensely and will therefore be more evident. Two, you will be able to identify him, having known him in life. Three, you can hunt for him, while he's hunting for you. Four—'

'Forget it,' said Dave, wearily, 'it all adds up to one word – bait. Well, if that's why we're here, then fine. We're cops, Danny and me, and we'll do our duty.'

'One last thing I want to ask Petra,' said Danny, 'before my mind goes numb. When the angel came down in 'ninety-six it killed a lot of innocent people. It said that it wasn't subject to the Ten Commandments, that since the victims' souls were not lost for ever then it was committing no real offence in the eyes of angels. Now the archangel has destroyed a lot of property on *its* descent, but no people. Why is that?'

'Why?' repeated Petra.

'Yes, why the change of angel policy?'

'The archangel wanted to minimize the risk.'

Danny looked mystified. 'The risk to *what*?'

'The risk to itself. The archangel didn't want to fall into the same trap as the angel. Angels are not used to being among live mortals and the last angel became contaminated, corrupted. During its presence here it became confused and strayed from the path of obedience and truth. It became tainted by our world.'

Dave nodded slowly, his mouth a grim line. 'I get it – it wasn't the angel's fault it turned into a demon, it was humanity's fault. The archangel's not worried about burning people, it's worried about its everlasting place in the order of angels. Jeez.'

Tired and needing sleep, he asked if he could be shown to his room. Danny remained at the table with Petra and Lloyd. Dave guessed that Danny would stay there until either he died of old age or Petra left, whichever occurred first.

Once in his room, Dave flung himself on one of the twin beds. 'Sleeping apart again,' he said, staring at the ceiling. 'Damn this gypsy life.'

He picked up the phone and called Vanessa, in San Francisco, delighting in the sound of her voice.

Chapter Seven

Manovitch gathered his disciples in a disused warehouse south of the river. Having successfully established a strong fortress he wanted to develop a specific line of attack against the holy men sitting around the table north of the river. He knew that if this Meeting was broken up the religious leaders would not get round the table together again for a very long time, perhaps never. Some had encountered strong opposition from within their own individual faiths, against a united front, and their opponents would use the breakdown of the Meeting to indicate that such a unification was against their own natural laws.

'Each religion follows its own gods, or version of God,' said Manovitch. 'The nays within the ranks will all start yelling that their leaders are wrong to want unification and they'll make damn sure there's no second try at it.'

A succubus called Skellank, sleek and beautiful like the rest of the creatures in the room, said, 'Why don't we just make an assault on the Meeting?'

Manovitch said, 'You think I haven't tried that already? I sent three of you over there yesterday.'

Skellank looked around the group for the missing faces, her expression registering that there were three less out of the two dozen who had met last time.

'What happened to them?' asked another demon.

Manovitch said, 'The archangel burned them.'

There was a shuffling, followed by a silence. These were demons who had already shown themselves cowards in the face of annihilation. They had risked the wrath and long arm of Satan and had fled the battlefields of Armageddon to hide down on the earth. Having run away from destruction once, they had no desire to court it again, even should they be forgiven their initial desertion.

'So,' said the handsome Bakan, 'what do we do now?'

'We formulate a sidelong approach,' snapped Manovitch. 'We must make life so uncomfortable for the bastards around that table, that they all run back to their respective countries. I need some ideas on how that can be accomplished.'

'Here's an idea,' said Skellank, her eyes glinting in the half-light. 'Why don't we take something of *theirs*, from that *book*? Why don't we take some punishment that's been meted out to sinners and *copy* it – only we do it better, see? We show those holy men around that table that any punishment handed out by the forces of God, we can do, only much worse.'

Manovitch nodded approvingly. 'I like that. I like that very much . . .'

Chapter Eight

The jet lag had taken its toll on Dave and by the time he managed to crawl out of bed it was eleven a.m. He took a shower, dressed, then went down to the dining room.

'Colombian?' asked Dave of the waitress, when ordering his breakfast.

'Don't know, I'll ask,' she said, obviously unused to requests for regional coffee.

'Kenyan,' she said, on returning. 'Or ordinary.'

'What the hell's *ordinary*? Instant? Damn, Kenyan, I guess,' he grumbled. Then, 'I'm sorry, it's not your fault.'

'You can probably get some Colombian coffee at a coffee shop,' she suggested.

'It's not that important,' he lied, 'bring me the Kenyan. And some toasted focaccia bread.'

'Some what?'

'Never mind.' He sighed.

At that moment he was joined by a bleary-eyed Danny, who probably looked worse than he felt.

'What happened to you last night?' asked Dave, innocently. 'Did you get any sleep?'

Danny's head snapped up as he sat down. 'Of course I did! Why do you say that? What are you trying to say?'

Dave blinked and shook his head. 'Nothing,' he said. 'I'm just asking how you slept, is all. What the hell, who cares anyway?'

Danny looked sheepish. 'OK, OK. I had a lousy night, if you must know. I woke at about three a.m. and couldn't get back to sleep again. What's for breakfast?'

'Not Colombian coffee, that's for sure,' grumbled Dave.

'Who cares as long as it's thick and black?' said Danny, smiling at the waitress.

The waitress said, 'A man after my own heart.'

'Coffee and toast,' Danny ordered.

'Brown bread, or white?' She sniffed, thereby proving to Dave that the hotel was not completely without its exotic choices.

'Brown, thanks.'

He was rewarded with a flashing smile, which obviously did not extend to anyone else at the table.

'You seem to be getting on well with the women over here,' said Dave. 'First that young lady last night, and now the waitress.'

'What do you know about last night?' said Danny, suddenly snappy again.

'Nothing,' replied Dave, 'but if you keep jumping down my throat like that, I'll begin to suspect.'

What he did suspect was that Danny had gone out on the town and found himself a local call girl. Danny had never been very successful with women and to Dave's knowledge had always gone to hookers for sex. He had even found love there, once, when he had married one named Rita. Rita had died in an automobile fire, another victim of the angel who fell from grace in San Francisco in '96.

'Will you be going to confession today?' asked Dave.

Danny, a Catholic who suffered terrible guilt pangs every time he sinned with a prostitute, said, 'No, I won't, if it's any business of yours, Lieutenant. What are you, my father?'

They ate their breakfast in silence after that, until they were joined by Lloyd Smith.

'There was another murder last night,' said Lloyd. 'A man was strangled and dismembered. They found his arms and legs scattered over the roadway and his head rammed on a spike of some iron fence railings.'

Danny said, 'You're telling us this for a reason. I'm sure there was more than one murder. What did the victim look like?'

'In life? Probably tall and lean, definitely angular-jawed.'

The other two men stared at Dave, who shrugged uncomfortably. 'Could be just coincidence,' he said.

'No,' replied Lloyd, 'all the bodies of the victims of this serial killer have had similar features to either you, Lieutenant Peters, or you, Sergeant Spitz.'

'I wish you'd say "lootenant" instead of "leftenant" – it throws me,' said Dave. 'So, what do you think? You think these guys were killed because Manovitch thought they were us?'

'No,' said Lloyd again. 'I think he killed them because they *weren't* you. I think he wants you badly, but when he gets one of you he'll keep that one alive until he secures the other one, using his hostage as bait. That's what Petra thinks and it makes sense to me. I think he's killing these others in a fit of pique when he finds they're not you two.'

'Did anyone see anything?' asked Dave.

'Yes, there were one or two witnesses. One of them is still in shock – the man's wife. She said the man who killed him was a youth, a tall, very good-looking, slimly built young man. After the killing the murderer climbed up the sheer wall of a house like a spider and ran away across the rooftops. It took a while to get this information out of her, you understand – she didn't stop screaming for at least an hour after they took her to hospital.'

'Shit,' said Dave. 'Anyway, that doesn't sound like Manovitch, sounds more like our friend the angel.'

'According to Petra, who as you know is in direct contact with the archangel, all demons – and dead souls – choose to be beautiful young men. Why not? I would if I had the chance to change bodies, wouldn't you?'

'I think I'd want to look like Clint Eastwood in *High Plains Drifter*, not like Rudolph Valentino in *The Sheik*,' said Danny.

'You speak for yourself, of course,' replied Lloyd. 'Valentino would do me just fine.'

'So, anyway,' said Danny, 'you think this is Manovitch, this serial killer who strangles then dismembers.'

'Petra is almost certain it is.'

'Where is she, by the way?' asked Dave.

Danny went scarlet and muttered, 'She'll be down in a minute.'

There was stunned silence around the table for a few seconds, then Dave whistled slowly. 'You mean, she's in *your* room? No wonder you look so ragged, buddy. You must have been up talking your heads off all night.'

Danny said to Dave, 'Don't be funny,' then he nodded and gave the Archdeacon a lazy grin. 'She likes me,' he said. 'Can you understand that?'

'You, er, seem a nice person.'

'Yeah, nice, but ugly. But Petra says she can see the beautiful me inside. She says I'm the most beautiful man she's ever met . . .'

Dave said, 'This is highly unprofessional.'

'Aw, come on,' replied Danny. 'It's not going to hurt anything. If she'd had a boyfriend you wouldn't have thought twice about it. Well, hell, I'm her goddamn boyfriend, so you can all chew on that for a while until she gets here. Here she comes.'

Petra came to the table in an African-style dress and turban. Dave thought she looked good enough to eat. He was incredulous that she should want to take up with his dowdy old pal, Friar Tuck. What the hell did she see in him – see *within* him? Danny was the salt of the earth, but he had little to recommend him in the way of looks or personality. There were ugly guys who got beautiful women, but they had something else – charisma or money or power, none of which Danny had. Simple niceness of character didn't usually set women's antennae quivering.

'Morning,' said Dave to Petra.

'Good morning,' replied Petra.

'You sleep badly, too?' Dave said, archly. 'Like my little buddy here?'

'That's enough of that, Dave,' said Danny. 'Let's get down to business. Petra, Lloyd tells us there's been another murder. We understand you have some theories about what's happening out there on the streets.'

'They're not theories,' she said. 'I know. Manovitch is frustrated. He's killing people because he can't get to you two – and because they're *there*.'

'So,' Dave said to Lloyd, 'what's on today's agenda?'

'First thing I want to show you is the weapon we've developed. You will all need to carry one, so we'll give you some practice. If you've fired a handgun, which I'm sure you have – perhaps not you, Petra? – this is a very similar firearm. Shall we go?'

They were driven to a firing range in North London, where they were shown the snub-nosed weapons. Dave was the first to try one out. He aimed at a bale of hay at the end of the gallery and squeezed the trigger. The gun bucked and the hay exploded in flame. Dave was impressed, as he watched a man douse the flames with water.

'Hey,' he said. 'What did you soak that bale in? Gas?'

'There was nothing on the hay at all,' said Lloyd. 'It was simply a dry bale. Now, would you like to try, Sergeant?'

'But the bale's still wet from the dousing.'

'Just point the weapon and pull the trigger, if you please,' replied Lloyd, 'but take two or three shots at it.'

Danny shrugged and did as he was told, squeezing the trigger three times in succession. Again, the hay burst into flames, burning perhaps not quite so fiercely as before, but burning none the less. It seemed that the incendiary bullets were able to ignite even a wet target.

'This is a good gun,' said Danny, stroking his cheek with the barrel. 'I want to keep this one.'

Finally, they were all equipped and ready for the streets.

'Now,' said Lloyd, 'you do some old-fashioned foot-slogging. I've sectioned off the city into a square search, a section each day. You'll be driven around slowly by competent drivers in separate vehicles – Sergeant Spitz and Petra in one and Lieutenant Peters in the other. We're using open-topped Road Rovers, so you'll be higher than most of the traffic and able to look over the top of it.'

'You mean, we'll be visible to Manovitch.'

Lloyd Smith shrugged. 'It's the only way we're going to get him to reveal himself. Don't forget, he's got to get close enough to use his hands – his only weapons at the moment – so you'll have the advantage.'

Chapter Nine

Dave said to his driver, 'Go east, young man.'

'You can't go in there,' said the driver, missing the Horace Greeley joke. 'We've cordoned off the dome. No telling what might happen if you approached the archangel.'

'Sure, I realize that, but I just want a closer look than the one I've had up until now.'

The fresh-faced young constable who was driving their car, was a Londoner by the name of Rajeb Patel. He turned the car down Theobalds Road and headed towards Gray's Inn. 'OK, I'll take you to the line. They might let us go inside a little way when we tell them who you are. Shall we get Mr Smith on the blower?'

'The phone? No, I don't want to cause any trouble. I'm just curious, that's all. Otherwise I shall feel a bit like the tourist who went to Pisa and didn't even take the time to drive past the Leaning Tower.'

'It fell over last year,' remarked Rajeb. 'People will go and see anythin' that's unusual. The archangel is attracting tourists by the thousand. You can get your archangel T-shirts all over London. Postcards. Guide-books. They've all got this picture of a naked bloke with wings and no Marquess—'

'No *what*?' Dave asked.

'Dick,' replied Rajeb.

Dave shook his head in bewilderment. 'How do you make that out?'

'Marquess of Lorne, *horn*. It's Cockney rhyming slang.'

Rajeb was grinning, his eyes still on the road. 'I'm sorry, Lieutenant, I happened to be born in Stepney and enjoy showing off my roots. That's why I'm not fond of the arch-angel, burning up my part of London. You know he even got St Paul's? And the Old Lady of Threadneedle Street?'

59

'Old lady?' said Dave. 'An old lady was burned? I thought no one died in the fire.'

'The Bank of England,' sighed Rajeb, as if he were dealing with an infant.

Dave shrugged and put on his dark glasses. There was a strobe effect from driving through streets lined with tall buildings as they headed towards the huge hemisphere of bright light. Finally they came to a barbed-wire fence. Armed soldiers were patrolling it and a road block across the main street going into the forbidden zone. A police sergeant carrying an automatic weapon held up his hand and Rajeb stopped the Road Rover next to him.

Rajeb flipped a wallet open. 'Patel, Sarge. North Division. I've got Lieutenant Peters here, from San Francisco? He wanted to have a closer look at the archangel.'

'I can't let you in,' said the sergeant. 'You must know that.'

Dave said, 'I know, Sergeant. Has anyone been in there lately?'

'You've always got your nutters, especially where religion's concerned,' replied the sergeant.

'Right. What happens to them? I mean, do they come out again, or what?'

'Nobody's ever come out,' confirmed the sergeant. 'They're probably all wandering around in there, blind as bats or – well – who knows?'

'OK,' said Dave, staring into the intense white light that filled the skyline ahead. 'That's all I wanted to know. Rajeb, take us where you will – cruise the metropolis. Do you *feel* anything? Any kick?'

'What do you mean?'

'I would have thought we would have felt *something*, some sense that something powerful was nearby. I mean, I'm awed by that light, but I don't *feel* anything.'

Rajeb took him south of the river. Dave concentrated on studying the crowds in the streets but felt a growing hopelessness with the task. How were they ever going to find Manovitch in a city full of so many people? Or, rather, how were they going to let Manovitch find *them*?

Maybe he had come down to earth as a dog or a rat – which would be apt, decided Dave – and not a human at all. It was so frustrating, having just to be there, waiting for the pounce, watching every direction, hoping they would recognize him before he got to them.

'Where are you taking us first?' asked Dave.

'Richmond,' answered Rajeb. 'There was a riot there a few days ago and several people were killed. It's still a bloody no-go area. Funny thing is, it wasn't one of your deprived boroughs, with poor housing and streets full of unemployed people. It was more one of your residential areas – stockbrokers, bankers and such. Most of the rioters were so-called respectable middle-class citizens. A man was known to address a crowd – whipped them up into some kind of hysteria. You know, like Hitler and the Nazis in the last century? That kind of stuff. Now the place is a bloody den of iniquity, full of villains.'

'Manovitch?'

'Sounds like it, dunnit?'

Danny was feeling both elated and fearful, as a man who is in love with a beautiful woman often feels, at least during the initial stage of a relationship. How could this be? he was thinking. How could this ravishing young black lady be interested in a short, dumpy, balding white man? But it seemed she was, for they had spent the whole night making love, frantically at first, then in a more gentle and thoughtful way, careful to please as well as be pleased, tender in their ministrations.

Her body was smooth, soft and curvaceous. She had hidden valleys and secret places he had never explored in his whole life before. Every movement she made excited him. Even now, as she walked about the room, the movement of her clothes was as fascinating to him as a strange and wonderful phenomenon in the heavens.

She smelt amazing, too – a musky smell, like a lioness lazing under a thornbush in the hot African sun.

'Have you ever been to Africa?' he asked her, as she collected last night's jewellery together.

She looked up and smiled. 'No, I was born here, in Britain.'

'Yeah, I think you already told me. I'm pretty dumb some-times. It's just – just the way you move and everything. You've got this kind of sway – I dunno. I just think you're beautiful, I guess.'

She looked up at him and frowned. 'Please don't keep placing so much importance on looks,' she said. 'They're the least significant aspect about me.'

'Yeah, yeah, I know,' he lied, kicking himself mentally for repeating the same mistake he had made earlier, 'but still, it's part of all that you are, isn't it? I mean, I can't ignore it.'

'I wish you would.'

'OK, OK, I'll try to think of you as ugly.'

She came to him and put her arms around him, kissing him passionately on the lips. Then she stared at him from a dis-tance at which he found difficult to focus. All he could see were her large brown eyes.

'Hey,' he croaked, 'are we going to get some work done, or not?'

'Yes, we are,' she said, giving him a final hug.

They went down to the foyer where they picked up the driver of their car, Stan Gates, a sergeant in the Metropolitan Police Force.

'Morning, Sergeant,' said Stan.

'Snap,' said Danny. 'Where are we going?'

'South of the river. I'm just going to cruise the streets, give you a feel for the layout of the place.'

'OK, let's go.'

'Have you got your weapon?' Petra asked.

'What?' said Danny, momentarily shocked, then, 'Oh, yeah, I got that all right.' He patted his shoulder holster.

'Then let's go,' she said, marching towards the revolving doors.

They crossed Waterloo Bridge and drove south-west. At every corner, every light stop, Danny expected to be jumped by his old enemy. But of course it was not going to be that easy. Manovitch was hidden among the millions and it was going to take a miracle to winkle him out. They had to wait for him to make his move, but in the meantime, being cops, they felt they had to be doing something, too.

After four hours, Stan drove home, via Oxford Street. While they were waiting at some lights a young man sidled up to the vehicle and looked Danny in the eyes. Danny's hand closed around the butt of his gun.

But the boy whispered, 'Want any copy watches, mate? Cartier? Longines? Copy Rolex?'

'No thanks,' said Danny. 'I can get 'em in New York.'

'What about some naughty software?'

'Get lost,' Stan Gates said. 'Before I nick you.'

They pulled away, leaving the youth disgusted and disappointed.

They continued to cruise up Oxford Street, studying individuals in the crowds. Danny was aware that Manovitch would not look like Manovitch, but he was hoping for intuition to assist him. Perhaps he would recognize some familiar habit or unconscious way of walking, or a tic or twitch, something perhaps even Manovitch didn't know he had.

'I don't care what Manovitch looks like now,' he told Petra. 'I'm sure I'll know him when I see him.'

Just as they were passing the Bendy Yellow store, Petra gave a shout. 'Look – there!'

Danny followed the line of her arm. A sleek-haired young man was looking at their car. He was dark and beautiful in a way that Danny remembered. Dressed in black, with a slick-looking overcoat that reached to his heels, he seemed exotic and out of place among the other people on the street. The man's eyes glistened with evil: he looked like some marvellous creature out of a Renaissance painting. What interested Danny more than anything was the young man's stance: he looked poised and ready to bolt, like a frightened cat.

'I see him,' said Danny.

The moment Danny spoke the words, the guy took off, heading towards Tottenham Court Road, then down a side-street. It was obvious that the car could not follow because

of the dense traffic. Danny jumped out without even opening
the door, giving chase. He had his new weapon in his hand.

'Hey, watch it, mate!' cried a big blond man, as Danny
brushed past him.

Danny ignored him, intent on catching the man with the
slicked-down hair, who ducked into a department store: the
kind full of ophite clocks and Persian rugs. Danny followed
him in, weaving among the opulent counters and wealthy
shoppers. At first, Danny thought he had lost his quarry, but
then he saw the black coat disappearing into a glass octagonal-
shaped container.

As Danny began running towards him, he saw the man was
in one of those terrarium elevators, which give the passengers
a view of the store as they go up and down. Danny looked
up to see the guy grinning at him through the green-tinted
glass. Danny hadn't any doubt he knew of an escape route
from one of the upper floors.

Shit, he thought, was that Manovitch up there?

Suddenly the grin disappeared from the ascending face, to
be replaced by a look of absolute terror. The man started
forward, pressing his hands against the glass walls, as if trying
to get out while half-way between floors. His eyes were large
and round, and his lips had a peculiar twist to them.

What the hell's going on? thought Danny. He wasn't
pointing his weapon at the guy. It was aimed at the ground,
in case of an accident. Yet Danny could have sworn the man
looked as if he were about to die, in a way that Danny had
seen once before, in '96. Instinctively, Danny shielded his
eyes with his hands.

In the next instant, there was a blinding white flash as the
interior of the elevator exploded in a shower of phosphorescence. Although the explosion was contained the light was
so bright, so incandescent, that Danny could see it through
taper-like hands. Several people in the store screamed.
Danny fumbled in his pocket for his dark glasses.

The elevator was like a brilliant lamp, hanging on the face
of the store, filling the whole place with effulgence.

Inside, something was burning as fiercely as an acetylene

torch: it was shaped like a giant wick and its heat began to melt the glass panels that surrounded it. Molten glass dripped down on to a counter covered with bottles of perfume. A counter clerk screamed as a drip hit him on the shoulder and burned into his body.

People were running blindly in all directions now, crashing into display stands and scattering the goods. Mountains of glass ornaments came crashing to the floor; piles of leather diaries scattered, sliding across the marble tiles; a stone model of the Egyptian Pharaoh Amenhotep teetered, then finally came smashing through a glass counter full of fripperies.

'Don't panic,' yelled Danny. 'Stand still, everyone.'

Of course, not a soul took any notice of him.

The elevator continued to ascend towards the glass roof of the building, like a nova star returning to its place in the heavens.

Once the glass had melted sufficiently to allow more oxygen in, the fire inside increased in intensity and by the time the sprinkler system had been triggered by the fumes, the creature within was almost burned to ashes.

Danny raced forward, grabbing the man who had been scorched by the molten glass, and dragged him away.

The sprinklers put out any incidental fires caused by the main source of the conflagration, which was now sizzling in a quick death high above Danny's head. It was obvious to Danny that a tragedy had been averted only by the safety system because many of the customers and staff were still crawling around in the mess on the floor, half blind and terrified. One or two enterprising shoplifters were stuffing things into pockets they could only know by feel. Cop though he was, Danny couldn't be bothered to arrest anyone. He was still stunned by what had happened.

What *had* happened? The guy had been running away from *him*, Danny Spitz, and then the poor bastard had internally combusted. Danny was too familiar with the scene to put it down to a coincidental phenomenon, a freak of nature. Someone had *made* that guy explode, just the way the angel used to burn demons in San Francisco six years ago.

Looking around him, it seemed to Danny that nobody was seriously hurt and, anyway, the paramedics were beginning to arrive. As he moved towards the doors, he heard someone mention something about terrorists but Danny knew better.

When he got out on to the street, Petra was there, ashen-faced. Danny, soaking wet from the sprinklers and dripping water, stared at her.

'Did you see it?' he asked. 'Were you here?'

'I – I just got here,' she said.

'Who did this?' asked Danny, gesturing back at the havoc inside the store.

'I think it must have been the archangel, don't you?' Petra said. 'I mean, isn't that the way it used to happen?'

'You mean when the angel was around? Yeah. I once saw the angel do that to a whole sidewalk café. Me and Dave were blown out on to the street when the place exploded. I think what saved the store here was that the guy was in the elevator. I hate to think what would have happened if he'd been walking through the drapery department.'

'The fire might have got out of control,' Petra replied.

'Might have? It *would* have – even if the sprinkler system had kicked in straight away. That was some human torch up there.'

'He wasn't human,' said Petra, quickly.

Danny stared intently at her, aware that water was overflowing the tops of his shoes.

'Not human? I keep forgetting you have this psychic connection. What was he, then? I suppose it's too much to hope that those are the embers of our old pal Manovitch, hissing away up there.'

'I'm afraid it wasn't Manovitch. It was just a demon.'

'Just a plain ole demon, huh?' Danny spluttered as the water dribbled from his bald patch down his chin. 'All that fuss for a common ole demon. Wouldn't you guess it? A deserter, eh, from the battlefields of Armageddon?'

'That's right,' said Petra. 'You know about them, don't you?'

'I used to have a good buddy among 'em, a demon called Malloch.'

'You had a fallen angel for a friend? A deserter from Satan's armies?'

'Well, I guess I'm overdoing it a little. He wasn't quite a *friend*. More of an ally, when we were trying to get rid of a mutual enemy. Poor bastard got incinerated by the angel. Actually, I think the angel had fallen himself by then, so it was one demon against another. There was this fancy trap rigged up – a fluorescent light tube filled with petroleum – and poor old Malloch was underneath when it was switched on . . .'

Stan had finally arrived at the doors with the car.

'Did we get him already?' asked Stan.

'Nah, just a common or garden demon is all,' replied Danny. 'Nobody important. Take us back to the hotel, willya? I got to get out of these wet clothes. We'll talk on the way.'

In the car, Petra said, 'The death of a demon *is* of little importance. It's Manovitch we want.'

'I know that,' said Danny, 'but I still want a debrief on this one. I'm still not sure exactly what happened.'

'I told you what happened,' said Petra, turning the full force of her brown eyes upon him. 'The archangel reached out and destroyed a fallen angel.'

'Why would he want to do that?' asked Stan. 'At all our briefings after 'ninety-six, we were told the world was crawling with demons, but they were relatively harmless – just villains on the run, so to speak, no more dangerous than a pimp or a pickpocket. That's what I heard.'

'You're right, Stan,' said Danny, patting the other man on the shoulder with a wet hand. 'Stan's right. The world is full of damn demons. Why would the archangel want to kill that one especially?'

'Destroy, not *kill*,' corrected Petra.

'Semantics,' Danny murmured. 'It was still a creature that could have been left alone.'

'When the archangel is told of the presence of a demon, then he destroys it.'

Danny looked at Petra. 'Who told him? You?'

She didn't answer this, but stared out of the car window.

'Anyway,' said Stan from the driver's seat, aware of a certain tension, 'that was some Roman candle, eh? What a way to go. Bonfire night.'

'Bonfire night?' questioned Danny.

Petra turned to look at him again. She wiped his face tenderly with a little lace handkerchief that smelled as if it had been dipped in the pools of heaven. It would have driven Danny crazy, had he been alone with her. He remembered the black silk underwear, flimsy and smooth, that smelled of the same perfume. He recalled wanting to drown in that fragrance just a few hours earlier.

'Bonfire night,' she confirmed. 'November the fifth. It's when we let off fireworks and burn the effigy of a man who tried to blow up the Houses of Parliament.'

'How long has this pagan ceremony been going on?' Danny asked.

'Since 1605,' answered Petra, smiling. 'Guy Fawkes was a member of the plot to destroy the Government at the time – the Gunpowder Plot we call it.'

'Come back, Guy Fawkes, all is forgiven,' said Danny. 'He could blow up Congress any time he chooses. Just at this moment the Republicans are in.'

'You're a Democrat?'

'You betcha. So you British have been burning the poor bastard's image every year for *four hundred years*? Four hundred times the guy has gone up in flames, just for trying to get rid of a few politicians? Hell, we've lost several presidents and nobody burns their assassins.'

'You're not as pagan as we are – or as unforgiving, obviously,' Petra said. 'When someone has a go at the upper classes here, they pay for it dearly. You can kill a peasant and no one bothers much, but when anyone has the audacity to attempt an assassination of the gentry there is a regular annual reminder of his fate, in case any other upstart wishes to try their luck.'

At that moment the car arrived back at the hotel and Danny

sloshed his way into the foyer. He took one look at the elevator, declined and went by the stairs. When he was in a hot bath, Petra came to scrub his back. That fragrance wafted over him again and sent him into dreamland.

Chapter Ten

Delia Marcole had been in the pits of the depraved and had always managed to emerge whole. Her faith, her utter conviction in the power of Good, had kept her clean. Now approaching her mid-thirties she had worked in the drug-infested inner cities since she was twenty-three, offering charismatic religion in place of heroin, giving the addicted something to replace their reliance on the white stuff they said they needed. It was nasty, dangerous work, but Delia had a calling and she followed that calling unflinchingly.

Delia was not afraid of injury or death, not *mortally* afraid. Her work of saving people from their own failings was more important than her life. Some called her a saint, but she was modest enough to brush this aside, embarrassed by it. Indeed she had been threatened, beaten up, slashed by knives and had acid thrown in her face, and still she would not give up what she felt God wished her to do – to help the helpless. She was one of those who had dedicated her whole self to others and she did so with a shining spirit, full of love and light.

It was midnight and Delia had just been to a house in a dubious street south of the river. Some of the street-lights had been smashed and the road was in semi-darkness. She was aware that she was being followed.

The sound of her own shoes clopping on the pavement helped to steady her heart. It was a comforting sound. She prayed as she walked, talking to One she was certain always listened. When her nerve was steeled, at the end of the street, she turned to face her pursuer. It was a man, a young good-looking man, who stopped and stared at her in the pale jaundiced light of the last lamp in the street. He smiled at her. His smile did not reassure her. Delia had been in the business of prising good people away from evil people for so long that she could sense when she was confronted by malevolence.

She knew better than to ask questions of a pursuing male, who would use the questions to intimidate her.

Instead, she said simply, 'Go away.'

'Go away where?' said the young man, with that infuriatingly greasy smile still on his face. 'Go away with you?'

'I have no money,' Delia said carefully. 'Take this.'

She threw her handbag at him. He caught it deftly and tossed it back, playfully.

'I don't need that.'

She thought she knew then what he was after and strengthened herself, straightening her back and glaring.

He smirked. 'You're right,' he said, 'but I'm not going to take you by force – I'm not going to rape you.'

She shivered. 'What then?'

He produced a wad of notes from his overcoat pocket.

'There's five thousand pounds here. I want you to let me fuck you among the rubbish in that garden. Five thousand. You could do a lot with five thousand. Save a lot of junkies from flushing their lives down the pan.'

She stared at the money, bewildered. Why would he want *her*? She was not particularly attractive. Her critics called her frumpy. She was slightly overweight, with no figure to speak of, she had never had a pretty face and the acid had left the skin pitted, scarred and ugly. And why among the muck and dirt of an overturned dustbin? She had heard of many perversions, but this was the first time she had encountered one as strange as this.

'I don't understand,' she said.

He leaned against the lamp-post and stared at her. 'You're not afraid, are you? That's good. Well, never mind why I want it.'

There was something she had to know. She lifted her chin and asked the question which she felt was the key to his motives. 'What if I was to say yes, but that I didn't want the money?'

His face creased in a frown. 'No, I must *pay* you.'

71

She relaxed a little. Now she understood what was going on. Someone was trying to trap her into an act of prostitution. Some local pusher bent on getting rid of this nuisance of a woman who was destroying his drug trade. Someone who wanted to ruin her by having her snapped screwing in filth in a public place, for money, by some tabloid photographer. Well, he was going to be disappointed.

'No,' she said, and turned to walk away.

The young man grasped her arm. 'No, listen – I'll make this ten thousand, twenty thousand, whatever you ask.'

'Let me go.'

'Look around you,' said the man. 'See all these houses – see that estate over there. You can have it. I can give it to you. Just do as I ask. Let me take you, over there in the darkness. No one will see . . .'

'Except your photographer.'

He shook his head vigorously, his blond hair flopping over his forehead.

'No photographer. Just the two of us. I know what you're thinking. Yes, I am trying to corrupt you – but it's for *me*, no one else will know. Just me.'

She tried to peel his strong fingers away from her arm, wondering if she should scream. Instinctively, though, she knew that if she tried to attract attention, he would kill her. She felt this in her heart. She could see it in his eyes. He would kill her without any compunction whatsoever, like swatting a fly. There was no compassion behind those eyes, no mercy.

'Don't try to run,' he said. 'It won't do you any good.'

'I know. You want to hurt me. Kill me, then,' she said defiantly. 'I'm ready to die.'

He stared at her again, then let go her arm and laughed. 'You're right, you *are* ready. Well, I don't give people what they *want*. I take things they want. I give them what they don't want – but I'm not going to help you become a martyr. Go on, get away from me. Take your ugly goodness and light with you – it sickens me. It turns my stomach.'

She was still a little afraid of him but was now determined

72

to find out why he was targeting her. 'What will you do now?' she asked. 'Shall I pray for you?'

'*Pray* for me?' spat the young man in disgust. 'What I shall do now is find another like you and persuade her to do what I want . . . or him. I have to recharge my batteries.' He laughed. 'You don't know what I mean, do you, you silly bitch? You think I'm a pervert.'

He walked off down the street, and Delia knew that she had had a miraculous escape. She had been but a fraction away from death. He had let her live, on a whim. The strength in those fingers told her he could have crushed her skull like a rotten apple had he so wished. It was a miracle for which she thanked God and then she hurried away.

She *did* know what he meant, even if she was a 'silly bitch' – she knew what the young man was after. He was a nefarious creature of the night: one of the Devil's brood. It was nothing to do with satisfying a sexual appetite. It was to do with *power*. Not him exercising power over her, but generating the power of evil by corrupting the good. She was nothing but a symbol to him, one of the icons of Goodness which he wished to desecrate to increase his potency, his power to perform necromancy.

Once he had debased her, contaminated her goodness, he would have killed her, she realized.

She hurried on, conscious of the sound of her own shoes on the flagstones.

Chapter Eleven

The debriefing for the day was in the Jasmine Suite, a room in the hotel set aside for the group's use. Everyone was present, even the two drivers, Stan Gates and Rajeb Patel. Danny began by telling the story of the demon who had been flash-fired that afternoon.

Dave winced as the story unfolded, remembering his own wife and child. Although he was now in love with Vanessa, the wounds of only six years ago were still raw. Department-store fires meant the recurrence of an age-old nightmare.

'. . . the next thing I knew,' said Danny, 'Petra was standing in the doorway.'

'Did you see this, er, demon?' Lloyd asked Petra.

'I was the first to notice it – just as the demon realized what I was . . .'

'*What* you are?' said Lloyd, frowning.

'Yes, my connection with the archangel. The demon sensed me there. I knew what it was – I can *feel* these things. I knew it was a demon. Then it ran away and Danny chased it. I followed a little later.'

Lloyd turned on Stan Gates. 'What about you, Sergeant?'

Stan was clearly not comfortable with all this talk of the supernatural and he looked as if he would rather be chasing down *real* villains, real people who didn't explode in white fire. Stan Gates liked haring around in a fast car with the siren blaring, knowing the man he was chasing was flesh and blood. He shifted uncomfortably in his chair, making it creak and setting Lloyd's teeth on edge.

'Well?' said Lloyd, more sharply than he intended.

'Ah, I saw the, er, victim – long black overcoat, greasy hair plastered over his scalp, funny-looking eyes. He was standing on the pavement staring at us, as if he recognized someone.

I thought at the time we had our man, that the presence of Sergeant Spitz had flushed him out, but the young lady's knocked that on the head. I didn't get out of the car – I've been told to stay in the car – so I didn't witness the, er, combustion.'

Lloyd said to Petra, 'You're absolutely positive this wasn't Manovitch.'

'Absolutely. Just as I'm sure the victim wasn't mortal either.'

Dave interrupted. 'Have we any reason to doubt that Petra here *is* in communication with the archangel? I just want to be sure she's not some fake medium trying to make a name for herself.'

Danny rose to Petra's protection, 'Hey—'

'No, listen, Friar Tuck, we all know you've been grabbed by the balls by this mystical young woman, but that doesn't mean she's on the level. She could even be fooling herself. We don't have any proof, do we?'

'No, *you* listen, Mother Teresa,' Danny said. 'Have a little faith, willya. Live up to your nickname.'

'Gentlemen, gentlemen,' said Lloyd. 'Let's not get overexcited. I'm personally satisfied that Petra has the power she says she has, but, of course, Lieutenant Peters is entitled to doubt. Now, let's look at the overall situation so far. We've got a vicious and wanton dead soul somewhere out there in the suburbs. So far as we know he's killed several people, but he has to remain hidden. On the other side we also have an archangel – only second from the bottom in the hierarchy of angels. Angels are divided into nine orders. In the first circle are seraphim, cherubim and thrones, in the second, dominions, virtues and powers, with principalities, archangels and angels in the third. What happens if this archangel fails? Perhaps a higher order will be sent, possibly from the first circle. What happens if a seraph comes down to destroy Manovitch?'

'Goodbye, planet?' said Danny.

Lloyd nodded gravely. 'So you see, we *have* to get him. Now, can we ask Petra how patient the archangel is likely to be?'

'The archangel says it's come down to earth to protect the conference from Manovitch.'

'Rock and roll,' said Dave, sarcastically. 'But this still doesn't prove who *you* are. You could be a demon for all we know – you're pretty enough. I guess there are such things as female demons, am I right, Friar Tuck? Succubi they call them, don't they?'

'Dave, don't push it,' said Danny. 'I know you're feeling sore because of me and Petra.'

'Sore,' Dave growled. 'Why should I be sore? I'm trying to protect you, you dope. We don't know a thing about this woman,' he stared directly at Petra, 'except what we've been told. Personally, I'm sceptical, and I want to see some proof of who or what she is before we go on.'

Lloyd asked, 'How do the rest of you feel?' Then to Petra, 'Forgive me, my dear, we do have to settle this.'

'Of course,' she replied, her features passive.

Stan Gates said quietly, 'I'm with the lieutenant. I'm old-fashioned. I need a little proof.'

Rajeb Patel nodded, to show that he felt the same way.

Petra said, 'Well you're not going to get it, Lieutenant, because I don't need to prove myself to anyone, least of all you. You'll have to take my word for it, just as everyone else does, and that's that.'

With those words, she rose from her chair and left the room.

Chapter Twelve

A man was standing on Westminster Bridge, looking down into the Thames. There was nothing very striking about his appearance: he was a grey-looking man in a grey suit. The suit was rumpled, as was the collar of his tieless shirt. His whole dishevelled aspect radiated despair: he was a man whose chronic depression had led him to the brink of a watery death, and he was about to step over that brink. A cold grey morning is a good time for a bitter, grey man to commit suicide: it gives him all the encouragement he needs to end his miserable life.

In his estimation there was nothing very fair about the city around him. Its majesty did not touch him, the sleeping houses did not move him, and though its mighty heart was lying still, Walter's dull soul could pass it by without a second glance. Only the sweet-willed, gliding river interested him.

Walter Rainforth sighed, thinking about his business, how it had flourished in the early years, and how it had begun to shrink in the nineties, until now it was in deep, irretrievable debt, ripe for the receivers, and Walter a bankrupt. Walter was a proud man, whose father had told him he was going nowhere, and now that curse had come true. Walter hated his father being right, but was glad the old man was dead and unable to witness his son's final humiliation. Walter wondered whether the old bastard was waiting for him, laughing, on the other side. That was a *really* depressing thought.

He climbed up on the parapet of the bridge and sat on the edge. Walter's wife would not receive any life insurance, because it would be suicide, but Walter didn't like his wife much, anyway. She had deserted him for a butcher five years ago. Walter had cried when she left but he had not changed his will. She was his only surviving relative. He had no one else to leave his debts to, apart from a stray dogs' or cats' home. Walter hated animals more than he hated his wife. It had to be said that just then Walter hated every creature that walked the selfish, remorseless earth – even himself.

'Hey, you!'

Walter turned to see a police car cruising slowly on the other side of the road. A constable was leaning out of the window. He fluttered a hand at Walter. 'Don't be daft, mate,' cried the policeman. 'You want to fall in?'

'Yes,' said Walter.

The police car stopped.

'You been on the piss, or what?' called the policeman. 'Don't be silly. Can't be as bad as all that.'

'It is,' said Walter. 'In fact it's worse.'

The policeman got out of his car and began to walk over the road.

'I'm going to jump,' warned Walter.

The policeman stopped in his tracks and retraced his footsteps back to the car. He said something to the driver, who picked up a microphone and spoke into it. Walter knew they were summoning assistance and he edged his bottom down off the parapet, gradually sliding towards the space between the bridge and the flowing waters below.

He would have jumped then, if the sun hadn't come up over the horizon, but it was such a beautiful sight it stopped him in mid-slide. He gripped the concrete and stared. It had been a long time since he had seen a big red disc rise out of the distant earth and send its rays over the waking world. Its roseate light caught the clouds and the roofs of the buildings. Even the archangel's dome had a pink tinge to it.

'"Red sky in the morning, shepherds' warning,"' muttered Walter. 'Well, it won't rain on me,' he added, with a certain bitter satisfaction.

He stared down again, at the now scarlet waters below.

'You all right?' called the policeman. 'Don't do anything silly.'

There was a barge below Walter, full of gas containers, going up-river. Walter winced. He might have jumped and just broken his back on those metal bottles, thereby making a bad situation a lot worse. Death was his goal, not hospital with a fractured spine.

The bargeman was looking down into the water, a puzzled expression on his face. Despite the situation, Walter was curious. The river was his final destination and if it perplexed someone he wanted to know why.

'What's the matter?' Walter called.

The bargeman looked up, and said, 'The water's all red.'

'It's the sun,' said Walter.

'No, it ain't,' replied the bargeman. 'It's the water – it's all thick and gooey. Smell's sickly-sweet too. It's *blood*. I swear it is. There's blood flowing down from up-river. What are you doin' up there, anyway? You better be careful, mate, you might fall.'

Blood? Walter gripped the edge of the parapet, clawing with his fingers to stop himself from going further. He could smell the blood now. Someone must be slaughtering cattle or something, up near Marlow, out in the country somewhere. Walter didn't want to drown in cow's blood. That was *disgusting*.

'Help me,' he called to the policeman. 'Help me, I'm slipping.'

The policeman, who had been edging forward in any case, dashed across the road. He caught hold of Walter's jacket just as Walter's bottom slipped off the parapet. Walter screamed. The policeman hung on, still clutching the bottom edge of the jacket.

Walter hung above the sluggish flow of the bloody Thames, his arms forced upwards by the weight of his body into a V-shape above his head. The policeman was leaning over the parapet, clinging desperately to the tail-flap of the jacket. Walter's arms began to slip down as he dangled there, gradually turning the sleeves inside out.

'Stop me!' screeched Walter. 'I don't want to die like this!'

The bargeman was staring upwards, amazed at the sight above, then he disappeared under the bridge on the stern of his craft.

79

The policeman tried to pull Walter upwards, but Walter slid further down his sleeves, until he was almost out of them, his fingers clutching the cuffs. He tried to get a grip with his shoes on the stonework, but just as his feet found a ledge, he heard the sleeves ripping away from the main body of the coat. He remembered that his business had been on the downward slope for so long, he had taken to buying cheap clothes from the market stalls.

'*Rotten* jacket,' he whined, as he fell forwards.

They were the last words he spoke before he fell into the sticky gore below. He disappeared under the surface of the Thames, swallowing thick gobbets of blood as he went. Then he kicked out, finding the liquid warm and buoyant, and rose to the surface. It was *horrible*. He hoped it was indeed animal blood, which was bad enough, but to be wallowing in *human* blood – that would have been unthinkable. Yet he *did* think of it.

'Oh, God!' he shrieked. 'Get me out.'

He swallowed another couple of mouthfuls as he rolled over on to his stomach. He began to float on the current. Then he felt something hard and sharp on the back of his shirt collar, and almost choked as he was dragged to the edge of a boat. Hands reached down and clutched at his slick red body, to haul him on board a river police craft.

'All right, we got you,' said a man. 'Are you all OK? Not hurt anywhere, are you?'

Walter sat up, coughing, on the deck and looked down at himself, covered from head to toe in gore.

'How the hell would I know?' he said.

'You all know *that* much of your Bible,' said Petra. 'You know the story of Moses and the Exodus. What we have here is a copycat. Manovitch is showing us his power.'

'The ten plagues of Ancient Egypt!' said Mother Teresa.

Friar Tuck said, 'With nine to come.'

From Oxford to the Nore, the River Thames ran thick and red. At the source, in the Cotswold Hills, near Cirencester, it was crystal water, but somewhere around Oxford it changed in colour and consistency to a liquid which resembled blood and owned all the chemical ingredients of blood.

Within the rest of London, all the smaller tributaries, most of them underground streams, were also blood. The Serpentine, the fountains in Trafalgar Square and elsewhere, all ponds, lakes, the rivulets creeping through charnel houses, the channels and gutters, the fluid that flowed from taps and toilets, all, all was blood, everywhere, blood. It gummed the pipes, it clogged the drains, it killed the koi in the marble pools of the rich. It filled the swimming pools and water tanks on the rooftops and sprayed red liquid from the automatic watering devices in parks and gardens. London was drenched in blood.

The only people who escaped the plague, having an isolated source of water, were those at the Meeting.

Lloyd told the others. 'The official communiqué states that an unusually fast-flowing Thames has scoured a hitherto unknown bank of red mud, which is mixing with the water.'

'Wasn't that the same excuse Pharaoh's advisers used the first time round?' said Dave, sourly.

'It's only a communiqué,' said Lloyd. 'Nobody believes it. People need something to talk about while they're queuing to get water from the tankers from outside the city.'

'Can you actually water the whole of London?'

'We're using Los Angeles as a model. You'll remember that three years ago the reservoirs there were poisoned by terrorists? If Los Angeles can supply water from the outside, then so can London. Besides, we don't expect it to last long.'

'What's the truth, then, about the source of the blood?' asked Dave.

The Archdeacon winced. 'The river at Oxford is choked with bodies – human remains – the blood is human. The reservoirs, too, have corpses floating in them. The gore seems real enough, except—'

'Except what?' asked Danny, feeling sick, remembering he had taken a drink of water in the middle of the night without bothering to turn the light on.

'Except that there's no one missing. There would have had

to have been a massacre to produce that many dead, a terrible slaughter, a *bloodbath*. The police say there were only the usual two or three murders during the night and the bodies are accounted for.'

Petra said, 'It's necromancy. Somehow Manovitch has managed to create enough power to produce those bodies out of nowhere. Satan has supplied him with his blood.'

'Then they're *not* real,' Danny said, relieved.

'Of course they're real,' snapped Petra. 'They're *there*, aren't they? That's still blood in your glass.'

Lloyd murmured, 'They'll be some deaths, anyway – disease . . .'

People had been screaming at Lloyd down the telephone – very important people – telling him to get some results soon, or else. He wasn't quite sure what 'or else' meant but he didn't like the sound of it.

'We don't seem to be getting anywhere,' he said testily. 'We've got to step things up a little. Has anyone got any ideas? Petra, why isn't Manovitch taking the bait? Is he frightened of us, do you think?'

Petra shook her head. 'He's not frightened of us, he's frightened of the archangel. He'll try to remain hidden, hoping for an opportunity to get at Dave and Danny. Revenge is secondary with him. What we've got to hope for is that he sees a chance and takes a risk.'

'But', said the frustrated Lloyd, 'we've advertised their whereabouts everywhere, even on television.'

'Perhaps he's living in some hole, some sewer somewhere, without access to such devices. He's a fiend, a dead soul used to the abominable conditions of hell, filth and squalor we can't even imagine, and any situation he's living in down here must be paradise in comparison. He certainly wouldn't be in some luxury hotel, with a TV in every room.'

'What about the newspapers? You can pick a newspaper out of a rubbish bin.'

'Have you thought that perhaps he can't read? Not only does the spirit regress in hell, but the fine intellect too. His mind has deteriorated into a savage twisted thing, the mind of a beast of darkness, and his former learning will be lost to it. His cunning will have increased tenfold – he's a warrior and a hunter – but he's probably an academic dunce.'

'He's not much of an opponent if he's illiterate,' sniffed Lloyd, who was a bit of a snob about education, having gone to Harrow himself.

'Tell that to Attila the Hun,' growled Dave.

Lloyd saw his point.

Danny said, 'While he's skulking around in dark corners, we'll only come across him by chance. It would be nice if he got impatient and went back to where he came from.'

Petra looked shocked. 'That would be disastrous,' she said. 'Inept as he is down here, Manovitch is a terrible force on the spiritual battlefield. If the angels are overpowered in the war on the plains of Armageddon, then Good will be lost, and Evil will rule the Earth.'

'I thought that couldn't happen,' said Danny. 'Not in the long run. I thought that eventually Evil *has* to lose.'

'Yes, *eventually* Good will triumph, but do you want to spend the next ten million years under the domination of Satan and his crew? You have innumerable generations of humans to think of, not just yourselves. We have to keep Manovitch down here, where he's vulnerable, however much it hurts.'

'There's a lot of evil in the world at the moment – wars and wrongful imprisonment, torture, we hear of new terrible things happening every day,' said Lloyd.

'That's *nothing*, nothing to what it will be like if the battle is lost on Armageddon. There'll be no force to stop the demons then. They'll come pouring down in their ten thousands. We all know there are a few here already, who cause little trouble, but that's because they're deserters, hiding from Satan as well as Satan's enemies. Victorious troops will be another thing altogether. Not even the weather will be left alone. It'll become unbearably hot in places, and bitterly cold in others. There'll be no respite, no temperate climates. They'll rape the earth and leave mountains of dead festering in the heat.

They'll destroy everything and put mankind back a million years. We'll be eating each other . . .'

'I think we get the picture.' Lloyd sighed. 'I wish we didn't get dragged into these otherworldly battles, but I suppose Petra's right. We must keep trying. Has anyone any new ideas to add?'

It appeared that no one had.

'One thing we ought to bear in mind,' said Petra.

'What's that?' asked Lloyd.

'The last plague is the most terrible. We've simply *got* to find Manovitch before then.'

Chapter Thirteen

Dave had taken to slipping from his bed and walking the streets at night. He guessed that Manovitch would feel more secure during the night hours and would therefore be abroad between the setting and rising of the sun. It made sense, then, to go out and seek the enemy during the hours when that enemy was on the streets, also searching.

In the last few days disease had swept through London, caused by the fetid blood which was still to be found everywhere. The hospitals were full of the sick, of whom some had already died. Many more would die. It was a revolting and insidious way to terrorize a city.

The holy men and women were holding fast, still thrashing out their differences around the table, though the situation was fragile and could shatter at any moment.

Dave was glad Vanessa was not in London with him. She had long ago acknowledged that he worked in his own way and neither wanted nor would tolerate any interference with his job as a policeman. Their relationship, even after several years, was still one that acknowledged the independence of the other. However, he knew that when he went out stalking the streets Vanessa would lie awake worrying until he returned to bed.

Two nights after the last of the blood had finally trickled out to sea from the river, Dave went on the prowl again. It was two a.m. when he was walking along a street in Kensington. It never got really dark in London, with the archangel's light acting as a lamp, but Dave had found that at night, without the heavy traffic and crowded streets, you could walk a hell of a lot further in a shorter time. Kensington was quiet and Dave could hear his own footsteps on the pavement.

Shadows were chasing each other down the alleys, where

several street people lay on cardboard mattresses covered in newspapers and ragged blankets. Cats, and one or two stray dogs, moved like pieces of darkness themselves, travelling between waste-bins, hoping for a discarded take-away. Occasionally a man or woman, or both, came down the street, hurrying to or from a party. Patrol cars went by, often at a fast pace, policing the city.

Because he did not know where to look, he looked everywhere, hoping for the sight of something unusual. At two thirty the wind began to rise, lifting the litter and sending it scuttling like live creatures down the concrete and asphalt. Trees rustled their leaves and creaked their branches. A sickle moon came out from behind a cloud, paled to distant silver by the light from the archangel. All very normal, all very usual.

Dave sighed, losing concentration for a few minutes, thinking about the absurdity of the assignment. There he was, stuck in a hotel at night, cruising the streets by day, looking for someone none of them could recognize. There was Danny, infatuated by a weird woman, thinking he had found love at last. And what about that guy Lloyd, becoming more anxious by the day, getting on everyone's back? It was all a big mess, with no real way to sort it out.

A piece of grit hit the back of Dave's neck.

What was that? Where had it come from? A bird? Birds didn't normally fly at night.

Dave stared upwards, scanning the windows and ledges above him. It all seemed peaceful enough. Then he thought he saw something – a dark shape – creeping across the rooftops. Was that a man up there? Dave slipped into a shop doorway, out of sight, and continued to stare at the roofs opposite. Yes! There he was again, slipping silently over the tiles, vaulting a parapet. Now he was on the flat roof of a store.

Dave thought about chasing the figure on his own and then wisely decided against it. It was not his personal safety he was concerned about, although that came into it, but that on his own he might lose his quarry. He needed back-up. It was important to run down the prey and corner it, where they could burn it. He shuddered a little at the thought.

Dave took his phone out of his pocket. He called Danny's number, then listened impatiently, as it rang, knowing instinctively that no one was going to answer. Next he called the network number, which was supposed to ring all the phones – Danny's, Lloyd Smith's, Stan Gates's, Petra's and Rajeb Patel's – and this time a welcome click told him that someone had answered.

'This is Patel,' said a voice, sleepily.

Dave said, 'Rajeb, it's Dave Peters. I've been out walking the streets and I've seen something. Get over here as quick as you can . . .' Dave stared about him and saw a sign a hundred yards up the street. 'Holland Park Road,' he said.

'That's W8, isn't it? Don't worry, I'll look it up on the way. Be with you in about ten.'

Rajeb lived in a small bedsit by Gunnersbury Park. He switched on the side lamp and jumped out of bed naked. As he was pulling on his underpants, Daphne woke up.

'What the hell are you doing?' she said.

'Got a call,' said Rajeb, struggling with his jumper. 'Look, dial 702 3658 for me, quick, woman.'

'Don't call me *woman*,' she said, sitting up. 'I'm not your skivvy.'

He grinned at her, melting her.

She picked up his portable, dialled the number, and when it was ringing handed it to him. Rajeb took the phone and barked instructions into it. When he was sure they had got the message, he flipped it closed and stuck it in his back pocket.

Daphne's blonde hair formed a curtain over her white freckled breasts. He couldn't help looking, even though he was in a hurry, and as always she noticed him staring.

'No bloody good now, mate, is it? You should have thought of that last night.'

'I was tired,' he said. 'I was out all day.'

'You should try teaching brats in Brixton how to add up,' she snorted, 'then you'd know about tired.'

Daphne was a school teacher. They had met in India while both were on backpacking holidays. Daphne admitted to Rajeb now that she had teamed up with him because she thought he was local and could help her with the language. In fact, having been born in Stepney like his parents before him, he didn't speak anything but his own brand of English.

'No Hindi?' she had said. 'No Urdu?'

'Nope.' He had smiled at her. 'Nor Tamil neither – shame, ain't it?'

'*Isn't* it. Bloody hell, you don't even speak English.'

'Yes, I bloody do.'

'Not correctly.'

Rajeb was a smart young man, though, and had had these conversations before. 'English is a dynamic language,' he told her. 'It changes with use. You use it to communicate. If everyone says *ain't* then ain't is correct. And everyone *I* know says ain't.'

'Everyone *you* know must be plebs.'

'Plebs?' he had said in mock horror. 'What kind of word is that? That ain't English, is it?'

She had faltered, realizing she had been caught out. 'It's – it's Latin, or at least, half a Latin word. Plebeians. They were the Roman lower-class citizens. The upper class were called patricians.'

'Ah, well, that's where you've got me wrong,' he told her, surprising her again, ''cos I'm a patrician. Me granddad was a rajah.'

Eagerly she asked, 'Was he really?'

'Nope, but you're easily impressed, ain't you? You should be ashamed of yourself. You're a bloody snob.'

When later he told her he was a London copper, she was even more mortified, but by then she'd fallen in love with him, so she couldn't do much about it. She had thought about not calling him when she got back to England, but soon she had found herself dreaming about his slim tanned body, his thick black hair, and his ready smile. She yearned for the sound of his voice murmuring in her ear and for the sound of his laughter. Rajeb had a pleasant, easy-going personality, which was a settling influence.

So she had called him on his work number.

'You know why I've telephoned you, don't you?' she said, anxious to retain a few vestiges of pride.

'Yes,' he said, infuriatingly, 'it's because I'm a nice bloke.'

'No, no, it's because I've got something of yours – that book you loaned me.'

'I lent you a book?'

'Yes, and I want to return it.'

Rajeb laughed down the phone. 'That's a good trick, love, I'll have to remember that. Keep something, so you can ring them up later and pretend you want to return it. Come on, admit it, it's my body you're after—'

'It certainly is *not*,' she yelled down the phone. 'In fact it wouldn't upset me in the least if I never saw you again.'

'Just a minute,' he said. She fumed while there was some murmuring going on in the background, then he was back.

'You were saying?'

'I *said*,' she growled, 'that I hope you drop dead. I thought the book was important to you and I've taken time out to ring you up, then I get all this rubbish back.'

'You're not in love with me?'

'Certainly not.'

'That's a shame because I'm very much in love with you – I've been trying to find you ever since I came back. You gave me a false number.'

This stopped her in her tracks, but her terrible pride would not allow her to admit her own feelings. She told him she had given him false information on purpose, to keep him out of her life, and then she slammed down the phone and burst into tears.

Ten minutes later her doorbell rang.

She opened the door to find Rajeb standing there, grinning.

'How – how did you . . . ?' she faltered, wiping away the tears.

'Had the call traced,' he said, his smile broadening. 'Clever dick, eh? I ain't a copper for nothing, am I? Hey,' he added in a concerned tone, 'you've been crying over me.'

'I've been peeling onions,' she snapped.

'Like hell you have,' he replied, and stepped inside the flat. Within ten minutes they were making love on her bed and within a fortnight she had moved into his bedsit. That was a year ago, and she hadn't regretted it – yet.

Rajeb left her sitting up in bed and took the stairs three at a time. His car was parked behind the flats. Soon he was speeding through the backlit night towards Holland Park Road.

Dave was standing on the corner.

'Where is he?' said Rajeb, jumping out of the car.

'Up there on the rooftops somewhere,' answered Dave. 'Did you call out the guard?'

'They're on their way,' replied Rajeb, 'but they may take a while. Shall we go up after him?'

'I think we'd better – we don't want to lose him now.'

There were no external fire escapes, so they went to the nearest doorway and kicked the door off its hinges. They ran through a hallway and up some back stairs, not sure where they were going but happy as long as it was upwards. A man appeared on a landing. He looked frightened.

'What do you want?'

'Police,' snapped Rajeb. 'How do we get on the roof?'

'You can't, not really. Out of the bedroom window, I suppose.'

They were shown to the bedroom and Dave jumped on to the bed of a terrified-looking middle-aged woman to reach a window on the other side. The curlered female crossed her chest with her arms as Dave stepped over her. 'Bert?' she whined.

'It's all right, love, they're coppers,' Bert told her.

Dave opened the window and looked down. The drop was three storeys. He eased himself out on to the windowsill and gripped the gutter above his head with both hands. Then he pulled himself upwards, praying that the gutter wouldn't rip away from the eaves. It didn't. Soon he was dragging himself up the slope of the roof on mossy tiles. Rajeb followed behind, more youthful and agile and a lot quicker than Dave. They crawled up, combat style, until they reached the peak.

Just beyond the roof they were traversing was a series of flat roofs. It was on the third of these that Dave had seen the figure.

'Over there,' he whispered to Rajeb.

Both men took out their weapons and eased off the safety catches. They slid down the other side of the tiles to land on the tarmac seal of the first flat roof.

Dave said softly, 'I'm going to close in on him – you stay behind me, about twenty yards – if I miss, then you'll have to nail him yourself. Don't let him get in close. He'll snap your neck within a second. If he's a demon he's got the strength of twenty men.'

'Right,' said Rajeb, a croak in his voice. 'Got it.'

Dave began to walk forward, slowly, his gun held in both hands and pointed to the front. No sound was coming from the third roof, but Dave had been watching it ever since he had caught his first glimpse of the sinister figure in black, and he was certain that whoever it was had not left the scene – not by way of the roofs. There were four large vent shafts, each contained by a wooden slatted housing. Any one of them could have hidden two or three men.

The closer Dave got, the more cautious he became. He had seen the strangled, mutilated victims of Manovitch's crusade, and he didn't want to be one himself. He didn't want his arms and legs scattered to the four points of the compass and his head jammed on a weather-vane, his open mouth catching winds from an easterly direction.

He glanced behind him once, to see if Rajeb was in place, and was pleased to see the young cop on the ball. Rajeb was exactly where he should be, his weapon at the ready. Dave began to close in on the third housing.

Suddenly, one of the slats opened, and a figure slipped out of the vent on to the rooftop.

Chapter Fourteen

'Hold it!' cried Dave. 'I've got a gun!'

He suddenly realized that an ordinary gun would not impress Manovitch. A demonstration was needed. He aimed at the far side of the roof and pulled the trigger. The gun bucked. A housing exploded in flame, sending slats of burning wood spinning through the air. Within a second or two the whole ventilator unit was blazing as furiously as any bonfire that ever burned a witch.

'Don't shoot!' screamed the figure, coming out from behind the air vent with his hands high. 'Don't shoot, for Christ's sake.'

'Step forward!' barked Dave, a sinking feeling in his gut. 'Now lie flat on the roof, arms and legs out.'

The figure in black did as he was told. Rajeb moved up beside Dave and while Dave continued to cover the figure on the ground, Rajeb went over to him. The vent was burning like a pyre now, its huge flame reaching up into the night. The silvery light from the archangel to the east was supplemented by this red, roaring torch. It was virtually daylight on the roof with both lamps.

'Shit!' cried Rajeb. 'It's Mort Darthy – a bloody cat burglar.'

'Damn,' muttered Dave, 'I somehow knew we hadn't got Manovitch.'

'You nearly killed me,' shrieked Mort, from his flat position on the roof. 'You nearly burned me alive, you bastards.'

'Shouldn't be out thieving, Darthy,' said Rajeb, 'then you wouldn't get caught up in these things. We thought you was a terrorist. In fact, we still ain't sure. For all we know, you could be the man we're after.'

'I ain't done nuthin' like that. I just been—' He stopped. 'I was just up here for some fresh air.'

92

'Yeah, sure you were,' growled Dave, bitterly disappointed. 'An honest man like you?'

Mort glanced up at Dave and said, 'A Yank? What's a bleedin' Yank doin' shooting at *me*? You ain't in bloody New York now, you know. You need a reason to shoot people in this country. What'chu got there, anyway? A fuckin' rocket launcher?'

The housing crackled and spat as it burned, the old paint going up with a nice blue flame. There were sounds of activity down in the street below now. A police van had arrived with the special squad. There was also an ambulance and several fire engines. Rajeb went to the edge of the roof and yelled down, 'It's all right, we've got him in custody. Someone put this fire out.'

The firemen threw up ladders, unrolled hoses, scrambled all over the building. Soon the fire was under control. The uniformed police took over custody of Mort Darthy and Dave left Rajeb to fill them in on the details of the arrest. Lloyd arrived on the scene, looking tired. Finally, so did Danny.

'Better late than never,' grunted Dave. 'Was your grandfather ever in the Seventh Cavalry?'

'Lay off, Dave,' growled Danny. 'I came as soon as I got the call. I had to wait for Stan.'

Dave grudgingly acknowledged to himself that Danny did not know the area and therefore needed his driver.

'Yeah, well, don't forget what we're here for Danny. I appreciate you're having a good time with the princess, but this is a job we're on, not a vacation.'

'Don't ride me. I'm sorry I'm late. Jeez, you think I wanted to miss the action?'

'I don't know,' Dave replied.

Danny walked away and sulked. Lloyd came up to Dave and asked, 'I take it we got the wrong fiend.'

'Yeah, this was your everyday robber-rapist-murderer fiend – nothing special.'

'That's a shame,' said Lloyd. 'Still, I'm glad you're on the ball, Lieutenant. From what I hear, he could easily have been

Manovitch. I'm sure we're going to get more than one false alarm.'

'I hope not – it's wearing on the spirit.'

Dave was more depressed than his manner showed. The trouble was, incidents like this brought them not one iota closer to Manovitch. It wasn't a case of following police procedural methods, painstakingly going over the clues, putting in legwork and picking over minute results, inching your way forward. They would find Manovitch purely by chance – or he would find *them*. Lloyd was right, Dave could do this kind of thing a thousand times over, and still be no nearer to finding his quarry.

Lloyd drove him back to the hotel, where he immediately phoned Vanessa, needing to hear her voice. He told her what had happened over the last two days, including his escapades that night.

'I'm glad I'm not with you,' she said, 'but I'm no front-line swat trooper's wife.'

'Quite right too,' Dave said.

'I take it from the tone in your voice that you didn't catch Manovitch.'

Dave slipped between the sheets and imagined her long warm body next to his own. 'I don't intend to *catch* him – I want to blow him off the face of the planet.'

'OK, I'll rephrase that. I take it you didn't blow him off the face of the planet.'

Dave sighed. 'No, it was a cat burglar. Isn't that a dumb expression? *Cat* burglar? To *act* like a cat, I suppose, not to *steal* cats. To creep around on rooftops and fool cops into thinking you're a dead soul.'

Vanessa said, 'Is that what happened? You didn't – you didn't burn him alive, did you?'

'Naw – I can't do what they really want us to do – shoot first and ask questions later. It's not in me. I'm a good cop, for Christ's sake . . .'

'Mother Teresa.'

'Yeah, Mother Teresa, if you like, but I can't set fire to a man just on the off-chance that it'll be the fiend I'm looking

94

for. Manovitch – I'll send him to oblivion in a second, but I can't burn innocent people, not even criminals.'

'That's what I love about you, Dave Peters, but I'm scared too. Manovitch won't think twice about killing you. He'll kill a thousand innocent people if he thinks he'll get you before you get him. Your chivalric code might be the end of you.'

'Well, I had good back-up tonight.'

'Danny was there, too?'

'Danny?' Dave snorted. 'He was wenching. I had Rajeb Patel with me. He's a good man. Better than Danny right now. Danny's head's full of petticoats.'

Vanessa said, 'Don't be too hard on him, Dave. Danny's a good cop, you've always said that. He's just caught up in something at the moment. It could happen to the best.'

'Why choose *now* to lose his head?'

'He didn't choose the time – and I think it's his heart that he's lost, not his head.'

'It's damn well both as far as I'm concerned. Damn Friar Tuck. Why can't he be like the real Friar Tuck and just worry about his gut?'

Vanessa said, 'The real Friar Tuck probably chased choir boys.'

'Well, if Danny can't be there for me, I'll have to do without him, but right now I'm inclined to send him back to the States. Useless bum.'

'You wouldn't do that,' whispered Vanessa, 'so don't go fooling yourself, Dave.'

Dave knew she was right, but he was feeling savage towards Danny, and he indulged himself with the thought that *he* was the lieutenant, and Danny the sergeant, and if things got any worse between them, he damn well *would* send him home.

When Rajeb Patel got back to his bedsit, Daphne was sitting at the kitchenette table.

'You want some tea?' she asked. She was wearing the pink candlewick dressing-gown he hated so much. It always made her look so matronly and formidable when she was annoyed, and did even less for her when she wasn't. He didn't dare

95

tell her how he felt about it, though: Daphne was not a woman who took well to criticism.

'Yep, why not? Thanks.'

When he had a steaming mug in his hand, he asked her, 'Why are you up? It's only five.'

'I was worried about you, of course,' she said, fiercely. She sipped her tea as if she were in a hurry to get somewhere and was irritated by having to make conversation.

'Were you? Worried about *me*?' He grinned.

She glared at him. 'You're so stupid sometimes, Raj.'

That wiped the grin from his face. 'I'm sorry. It's me. I can't be any different. I can't be what you expect, Daphne, I can only be what I am. If you think you can change me, forget it. It doesn't work like that, you know. People can't change each other. They can compromise a little bit, but they can't be someone else. I have to treat things like this frivolously, or it doesn't work for me. I'm sorry it annoys you so much.'

She burst into tears. They streamed down her freckled face and dripped on to her dressing-gown. He got up and hugged her. Her 'crying' breath smelled sour and musty. That didn't bother him. Nothing intimate worried him.

'Look, girl,' he said. 'What're you trying to do? I was a copper when you met me. I don't want to be nothing else. I don't know how to be anything else. I wouldn't tell you not to be a school teacher, would I? You'd bash me if I did. I don't even dare tell you little things . . .'

She pulled her head away from his shoulder, her nose red and sniffly, her cheeks stained with tear-runs. 'What little things?' she asked, suspiciously.

'Well, just things that get on my nerves – same as some of the things I do get on yours.'

'Like what? What things?'

'That dressing-gown,' he blurted out. 'I hate it.'

She looked down at herself in amazement.

'My mother gave me this for Christmas, five years ago.'

'It don't matter, does it? I still hate it. I couldn't care less if the Dalai Lama blessed it first, or one of the three wise

96

men gave it to Jesus for his birthday. I'd still hate it. It makes you look like something out of a squalid soap.'

'Oh, does it?' she cried, hotly. She pulled it off and threw it on the floor. 'Right, you can tear it up for cleaning rags then, can't you? Go on.'

He reached down too eagerly for the offending item, intending to get to work on it instantly with a pair of kitchen scissors, but she snatched the dressing-gown back. 'On second thoughts, if I want to wear it, I bloody well will.'

'Shit – so close,' he muttered. Then he said, 'Bugger this, it's only a dressing-gown.'

He snatched it back again, ran to the window, opened it and threw the garment out. 'There,' he said, 'and good bloody riddance. You look like Cinderella now, instead of one of the bloody ugly sisters.'

Daphne stared at him, rage and horror fighting for control of her features, then she suddenly burst out laughing. 'You silly sod,' she cried. 'You silly dope.'

Rajeb always cooled down as quickly as he became heated.

He laughed loudly. 'Too right I am. We're like a couple of kids, ain't we? Fighting over a bloody dressing-gown? Come 'ere.' He went to her. She was dressed only in a low-necked T-shirt now – a longish one that she used as a nightie. There was a picture of Bugs Bunny on the front, chewing a carrot and asking, doc, er, what's up.

Rajeb kissed her slowly, smelling the sleep on her, and she melted into him. Her various odours always excited him. She had a thousand fragrances, all different, some weak, some strong, and almost every one turned him on. He pressed against her, the contact with her warm body giving him an erection. Then he reached down and pulled up the T-shirt to reveal her shapely form, squeezing the little puppy fat around the waist which he liked to tease her about. He bent his head and kissed her nipples one at a time, enjoying as always the geography of her body, the freckles like scattered constellations on the downward slopes of her breasts. This was a country he alone was allowed to explore and the privilege thrilled him.

He liked the contours, the blemishes as much as the smooth, pure stretches of skin. That small mole there, and that tiny scar, they were his discoveries. He knew her body even better than his own. He knew every crevice, every valley, every mount. He knew its dark forests, hiding untold pleasures. He knew its deep, folded, slippery places, where pleasures became ecstasies, where fantasies became realities for brief spurts of time. He knew where the orchids grew – their secret cups were his – and his fingers examined their silken petals, tenderly, gently.

'Just a minute,' she murmured in his ear, 'my bum's hurting – it's on the edge of the table.'

He realized he was pressing her back too hard and let her up. She went over to the bed and threw herself on it, lying on her back, the T-shirt still up around her armpits where, as a matter of principle, she did not shave. As always, her posture at such times sent a jolt of urgent need through Rajeb's loins, until he was almost beside himself with lust.

'Come on, then,' she smiled, as he struggled out of his clothes, 'hurry up, I'm going off the boil.'

Finally, all the armour was off and the knight bared to the flesh. He threw himself on the bed beside her. She pushed him on to his back and slowly lowered herself on him, her legs wide apart. 'I don't know who's skewering whom,' she murmured, 'but it's nice. I feel like a tropical fruit, all warm and damp.'

She knew talking would turn him on even more.

'Oh, God,' he murmured, closing his eyes as she lowered her breasts on to his face. 'You're so beautiful . . .'

They moved together then, their rhythms intuitive and instinctive, like the rhythms of nature.

Luckily they had both reached their climaxes before the telephone rang.

'Patel here,' Rajeb groaned into the portable. 'What?'

'Just wanted to say thanks,' said Dave Peters's voice. 'You did good tonight.'

'You don't know the half of it,' replied Rajeb, as he looked

up at Daphne, still astride him and grinning down at him.
'Not the bleedin' half of it, mate.'

'Not sure I understand, but thanks, anyway.'

'You're welcome,' said Rajeb.

Out in the street a bag lady discovered the cast away dressing-gown and decided it was her birthday.

Chapter Fifteen

Danny was missing his home city. He was missing Mario's restaurant, Fisherman's Wharf, Russian Hill, Chinatown, and Hunter's Point, all those familiar places. Danny was a home boy, born in Davis, but raised in San Francisco after his father got a job as a civilian worker at the Presidio. Lake Tahoe, LA, and Yosemite Park were the boundaries of his world and beyond these pales was the emptiness of outer space.

Danny was on his knees in church. He had meant to go to confession, but at the last moment he became shy. The priest was a foreigner, an Englishman – or maybe even an Irishman, Scotsman or Welshman – but he wasn't an American. More specifically, he wasn't from San Francisco. Danny didn't want to ask a priest who was not from San Francisco to forgive him his sins. It didn't seem right. His sins were the sins of a San Francisco cop, and a San Francisco priest, someone who understood how San Francisco cops functioned, what they had to go through, and the micro-climate they worked within, was the appropriate intermediary between him and God.

So, he prayed instead, and sat through some of the service, with Petra at his side. She was, he was thrilled to discover, a Catholic like himself. She had been schooled at a convent, in Birmingham – England, not Alabama – and though she told him the nuns had given her a hard time, she was still of the faith.

A little way into the service, Danny got up and went outside. Petra followed him a little later.

'What about mass?' she asked him.

He didn't answer this question. Instead he said, 'Is there anywhere we can get a cup of coffee?'

'There's a stall just down the street. It won't be very good coffee, though. Not what you're used to.'

'It'll do fine.'

They walked to the burger stall, just outside Embankment underground station, and Danny bought a coffee.

'Hold it,' he said to the vendor, 'I just want to check the water.'

The vendor made a face. 'I always use bottled water. There's no blood in *my* coffee.'

'OK,' said Danny, 'can't be too careful.'

People were still falling ill from contaminated water. The graveyards were full of them. After the blood-river incident the cops and army had made a house-to-house search of the Richmond area. They had arrested quite a few suspects, but there was no sign that any of them was Manovitch. Dave said there was no way Manovitch would allow himself to be taken into custody. There would be a holocaust first.

Petra didn't want anything. She watched him while he licked the excess coffee powder from around the rim.

'Habit of mine,' he murmured, when he caught her staring. 'Sorry. It drives Dave crazy.'

Petra nodded. 'You and Dave, you're very close, aren't you?'

They walked down to the river and stood staring into the dirty water.

'We have been – we used to be. I guess he doesn't like me much at the moment. I'm not doing my job very well.'

'It's because of me, isn't it?'

He looked at her and smiled his roly-poly smile. 'You're part of it. I think he's jealous.'

'No,' said Petra seriously. 'He's not jealous. He's not even envious. He's happy with that woman he lives with in San Francisco – Vanessa, isn't it?'

Danny crushed the cup which was still half full of coffee: it covered his hand and splashed his suit. He knew he was acting childishly, but it didn't seem to matter in front of Petra. She seemed to know his innermost self. He believed his spirit, his personality, even his thoughts, were naked before this strange and beautiful woman. She had the kind of insight a medium would give her third eye for.

'Dave stole Vanessa from me, you know that, don't you?'

Petra said, 'You can't *steal* anyone from anyone – people aren't things. Were you and Vanessa lovers?'

Danny felt uncomfortable at this question. 'No, we were never lovers . . .'

'You were engaged to be married then, but were waiting for the wedding?'

'No, we – we were just friends. Good friends.'

'Good friends are good friends. You should place a high value on friendship. It often has greater status than an affair. Emily Brontë thought it did. Is Vanessa still a good friend?'

'Yeah.'

'Then how did he take her away?'

Danny stared down into the water. 'You make it sound so simple,' he said. 'It isn't as simple as that. I met Vanessa first, we became good friends, then Dave came back from Washington and, before I knew it, they were in the sack together.'

Petra put a hand on his shoulder. 'Sounds like she fell in love with Dave, but not with you. That's OK, isn't it? You can't make people fall in love with you, Danny. I'm in love with you – isn't that enough?'

'You are?'

'You bet.'

Danny beamed, but something was puzzling him.

'You know, the way you say some things . . . you often sound American. You sure you've never been to the States?'

'Oh, come on, Danny, we get fed your television, your cinema, your cdi's – the US culture spreads its nets wide. It's not surprising you find certain aspects of life over here familiar, is it? You Americans are a strange mixture. You export your culture as if it's the only one worth having. You even cannibalize it – your songs are about US towns and cities, and most of your films and books are about the American way of life. You're so parochial yet you rule the world. Don't you find that strange?'

'There's a bunch of criticisms in there I'm sure I should get mad about.'

102

'And the other thing is, you can't stand being criticized,' Petra added.

'Who the hell can? Not the British, not the French or the Italians.'

She shook her head. 'But you Americans are so sensitive about it.'

'We are not. We're willing to listen to any lousy, rotten, son-of-a-bitch putting us down – for at least ten seconds.'

'Ten seconds is right.'

'Just don't say anything about TEXAS!' he growled, in mock anger.

She laughed. She really was a remarkable woman, and nettled as Danny felt about what he saw as an attack on his country, he could not let her see it upset him. Instead, he put his arm around her shoulder, possessively.

Danny did not see how Dave could *not* be jealous, even though he had a woman he loved. Just because you possess a diamond ring, doesn't mean you're not going to envy the owner of the Star of India.

'I still don't understand why you find *me* attractive,' he said to her.

She rolled her eyes to heaven. 'Are you still on about the superficial side of people? What does it matter *what* you look like? It's *you* that matters. I keep telling you.'

'You keep telling me, but I still find it hard to believe. Physical attraction must come into it, surely? It's got to, somewhere.'

'Only for shallow people. Not for people like you and me, Danny. I'm sure you'd love me even if I was, oh, say, short and dumpy and frizzy-haired . . .'

Danny had loved a woman just like that, once, but she had been killed by a fallen angel.

'Yeah, I guess I would.' He grinned, happy that he did not have to lie about it.

'While we're here,' he said, staring at Petra, 'I'd like to see some things. You know, some sights? I want to see Bucking-ham Palace too, and the Tate Gallery, and Big Ben, and the Tower of London . . .'

103

'Not the Tower, I'm afraid,' she said. 'It's closed for repairs – has been for over a year.'

Sergeant Stan Gates was a loner. He was strongly attracted neither to women nor to men, and consequently he told people who showed any curiosity about his relationships – or lack of them – that he was married to the force. It was the truth. The police force was his life and every waking minute was devoted to it, whether he was on duty or not. He liked a pint of beer in his favourite pub – the Princess Louise in High Holborn – and he enjoyed chatting to some of the customers in there, but his mind was never far away from his job.

Stan Gates had been born in York, but his family moved to London shortly afterwards and, like Rajeb Patel, he looked on himself as a Londoner. He had been raised in Hornsey, in Green Lanes, a multicultural area. Most of the kids Stan went to school with had been Greek Cypriots. He had enjoyed his childhood, hanging around the kebab take-aways, running riot in the streets with kids of all shades, from white through to black. They had a hell of a time, nicking cars, pinching fruit from the street stalls, filling the concrete and brick alleys with their yells.

At fourteen he'd been arrested three times for various misdemeanours, and then he met a cop who told him he was a dickhead for wasting his life. Boysie Robertson, a police training sergeant, had said to Stan, 'You think you're smart, don't you? You might be, but you're not as a smart as me, mate. I'll prove it. You think you could beat me at Karate Kid?'

Now, at the time Stan was a champion player of arcade video games and Karate Kid was one of his favourites. 'Yeah,' he sneered.

'Right,' said Boysie, 'you lose and you have to come away camping next summer – six weeks with the police cadets.'

'You're on,' Stan cried.

To his incredulity he lost. Boysie beat him seven games to nothing. He couldn't believe it. Old people couldn't beat young people at video games. He said as much.

'I keep in peak condition,' Boysie told the juvenile. 'My reactions are sharper than yours.'

Still, Stan felt he had been cheated somehow, and vowed he wouldn't go to the police cadet camp with Boysie. Yet, when the time came, Boysie turned up at his house, called him a welcher, and took the reluctant young Stanley to Southport. There he found himself joining in all the games, all the training, all the activities, and, surprisingly, enjoying himself. He never looked back from that time and inevitably he joined the force as soon as he became old enough, much to the dismay of his parents.

'We've never had a copper in the family,' his father grumbled. 'I dunno that we want one, either. You'll be coming home in your uniform, won't you? What'll the neighbours think? They'll all move away, I'll be bound.'

Family considerations were not the kind of thing that swayed Stan's decisions. He wanted to be a policeman and that was that. His father allowed himself to be mollified once Stan went into plain clothes. By then, however, his mother had got used to the uniform and was disappointed that her son would no longer signal his arrival using the siren on his car. Special duties meant that he was incognito most of the time.

In civvies Stan returned to his London-boy look: immaculate hair cut short, parted on the left, a definite hairline standing stark of a shaven neck; no sideboards, no moustache, clean-shaven face (smooth-as-a-baby's-arse); padded-shouldered sharp suits, plain button-down-collar shirts and Windsor-knotted ties; silver cuff-links during the day, gold at night; expensive watch, chain link strap; gold signet ring on his right hand, second finger; good Italian leather shoes with a cut-out pattern, nothing fancy, usually brown; sober socks. A clean, *hard* look. Frightening if you were a scruffy git from one of the bad housing estates like the one on which Stan had grown up. Stan, like most of his kind, had gone overnight from baseball caps worn backwards, overlong jeans and woollen jackets to the kind of thing he now wore and would wear until he reached fifty-odd.

As he stood, drinking his pint of bitter in the Princess Louise, the day after the Thames had lost its blood, Stan Gates thought about his present duties. At first he'd been disappointed to draw the short, bald cop. The other had looked lean, mean and efficient – just the sort of guy that Stan liked to work with. But Danny's reaction to the demon in Oxford Street had impressed Stan. It had been quick, clean and without any trace of fear or hesitation. Stan's opinion of Danny had changed since that afternoon. He still admired the other one, Dave, but realized why Dave had chosen Danny as a partner.

'Another one, please, Jim,' Stan said, slamming the straight glass down on the counter.

'Coming up, Stan,' replied the barman.

A man at Stan's elbow asked, 'You workin' on a big case at the moment, Stan?'

He turned to see Willy Prebble, a local locksmith.

'At the moment? I'm *always* on the job, Willy, you know that. Right now, though, I'm driving a Yank around the Smoke – a cop like me from San Francisco. He's not much to look at, but he's got it all here.' Stan tapped his temple.

'What're you doing? Chasing after someone?'

''S'all to do with Holy Mick,' Stan said, nodding in the direction of the brilliance most residents believed to be the Archangel Michael. 'There's a character connected with him that needs a little justice administered – and I don't mind telling you, Willy, I'm the one what's going to give it to him.'

Stan patted his shoulder holster significantly and was gratified to see Willy's eyes widen a fraction.

'You're going to *do* someone?'

'Some *thing*,' corrected Stan.

'An animal?'

'You could say that,' Stan replied, thinking he had said enough. Willy's mouth was as big as Avonmouth and it would be all over Holborn by tomorrow morning. Still, where was the harm in that? It was no secret that they were out to get the creature from hell called Manovitch.

106

Chapter Sixteen

It had been nearly two months since Lloyd Smith had heard from his nephew, Holden Xavier. Xavier wasn't Holden's real name, of course – neither was Holden for that matter – but Lloyd had long since ceased to concern himself over the vagaries of his nephew. Holden was a mystery to him, with his passion for snapping pictures, and Lloyd simply accepted his nephew for what he was. He loved the boy as he would have loved his own son, had he and Emily ever had children. Unfortunately for them both, Lloyd was infertile, and until Holden had come to England, Lloyd had not known what it was to have a young person to consider, to understand and, eventually, to love.

Holden, young at twenty-five, tall, lean and blond, good-looking, an excellent gourmet cook, had wonderful artistic and decorative taste, earned good money, was cultured, and was great fun. Lloyd missed him when the boy didn't contact him for some time, and needed one of their talks about poetry, or music, or . . . anything. He missed most of all Holden's soft accent and disarming enthusiasm for all things bright and beautiful, all creatures great and small.

All creatures, that is, except the frog.

When the plague of frogs was in its second day, with millions of the creatures invading London from the river, Lloyd decided he would break his promise not to call on Holden at his home and visit him there. Lloyd's messages left on Holden's answering machine went unreturned and he could never get Holden directly, either at his flat or his studio. Perhaps Holden was embroiled in a really time-consuming torrid affair – he was an obsessive personality – and had nothing left for outside influences. Well, be that as it may, Lloyd wanted to find out if his nephew was all right, and if he was interrupting something exclusive, then it was just bad luck on Holden.

Unfortunately, Holden lived in Surbiton, and though Lloyd knew it was a dangerous area to enter these days, he was willing to take the chance.

The frogs were everywhere: on the pavements, in the roads, down alleys, in houses, on the underground platforms, in the trains, in beds, pockets of suits, handbags, cupboards, underwear – everywhere. They were common frogs, *Rana temporaria*, three inches long and a variety of colours ranging through grey, yellow, brown, orange, red, black – speckled and marbled – and much to the chagrin of Thai and French restaurants, inedible. They were clogging the sewers and toilets, causing flooding and overflows. London stank. They were shorting electric equipment, and jamming mechanical devices by crawling inside them. London was coming to a halt. They were getting into larders and pantries, into pies and cakes, and their repulsive faeces were decorating every surface. London was disgusting.

Probably the most upsetting thing about them was they squashed underfoot, wherever one trod. Lloyd hated them. Every step he took made him shudder as his Italian shoe leather squished anything up to four frogs flat, their guts squirting everywhere, getting into his trouser turn-ups and on to his Scottish woollen socks. They caused a deadly slippery surface, as bad as ice in winter, and the hospitals were full of old people who had fallen and broken their hips. Their bloated carcasses rotting in the sun filled the air with foul gas and made Lloyd feel like vomiting. Disease was bound to follow in the wake of so much pollution.

Yet still they came, more and more of them, hopping up from the banks of the river Thames, as if the murky waters held an infinite number of them. They swarmed over buildings and graveyards, over the statues and monuments. On the day that Lloyd had decided to pay a call on Holden, yet another invasion was beginning. The presence of so many frogs had attracted creatures from the countryside in search of food and London was surrounded by an advancing army of snakes and rats, hedgehogs and herons, who had come to gorge.

'Horrible creatures,' muttered Lloyd as he walked along, bursting dead swollen frogs with soft explosive cracks. 'Never liked them when they were in their ponds, let alone on the streets.'

'You should try sleepin' in 'em,' said a bag lady, overhearing his words. 'They're soft, but they're bloody well messy.'

'I'm sure you're right,' said Lloyd, hurrying on.

'And they jump about!' she yelled after him.

Lloyd had no desire to stand and chat to a smelly old bag lady in a sea of frogs. All he wanted to do was get to Holden's flat in Surbiton. The taxi he had been in had ground to a halt when frogs got into the engine and another cab had not materialized, so he had been forced out on foot. Yuk! It made him want to puke. He noticed an army group trying to clear the streets, but they were fighting a lost battle.

Lloyd reached the block of flats where Holden lived. He rang the bell. There was no answer. He rang again. Still no answer. Lloyd stared at the door and then took out his key ring. He had a key to the flat if Holden had not changed the lock, which he did not appear to have done. He had never used it before, because he would have been terribly fazed if he had walked in on some love-making scene.

The key worked. Lloyd entered the narrow hallway. A thick, ugly stench hit him and he held his nose in disgust. There was a huge pile of letters on the floor. He stepped over it and continued into the depths of the flat.

'Hello – anyone home?' he called.

There was no answer. Lloyd went into the living room.

'Hello, hello,' he called.

No answer. The flat was obviously empty. Lloyd looked around him. The place had that unlived-in look to it. At least the frogs hadn't managed to get in, but it all looked a bit dusty, as if no one had been around for a while. Had Holden gone away? Perhaps he'd been called back urgently to America for some reason. The death of a relative? But then Lloyd would have heard of that too. An assignment from a magazine in some exotic location? That was more likely.

A terrible stink was coming from somewhere. It wasn't rotting frog – Lloyd knew what that smelled like – it was much worse.

Lloyd went to the answerphone and pressed the replay button.

'Hello, Holden, this is Lloyd, your uncle, here,' came back his own voice. 'I've been trying to get in touch with you for some time now . . .'

It was the call Lloyd had made that morning.

Holden would have said, 'How many people called Lloyd do you think I know, Uncle? You don't have to announce your relationship every time you call.'

Lloyd pressed the fast-forward button, then replay, to hear an earlier message he had left. The tape had gone through once and was rerecording itself. Holden *had* been gone a long time.

Lloyd collected the mail from the hallway floor and found two dead frogs among the letters. It was mostly business mail and circulars, with one or two letters from the States. The oldest dated back some two months previously.

'There's something strange going on here,' muttered Lloyd to himself.

It suddenly struck him that Holden might be lying dead somewhere in the flat – that smell . . .

Lloyd went reluctantly into the bedroom, half expecting to find a rotting corpse between the sheets, left there by a premature heart attack or perhaps by a murderer picked up casually at a singles bar.

The bed was neatly made. There was no body.

The bathroom, the spare bedroom, each room revealed nothing in the way of an explanation. Finally Lloyd came to the kitchen where the smell was definitely strongest. He gagged as he entered. On the draining board was a package, oozing vile green fluid. It was this that smelled so bad. Gingerly, Lloyd opened the packet, using a kitchen fork. The paper fell away like wet tissue to reveal rotting prawns.

Lloyd was sick in the sink.

110

He left the flat determined to get to the bottom of the mystery and decided he would go next to Holden's studio in Richmond. It took him four attempts to get a cabbie who would take him into the area where so many murders had occurred recently. Mostly they shook their heads and drove off without waiting for him to explain.

The cab, driven by a big, tough-looking black woman, ploughed its way through the mass of frogs, crushing thousands of them under its wheels. They stuck to the tyres and flew up into the wheel arches. Their gore splattered on the windscreen and the driver had to keep pressing the wash button and using the wipers, smearing the glass in front of her. Lloyd couldn't understand how she could see where she was going, but she just looked bored and faintly contemptuous of the whole business.

'Not very pleasant, is it?' said Lloyd. 'The frogs, I mean.'

The woman cocked an eyebrow and declined to answer, staring dully at the mass of green and red before her.

The cab swished through as it might through slush during a thaw after snow, leaving a trail of slime behind it. Finally, it arrived.

Again, Lloyd's keys worked the locks, and he entered the studio flat with its huge skylight window. Again he gagged with the stink. Foul odours were becoming the bane of his life. This time he stared around him in horror, to see that the studio was in a terrible mess, covered in excrement – human excrement by the look of it – and urine stains. It was the ugliest moment of Lloyd's life. He almost wept. All Holden's beautiful photographs, those of the down-and-outs, with their marvellously creased faces, the Epping Forest shots at sunrise and sunset, the Avebury Ring, misty with the sheep wandering over the hill, the street children, they had all been desecrated – yes, that was the only word to use – desecrated by some maniac in Holden's absence. Even the monochrome portrait photographs of Lloyd himself were smeared with brown, his silver hair covered with the mess, his pale narrow face splattered. Lloyd had felt a great sense of honour to be photographed by Holden, for even though they were relatives

Holden would not have compromised his art for the sake of family ties. Holden had said he wanted the photos because Lloyd had the distinguished look of a senator of Ancient Rome. 'You're a patrician, Lloyd,' he had said. 'You were born two thousand years too late . . .'

Now someone had turned him into a filthy plebeian.

Lloyd suddenly became angry. Whoever had done this should not be allowed to get away with it. The police would be brought in. They would find the perpetrators! Lloyd took his phone out of his pocket and dialled Stan Gates, asking him to get there as soon as possible. Stan Gates was a good man. He would find out who had done this terrible thing to Holden's studio.

Lloyd had hardly had time to put the phone back in his raincoat pocket, when he heard a sound above him. Startled, he looked up, to see someone entering the flat by way of the skylight.

It was . . . it was *Holden*.

Holden dropped to the floor, as agile as a cat, from twelve feet up and stared at him. Holden's clothes were ragged. They seemed to be too small for him. And he had no shoes on his feet. He had grown a dirty-looking beard and his once-groomed hair was long and unkempt.

'Holden?' said Lloyd, warily, for his nephew looked very strange and frightening in some way. 'What – what are doing, coming in that way? You look terrible. Your eyes. What's happened here? Were you chasing a burglar on the roof? The man who did this? Is that what you were doing up there?'

Holden sneered at him, his eyes narrow and sharp.

'You look so – so *dirty*,' said Lloyd. 'You were always such a *clean* person. What's happened to you?'

Holden crossed the room remarkably swiftly and grabbed Lloyd by the throat with one hand. He stared with eyes like flints into Lloyd's own and then his head jerked sideways and he examined, across the room, a photograph. Lloyd saw that Holden was studying one of the portraits of himself.

Lloyd's hands tore at the fingers that seemed incredibly muscular. Holden had never struck Lloyd as being particu-

112

larly strong – or brutish – as he seemed now. Lloyd didn't understand what was happening.

'Don't hurt me, Holden,' he said. 'I – I came up here because I hadn't heard from you – I was getting worried. I promised your father and mother I would keep an eye on you, you know. It's been nearly two months since we last had lunch together. Please, please don't squeeze my neck like that . . .'

'You know him,' said Holden. 'He knew you. He took your picture.'

It was Holden's voice, the tones and accent, but somehow they were not Holden's words.

Lloyd began to get angry again, this time for a different reason. 'Are you sick, boy? What's the matter with you? Holden, you're choking me. Please.'

Holden tore at Lloyd's clothing as Lloyd struggled, his mind unhinging, his brain going into panic. What was happening? Was this really his nephew? The boy had gone crazy. Lloyd felt sure he was going to kill him. The whole situation was insane. Lloyd felt himself beginning to hyperventilate as he was thrown to the floor, now naked from the waist down.

'Help!' he shrieked, breathlessly. 'Somebody help me!'

Holden lowered his own trousers and Lloyd's eyes bugged as he saw the huge ugliness which was Holden's.

'Oh, my God,' whimpered Lloyd, 'what's happened to your genitals? Why are you looking at me like that? Oh, Lord, that *thing* . . . oh, no, please, Holden, tell me what's happened to you. Oh, Christ . . .'

Lloyd was flipped on to his back and then he bit his tongue hard and his eyes started with the incredible pain. He was being penetrated and his flesh began to tear. Now there was no hyperventilation, only unbearable agony. His whole lower body was afire with pain: pain that went right through to his skull and gave him a massive migraine within seconds. Holden was piercing his shoulders and neck with his nails, nails which felt like talons, as he rode Lloyd like a horse.

'AAHHHHHHHHHHHGH! GA' . . . HEL' UUGHHAAA – DON'T HURT ME ANY MORE—'

113

Drool splattered on Lloyd's back, as Holden grunted heavily like a pig. The thing Lloyd dreaded the most in the whole world, was happening to him now, and the person who was doing it to him was his Holden, the young man he loved more than any other human being on Earth. Holden was raping him with some grotesquely malformed penis.

Holden was ripping him apart.

Lloyd's heart was racing, pounding, below the pain.

Holden continued to hurt him, badly, until he passed out, unable to endure the pain, degradation and terror any longer.

Chapter Seventeen

Daphne had been waiting at the school for over an hour. The children had gone home, she was feeling weary and ill-used, and she was beginning to hate politicians. That morning the Minister for Education had been on the television, attacking teachers for not maintaining discipline in the classroom, for failing to give children a decent education, for not administering examinations on time, for – Daphne felt – most of the ills of mankind.

The Minister, like most of his kind, had had a private education, his children were at public school, he knew virtually nothing about primary and secondary education of young people in a multiracial society, yet he continued to pontificate, talking about 'old-world values' whatever they were, and demoralizing the teaching profession, lowering its status in the eyes of the rest of society. 'Children today', the Minister had said, 'are leaving school without even being able to *spell*. These illiterate children, heaven help us, will become our new captains of industry . . .'

Daphne sighed. They always homed in on the spelling, as if it was the greatest crime in the universe not to be able to spell. She doubted whether the Minister himself was any good at spelling, but he didn't have to prove it with an army of civil servants between him and the public. He certainly didn't know the meaning of *illiterate*, if he thought it meant not being able to spell.

'Screw them all,' she muttered, as she continued to fill in the endless forms required by administrators on each and every child, in order to prove she was doing her job.

The frogs didn't help matters. Daphne felt it was a wonder the Minister of Education hadn't blamed the plague of frogs on teachers. She smiled grimly to herself as she recalled the point in the interview when the interviewer had mentioned the plagues and the Minister for Education had said, 'Dreadful, dreadful – but we must work through it. Children must be taught, whatever the conditions. We've got the next one to contend with yet, haven't we? The swarms of flies . . .'

Her children would have corrected the Minister for Education in an instant. It was not *flies* but *lice* which were expected after the frogs. The Minister was not only bigoted, he was ignorant, too, as most had been in the past. They continued to disrupt life in the classroom without improving it one jot. 'I hope the lice eat him alive,' muttered Daphne, 'while he's looking for flies to swat.'

A car horn sounded out in the street.

That had better be Rajeb, she thought, as she gathered her things together.

It was indeed Rajeb, over an hour late. He shrugged as she waded through the frogs towards the car. He was trying to look boyish, trying to disarm her before she laid into him. Despite her annoyance, she melted.

'Nasty little green things,' he said, as she got into the car.

'Actually, I don't mind the frogs, it's people I hate,' she told him.

She saw by his face that he thought she meant him, so she added, 'I'm talking about politicians, if they can be called people.'

'Oh,' he said, and his face visibly relaxed as he drove through the streets of frogs. 'Yeah, you're right there, love. Bloody idiots, ain't they?'

'Ain't they just,' she agreed, and he smiled.

'You know what happened today?' he asked her. 'You might not like this story.'

'No, I don't know, but you're going to tell me,' she said. 'I can see it in your eyes. And it's going to be gory – I can tell that, too.'

He grinned at her. 'Too right. You know the boss, Smith? He was raped in a photographic studio.'

A shudder went through Daphne, but something stiffened inside her. 'That's not big news, women get raped every day.'

116

He glanced sideways at her. 'Yeah, I know what you mean, love, and I agree with you. Just because it's a man it's not more important – but this was Lloyd Smith, the Archdeacon. If it had been Jessica Jameson, the Minister for Health, it would still have been big news, wouldn't it?'

'I suppose so, but there's more to it than just that, isn't there? Otherwise you wouldn't be like a cat on a hot tin roof.'

'Elizabeth Taylor and Paul Newman – brilliant,' he said.

'Tennessee Williams, actually.'

'No, seriously, you're right. Let me tell you what I heard. You know Stan Gates?'

'I know *of* Stan Gates, you speak about him.'

'Right. Well, Stan answered a call which Smith sent out from his nephew's apartment. It could have been *me* answered that call—'

'Get to the point, Raj.'

He gave her a hurt look. 'I was thinking. Anyway, Stan arrived at the studio to find Smith being raped by his nephew. Had to kick the door down to get in. Blood all over the place. The nephew tried to escape out the skylight and Stan shot him—'

'He killed him?' Daphne said, shocked.

Rajeb shifted a little in the driver's seat as he steered the car around a parked lorry.

'We got these special guns, see, for burning demons or whatever.'

'They don't shoot ordinary bullets?'

'Nah, not really. They shoot these incendiary rounds. Stan said the guy just exploded in flame. He said – Stan, that is – the guy still carried on climbing out of the attic, rolled down the roof like a ball of fire and fell down in the alley at the back where he just burned to a crisp.'

Daphne's stomach turned over. 'That's horrible.'

Rajeb looked at her quickly. 'He raped a bloke, don't forget.'

'You don't kill men for raping women,' she said firmly. 'Until recently only a few of them were even convicted, and then they only got a couple of years.'

117

'Yeah, I know what you're saying, love, and I agree with you, but Stan said this bloke attacked him, would've killed him, if he hadn't been able to protect himself. The guy threw a roof slate at Stan which stuck in the door like a knife – must have been a really strong bastard. Stan just reacted. Anyway, Smith said Stan did the right thing.'

'Well, he would, wouldn't he?'

'I suppose so. If anyone tried that on me, I'd want his head torn off and rolled down the gutter. Smith was terrified that his nephew had caught some disease, too, which could be passed on. Said his dick was like Nelson's Column – bloody massive thing, swollen out of all proportion.'

'Raj, I really don't want to know all the details, thank you very much.'

He nodded at her. 'Nasty stuff, eh?'

'Ugly is more like it. Now, can we just get home and have some tea?'

Daphne scratched her groin, caught herself doing it, and stopped, embarrassed.

Rajeb said, 'What makes a bloke's dick swell up like that, I wonder. I never heard of a disease like that, have you? Not a social disease, anyway. They usually rot you, don't they? Or kill you. Do you think it was elephantiasis, something like that? I saw that in India. People's legs as thick as tree trunks. Bloody horrible.'

'Raj, I really, really don't want to talk about oversized penises, if you don't mind.'

'Yeah, know what you mean, love. Morbid, ain't it?'

Daphne sighed and shook her head. 'That's not quite what I meant, but let's drop it. It sounds an awful business. I'm sure Lloyd Smith didn't want his nephew killed, despite what he had done to him.'

'Oh, yes, he did. He screamed at Stan, "Kill him!" He wasn't happy to find the body was just a lump of charcoal, though. He wanted the nephew examined – he wanted to know why his dick—'

'Yes, yes. I've had a lovely day, too. Now let's go in and make some tea.'

They had drawn up outside their flat.

She scratched her head as she got out of the car and stared east, at the big bowl of light that was the archangel. She reflected, as she scratched, how much life had changed since the archangel had arrived, and yet how *little*. There were rivers of blood and frogs, and demons running loose in the city, and wasteland where banks and churches used to be – all sorts of things had changed – yet ministers still pontificated, rapists still raped and Rajeb still insisted on telling her about the sordid aspects of his job.

Perhaps the latter was necessary. Perhaps she was acting in the role of a counsellor to him, helping him unload the ugliness of his job. She wasn't sure that was healthy. Perhaps he ought to go to a proper therapist for this sort of thing . . . Shit, her groin itched – so did her head – she scratched them furiously. Had she picked up a flea in Rajeb's car, fallen from one of his criminals?

'Have you been carrying any street people in your car?' she asked.

'Me, no, why?' he said, climbing the steps.

She saw him scratching under his left arm.

'Why are you doing that?' she asked, a horrible thought dawning on her.

'Doing what?'

'Scratching like that?'

'Was I?' he said, looking surprised. 'I'm sorry, it's very working class to scratch, ain't it?' he joked.

'I'm doing it, too, you dope,' she growled, scratching furiously.

He looked at her. 'Oh, fuck, it's started. The third plague. *Lice.*'

They rushed indoors, tearing off their clothes as they got inside.

'Have a look at me,' she shrieked. 'Down there.'

He dropped to his knees and inspected her groin. After a second or two he could see a tiny grey creature scuttling around in the forest of her pubic hair, busying itself with the nefarious activities of a human louse.

119

'Razors,' he cried, straightening up. 'We got to shave our-selves.'

'I'm not shaving my *head*,' Daphne yelled, distressed. 'I don't want to be bald.'

'We'll get some stuff, then. You go down to the chemist and get some now.'

'You go.'

He stood there, undecided, and she cried, 'What are we quibbling about? *Everyone* will have them. Get down there *now*, quickly, before they run out of stuff.' She scratched her head like mad. 'And hurry, for God's sake.'

Rajeb pulled on his clothes and rushed out. Daphne was dying to take a shower but knew she would have to wait for the treatment, whatever it was. She hoped it wasn't that purple stuff she had seen on some children's heads. It was so *conspicuous*. 'Oh, Lord,' she moaned. 'I hate this.'

While Rajeb was gone she went to the bookshelf and took down an encyclopaedia. '*Pediculus humanus capitis, pediculus humanus corporis, phthirus pubis*,' she read out loud. 'The three types of louse that infest the human body. Oh, shit, I hope the stuff Raj gets works on all of them. I can't stand it.'

On the way to the shop Rajeb saw other people in the street, scratching themselves. The lice obviously upset the more fastidious people and those with obsessive natures were to suffer the most. Rajeb saw one man crawling with lice, running all over his face, the backs of his hands, his neck. A policeman watched, horrified, as a businessman began clawing at himself with long nails, trying to get rid of the irritation. Claw-marks began to appear on the man's face, as he stripped the skin from his cheekbones, and blood ran down inside his shirt.

'Aaaarrrrrghhhhh,' screamed the businessman, becoming more feverish in his scratching and clawing. 'Can't stand it – can't stand it. Bastards. Bastards.'

He ripped open his shirt and began raking the pale skin from his chest.

Rajeb said, 'For Christ's sake, mate, you'll bleed to death.'

120

But the man was deaf to any advice. All he wanted to do was get rid of the lice. His nails dripped with his own skin and blood. He began rubbing his back and chest against a rough-cast wall, scraping further flesh from his body. Eventually, he ran down a side-street, still screaming.

This was just the first of many similar cases of self-mutilation that Rajeb saw. By the time he got to the chemist his own lice were torturing him almost beyond endurance, but he was strong enough not to give in to the scratching.

As he came out of the shop a well-dressed woman stepped from a car with a look of utter disgust on her face. She might have been a model for *Vogue*, had her features not been so distorted. She appeared to have been shopping in the smart West End stores, because bags of new clothes were falling out of the vehicle. She staggered a few paces, clawing at herself, then with an expression of utter loathing, took something from her handbag. Rajeb saw that it was lighter fuel. She began pouring it over herself.

Then she took out a gold cigarette lighter.

Rajeb ran towards her, shouting, 'No!'

Before he had reached her, she was alight and running, the wind fanning the flames. She was screaming, too, in a very high-pitched tone, like a rat dying in pain. At the end of the street she fell under a truck driven by a demented driver and was mercifully crushed under its wheels.

Rajeb ran all the way home, hoping that Daphne was not in the same state.

She was scratching herself raw by the time he arrived back with bottles of fluid and powders and even tablets that did something to the blood which destroyed the life cycle of the louse. They swallowed the tablets straight away, knowing they would have to wait days, perhaps weeks, for them to work.

They treated each other's bodies with liquids and powders in an extravagant display of overkill. When they were finished, Daphne felt a little better. Dropping white powder like a snowstorm, she went to find some fresh clothes in her wardrobe. She opened it up, took out a white blouse, then shrieked as she saw it was covered in nits. She threw it across to the corner of the bedroom.

'They're all over my things!' she yelled.

Rajeb rushed to her side and inspected her clothes, then his own, finding them crawling with lice.

As were the bedsheets and duvet.

When it was inspected closely, so was the carpet.

There were lice in the cracks of the walls, behind the skirting boards, in the cupboards, even in locks.

'What did we do to deserve this?' he groaned. 'We'll be eaten alive.'

All over London the cry went up, 'We'll be eaten alive.' Experts were called to the television news desks, to explain that very few species of lice actually *bit* anyone: they mostly only sucked blood. Strangely, this did little to reassure the population at large. It certainly did little to stem the suicides, some of them quite horrible, mostly among fussy old gentlemen and prissy old ladies, to whom lice were an utter disgrace and brought them unbearable shame.

There were those experts who offered other comforting thoughts, such as, 'Well, you know, cats and dogs have lice all their lives. We try to treat them, of course, but you can't eradicate them completely. Perhaps we shall now join our pets in maintaining parasites. Some conservationists think this is a good thing – after all, lice are creatures, too – we wouldn't want to see them become extinct like the elephant, now would we?' The interviewer stared hard at the expert, while cracking a tiny creature between his finger- and thumb-nails, hoping like hell it was high on the list of endangered species.

There were those who fled the city, in a desperate attempt to escape, taking their lice with them. There were a miserable few days ahead, and everyone knew it. Chemical companies were about to make a fortune. Those astute in financial matters had already bought shares.

London was crawling.

A Glaswegian busker was dragged in off the street to read Burns's 'To a Louse', on national radio. Very few people understood him, especially since he'd oiled himself well before the performance, but they caught the spirit of the thing. People started seeing themselves as others saw them and the sight was humorous rather than ugly.

The only people who were not concerned and who carried on their daily lives without a hiccup, were the bag people, the street people, the embankment tramps. To them life went on as normal, and they couldn't see what all the fuss was about. Many of them had had companion lice, almost pets, for as long as they'd been on the road.

And the monkeys, of course, in London Zoo. They, too, must have been mystified by the commotion. After all, it created social contact to be able to delouse your partner or friend, carefully picking through the hair, chattering as you did so. It was a great way to spend an idle hour or two and almost as therapeutic as a group hug.

Rajeb said as much to Daphne, as he picked through her scalp late that evening, and she hit him hard on his infested parts.

Chapter Eighteen

Even the hospital beds were crawling with lice, but humans are remarkably adaptable creatures. Some days after the vermin had arrived, people who would have sworn that they would go mad if just one louse was found on their person, now scratched and slapped irritably but patiently at their parasites and were simply reluctant, but resigned, hosts. You did what you could to keep their numbers to a minimum, but you couldn't go rushing around hysterically screaming through the streets for ever.

The ozone layer took a heavy hammering from army surplus anti-lice spray cans. The one source for these items was the A & N Stores, the military being the only large body who had planned for an invasion of lice over the last fifty years. Since the cans had been manufactured in the middle of the last century, they were not environmentally friendly.

Danny and Dave sat by the Archdeacon's bed. Lloyd was lying back, beads of sweat on his forehead, his hand gripping a handkerchief as hard as if he were trying to squeeze water from a stone.

'It hurt,' said Lloyd, miserably. 'Twenty-seven stitches.'

'I'm sure it did,' replied Dave, 'but at least you're alive.'

'Oh, God, that poor boy, burned to death. Yet he hurt me so badly. He must have been insane.' Tears streamed down Lloyd's face, denying the words he had just uttered. 'What I find hard is that the pain he's caused me wipes out any good feelings I ever had. He was like a son to me.'

Grief mingled with pain, causing a complex emotional turmoil in Lloyd Smith, a situation that both Dave and Danny felt embarrassed at having to witness. Lloyd wanted to hate the person who had caused him such agony, but that person was a young man he had cherished, and love battled with hate. Lloyd was obviously exhausted emotionally as well as physically.

When Dave felt he could, he continued. 'Now,' he began. 'I want to ask you about something. You described your assailant as being a gentle, kind person . . .'

'He used to be – that's what I can't understand.' The tears were welling in Lloyd's eyes again. 'I mean, I thought I knew the boy well. I can't believe how much he's changed in a few months. He was like some beast – yes, that's it, it was as if some terrible creature were lurking inside him. His eyes – they were hypnotic – insane eyes. And there was this tremendous energy about him – it's hard to explain – as if he had a wild animal locked inside him, fighting to get out.'

'And his, er, parts were . . .'

'Enormous. Twenty-seven stitches, I had. That tells you something.'

'You were torn,' said Dave, 'like some of the male and female victims from the South Bank.'

Lloyd Smith's eyes suddenly opened wide and he sat up quickly, even though it was obviously an effort.

'Manovitch?' he cried.

'I'm surprised', said Danny, 'that it hasn't occurred to you before now.'

Lloyd said, 'Well, I just didn't think – he looked like Holden. Why would Manovitch want to copy someone else's appearance? Unless—'

'Unless he *became* that other person,' Danny finished for him. 'Perhaps Manovitch preferred to possess a body already formed rather than create his own, as the demons do. Maybe as a dead soul he's *unable* to fashion his own body.'

Lloyd's eyes filled with tears again. 'Poor Holden. To be taken over like that by some foul creature, used, and then – and then to be burned alive.'

Dave said kindly, 'I doubt whether the original owner of the body was even aware of dying, or felt anything. Holden probably lost his life the day Manovitch entered his body.'

'I'd like to think that was the case,' said Lloyd. 'I hope Holden didn't suffer. And I'm glad it wasn't him that did this to me. Once I had lost Emily I thought more of Holden than anyone else in the world. He was a selfish young man, of course, but all young men are selfish. It's part of what they are. He could be really thoughtful when he wanted to be.'

He turned and stared at Dave. 'And if what you're saying is true, we have caught our dead soul by accident? Manovitch is nothing but a pile of grey ash. Is that too much to hope for, do you think?'

'No, I think it's entirely likely that Holden was Manovitch. We were only ever going to get him by accident. Happily that accident has occurred sooner rather than after more deaths and disembowellings.'

Lloyd began to look a little better. 'You think we've destroyed Manovitch?'

'Yep, and the Meeting is still going strong. I think Manovitch made the holy men more stubborn. They won't give in. And I think it's time Danny and I went home to San Francisco.' He didn't add, 'Before Danny makes a complete fool of himself', but he wanted to.

'We need to have a meeting, to find out if the others feel the same,' said Lloyd. 'I should be out of here in two days' time – maybe even tomorrow. You can wait that long, can't you? If what you say is true the archangel should be gone before then, shouldn't it? After all, what's it waiting around here for if the creature it came to destroy has been obliterated?'

Dave felt disappointment surging through him. He really did want to be on his way home. London was OK, but it wasn't San Francisco, and he disliked living out of a suitcase. A fairly conventional man at the core, Dave found enough vicissitudes in the disturbed routine of a detective in his own home town to satisfy his need for variety. Still, there was some sense in what Lloyd Smith was telling him. He was not 100 per cent sure that the body in the alley was Manovitch's. It might be that of some other rogue demon unwisely drawing attention to itself.

'How do you feel about this, Danny?' Dave asked his partner.

'I think Lloyd's right. We can't make the decision here and now. We need to discuss it with everyone else.'

Dave shrugged in defeat. 'OK. See you in the Jasmine Suite, Lloyd.' He stood up, scratching himself vigorously. 'Hopefully by then the lice will have gone into retreat.'

'It's flies next,' warned Danny. 'A plague of flies.'

'They won't come,' said Dave firmly. 'I think we've got our fiend. There won't be any flies.'

Lloyd nodded. 'We'll see. And now,' he sighed heavily, 'I have the unpleasant task of ringing my brother in California, to tell him his son is dead. I want the other business, the rape, to remain a secret, Lieutenant, you understand? I don't want my brother finding out – there's all sorts of ugly connotations – well, I just don't want him knowing about this. I intend telling him that Holden died in a studio fire. It's almost the truth.'

'I understand,' Dave replied. 'You have my promise that it won't go any further than us. What about the media?'

'I've already dealt with them,' said Lloyd. 'Gates has told them exactly what I've just told you.'

'Manovitch is still out there,' Petra announced.

'How do you make that out?' asked Dave, sourly. 'From what Lloyd tells us, there was some kind of supernatural creature in Holden Xavier. He was possessed.'

'I don't deny that,' said Petra. 'There was more than likely a creature from hell inside Xavier – but even if it was Manovitch, he escaped. The archangel says that Manovitch is still in existence. He still stalks the streets.'

Dave buried his face in his hands. 'Oh, *damn* it to hell,' he groaned. He looked up sharply. 'Listen, you could be a nut for all we know.'

'Hey,' cried Danny, glaring at him, 'don't call Petra a nut. She's no nut – she's not a liar either. Listen to her. She knows what she's talking about.'

Dave snapped, 'Danny, I don't think your judgement of this woman is reliable.' He turned to Lloyd to avoid further confrontation. 'How does everyone else feel about this? C'mon, let's hear it.'

Lloyd said, 'Was the archangel still there when you came down to breakfast this morning?'

Dave nodded. 'Yeah, but—'

'Well, in my opinion,' said Lloyd, 'the archangel would have gone the instant Manovitch had been destroyed. The fact that it's still planted firmly in the City indicates to me that its work is not yet over. What about our own policemen? How do you feel? Sergeant Gates?'

Stan Gates stared around the table. 'Personally, I think the fiend has gone up in smoke. I agree with the lieutenant.'

'Constable Patel?' asked Lloyd.

'I'm with you, sir. I don't think we've got the creep yet – I think he's still around.'

Lloyd moved in his chair, obviously still in great pain. 'Right, then, this isn't a democratic meeting. Whether or not to dissolve the project is my responsibility but I'm grateful for your comments. On reflection, I don't think we have enough evidence and therefore I think we should wait until the situation develops one way or the other. If the flies come, we'll know Manovitch is still out there.'

Danny looked smug, which infuriated Dave.

'There's just one thing I'd like to add,' he said evenly. 'I'm sending Sergeant Spitz back to the States.'

There was a stunned silence, then Danny half rose out of his seat. 'You're *what*?'

Dave's face hardened. 'You heard me. I'm your superior officer. I think you're prejudicing the project with your behaviour and I'm ordering you to return to San Francisco. No discussion. Be on the next flight. I'll fax the office to make sure they expect you.'

Black-faced with anger, Danny slammed his fist down on the table top, making the water glasses jump. 'I *won't* go, damn it. You can't tell me what to do, you . . . *Jesus Christ*. Twelve years we've been partners. How can you do this to me? Your own partner.'

'I'm doing it *because* we're partners, Danny—'

'Don't call me Danny – it's Sergeant Spitz.'

'—and because I hate to see you making an idiot of yourself.

128

The only way you're going to get out of this is to resign and you'll *still* have to go home to do that first. You're only in Britain at the invitation of the Government for a specific job of work. That job is over.'

'Fuck you!' roared Danny.

Dave went scarlet, but he ignored the outburst and turned instead to Stan Gates. 'I'd like you to drive him to the airport. Would you do that? Buy him a ticket and put him on a plane.'

Petra said, 'Could I have a word with Danny outside?'

'Help yourself,' replied Dave. 'Have several.'

Petra took the steaming Danny by the arm and guided him towards the doorway, his face still full of thunder.

Once they were out of the room, Rajeb turned to Dave. 'You sure you're doing the right thing here?'

Lloyd nodded. 'I'd like to hear the answer to this too. Why the sudden change of policy, Lieutenant? It's something more than the woman, isn't it?'

Dave hunched inside his suit. 'It is and it isn't. I don't have to explain my actions to anyone but my superiors back home.'

Lloyd shrugged. 'Well, if you don't mind, I'm going back to my room. I find these hard chairs most uncomfortable. Let me know if Sergeant Spitz manages to get a flight, won't you?'

He rose awkwardly and hobbled out.

Rajeb asked. 'Do you want me any more today, Dave, or can I take some time off? My girl has a couple of days off and if we're just waiting around . . . ?'

'Go. Enjoy yourself.'

'Sarge?'

Stan Gates nodded. 'Yeah, OK, but you're still on standby. Call in every six hours.'

'Will do. See you.'

Rajeb left the room, just as Petra returned. 'Danny is ready to go now,' she said. 'I helped him pack his suitcase and we've said our goodbyes. I shan't be coming to the airport with you.' She turned to Dave. 'He's all right now.'

'Good,' said Dave, gruffly, not looking at her.

Stan got up and left and Petra said she would see Dave at the next meeting.

He was left sitting alone at the table. 'What a crock of shit,' he said, staring bleakly at the flock wallpaper.

After a while he put on his dark glasses, went out and headed east down Theobalds Road, walking towards the great dome of light which housed an undelineated being: mysterious, invincible, holy, holy, holy, a lord of hosts. Why hadn't Manovitch tried to take on the archangel down here on Earth? Presumably because he couldn't, or he would have done so before now. Perhaps an archangel was unassailable, especially on foreign soil. Angels could be destroyed by Manovitch and his army of dead souls, but not archangels?

Dave sighed. Rajeb was right: he was confused about his own motives for sending Danny back to the States. It had almost been an impulse thing, a decision of the moment, and he couldn't explain his reasons, not with any satisfaction, even to himself. It just seemed the right thing to do. Sure, there was the Petra aspect to it all – damn it, Dave was human, after all. If Danny had picked up a normal woman, Dave would have been pleased for him. But he had found this surreal creature from some work of fiction. Well, she seemed to have Danny tamed and in her pocket, that was for sure.

When he reached the barrier, Dave stopped, leaned on it and looked into the blinding white hemisphere. It dazzled the mind, this dome of brilliance, as well as the eyes. There was about it a unique quality of purity. He felt similar to the way in which a wanderer in an unexplored region might feel, suddenly coming across a magnificent waterfall, so clean, clear and untouched by the world that it must have come from the mouth of the Creator himself.

There was something inside that dome which reached out to Dave. Mingled with his awe was a sense of warmth and security. This light, this glow from a firefly of God, was, of course, nothing beside the light at the centre of the universe, the Creator's own light. It was a candle flame against a sun. Yet it had brushed that sun, and had that sun's blessing, and the peace that had rubbed off on it could be felt and wondered at by a plain cop from the streets of San Francisco.

130

Dave stood there for a long time, just staring into the dome, soaking up its tranquillity.

Walking back to the hotel, he noticed the London architecture around him. He could not get a 'feel' of London as a whole. It was such a mixture of styles and periods. There were bland modern office blocks next to magnificent Georgian buildings. Egyptian obelisks, bronze lions, grand palaces, corner shops, massive colonnaded museums, tiny news stalls. There were dirty alleys, like Wild Court, inside which forgotten single trees struggled for light, contrasting with those like Sicilian Avenue which boasted restaurants and shops. Dave couldn't get a grip on London. It was too diverse, too much a mish-mash of thrown-together buildings and streets for an overall vision.

'Well,' he told himself, 'Danny won't miss it. The bum hardly saw outside his own bedroom.'

That wasn't quite true, but Dave needed to comfort himself with the thought that he was doing the right thing. He would have liked to have gone back himself, but the job wasn't over yet. Manovitch – he had to admit it privately – was probably still out there.

Chapter Nineteen

Petra left the hotel and walked to Holborn underground station. She took a Piccadilly line train to Leicester Square and then the Northern to south of the river. Finally, she took a bus to a certain street in the Elephant and Castle. Even before she had boarded the bus she had wrapped a scarf around her head and the lower half of her face. She did not want to be recognized.

It was dark when she walked down the short grubby backstreet and quickly ducked into a side alley. She paused and listened for a while before climbing a fence, in her elegant expensive clothes, to drop into a rubbish-cluttered back yard on the far side. She had wisely put on low-heeled shoes before setting out and they served her well as she negotiated the morass of cans, bottles, rags and other litter in the yard. There were rusted pushchairs to circumnavigate, and bicycle frames, and all sorts of junk thrown out over a number of years by the various families who occupied the five flats into which the house had been separated.

Petra's destination was the second floor. She noticed that the curtains were still open, though a light was on in the room behind them. Petra climbed on to the dividing wall between the properties, to crouch against the main wall of the house itself. Once there she cautiously stared into what was the living room.

Though cheaply furnished, with overstuffed sofas and an old oak table, the room beyond the glass was spotlessly clean. Sitting at the oak table was a boy of about twelve. He seemed to be poring over school books, no doubt doing his homework. His hair was a mass of tight black shiny curls above a broad handsome face. There was a deep frown on his forehead, as if concentration was intense.

132

On the wall behind the boy, who had been christened Abibi but whom everyone called Abby, was a map of Nigeria. Abby had never been to Nigeria. Neither indeed had the person who had sketched that map, which was signed *Petra, aged 13 years*. Nigeria was a land shrouded in mystery for both these people: the homeland of their grandparents. They knew many stories about it, of mythical animals who talked to humans and each other, stories of tribal passion, of war, of lost golden kingdoms. They had both been fascinated by the country of their ancestors and had sworn to visit it one day, once there was money and time enough.

Petra gazed at her younger brother fondly, wishing she could burst through the glass that separated them and hug him close to her. She did not, however, wish to worry him: he thought she was dead. She had told her parents she was going out to Nigeria, to seek her roots before her disease overtook her completely, and later they had received a message to say she had died *en route*. They were too poor to have the body shipped back to England, so they accepted that she had gone and planted a tree in a local graveyard, to remember her by.

Suddenly, the door to the living room opened and a portly woman entered carrying some shopping. Her mother had hardly changed since Petra had last seen her. She was one of those women who had been born looking forty and had stayed that way though she was a decade older.

'Abby, are you workin' hard?' Petra heard her mother ask.

'Of course,' Abby replied, almost irritably. 'Can't play football in the dark, can I?'

'You think about your school work,' said his mother, heading towards the door to the kitchen.

The boy cast his eyes to heaven, as if he alone in the world had parents who were not only dense but beyond redemption.

Petra smiled to herself, thinking of the times when she, too, had been sitting at that same table and wishing she could be out playing something with the other girls in the street. She had thought then that her parents were cruel, keeping her working while others let their children run wild. Later,

of course, she revised her opinion. When she had landed a
job as a top fashion model, they had been so proud of her.
Petra had taken her mother on a shopping spree in Paris and
it filled her eyes with tears to remember how close the pair
of them had been at that time.

A man entered the living room in working clothes. He was
tall, serious-looking, and had a scar on his left cheek.

'You workin' hard, Abby?' said the man, folding a newspaper and tucking it under his arm.

Once again the long-suffering Abby rolled his eyes and
groaned. He didn't even bother to answer, but bent over his
books again.

Petra worked hard to control the lump in her throat. How
her daddy had cried the night she died! He had sobbed his
heart out. This man, who looked as hard and tough as a piece
of railway track, had collapsed and melted in her mother's
arms, soaking her dress with his tears. He looked care-worn
now, and he was shuffling a little in his carpet slippers. Petra
had seen her grandfather shuffle like that, when in the begin-
nings of Parkinson's disease.

Her mother came back into the room.

Petra stayed quite a while, just watching, enjoying seeing
her family react to each other. They had been, and still were,
a happy group – as families go – and there was genuine love
and affection at the core. Her daddy had once had a Nigerian
coin cut into four. One quarter of that coin still hung on a
pendant chain around Petra's throat. When she had been
whisked off to hospital with a suspected cardiac arrest, the
staff had wanted to cut it off her, but she had screamed at
them to leave it on. She could see her brother's quarter,
dangling from his neck, hanging over his books.

She would have loved to go in and hug them, but Petra
was no longer Petra, completely, and there was a conflict
within her which could not be controlled by her alone. She
was given licence to observe her family at their evening activities, but that was all. She could not show herself or let them
know of her presence.

When she had tortured herself enough, Petra slipped from

the wall and across the rubbish in the yard to climb over the fence. She dropped down to the other side and was wiping her hands on a handkerchief when a figure appeared alongside her. She gasped in surprise, stepping back quickly.

'What the hell are you up to?' said an American voice.

Petra gulped hard. 'Lieutenant Peters?' Anger replaced shock and Petra said defiantly. 'Have you been following me?'

'Yes, and I don't apologize for it,' said Dave. 'I wanted to find out what my buddy had got himself into—'

'We can't talk here,' she said, walking past him and out into the side-street. 'Let's go for a coffee somewhere.'

'What I'd like to know, is—'

'*Not now*,' she snapped, walking on.

His head jerked back but he followed her silently just the same, keeping pace with her trotting walk, until they were on the main road. She hailed a taxi and he got in beside her. She gave an address on the north side of the river. Ten minutes later Petra pointed to a café on the corner of the Strand.

'In there,' she said, perfunctorily.

When they were at last sitting down, a coffee in front of each of them, she said, 'Now, just what is it you want to know about me? I'm not sure you're entitled to know anything, but if the question is put politely, then I may answer it.'

He stared at her with those hard eyes of his. 'First, I want to know what your interest in Danny is.'

'I should have thought that was obvious. I'm in love with him. He's a wonderful person.'

'I find that hard to believe.'

She looked at him archly. 'You mean, that Danny's a wonderful person?'

'No, that *you* should think he is.'

Petra sipped her coffee and smiled. 'You mean, I could have any guy I wanted, so why choose a short, balding man with a penchant for call girls and confessing to priests?'

He raised his eyebrows at this, but nodded slowly. 'Yeah, that's about the size of it.'

'Well, the truth is, Lieutenant Peters, that people like me,

135

a rare beauty – and I have no false modesty about that – are very often lonely. We're still only one person, a person who needs a close relationship as much as anyone else, with someone they regard as a soulmate. Believe it or not, Danny and I *are* soulmates. I couldn't care less what he looks like – that isn't important to me in the least. If I wanted a pretty boy, or a muscle man, I could have chosen one of the male models I worked with. They are usually as empty-headed as mannikins, and that's why they would not have done for me. Danny is quite the opposite. His head is full of bright things. Now, does that make sense, or not?'

'It makes sense to a certain degree, but I wouldn't have called Danny an electric personality either.'

'That's because you're a man, and not a very spiritual man either.'

Dave looked sour. 'I resent that.'

'You may resent it,' said Petra, 'but it's true. In comparison to Danny, who is a *very* spiritual man, you have little to offer in that respect. The nickname they call you by, Mother Teresa, to me that's a misnomer. You're practical, probably kind and generous, and I know you're intelligent and quite emotional at times, but you're not spiritual – not to any great depth. I won't use the word *shallow* because that's the wrong term, but your depths are not metaphysical.'

Dave felt affronted by this. He considered he was as spiritually sound as the next man. He might not practise matters of the spirit, or give them much attention, but he certainly believed he was no more secular than Danny.

'They call me Mother Teresa because of my integrity,' said Dave stiffly, wondering how the hell this interrogation got turned round in the first place.

She sighed. 'You really don't understand what I mean – what most people mean – by the word *spiritual*, do you? You can't just *be* it, you have to practise it, learn to become it. How many times have you been to church in the last ten years?'

'How do you know I'm a Christian?' he asked, shrewdly. 'Maybe I'm a Buddhist?'

136

'How many times do you meditate in a day, then? Or have *anything* to do with spiritual matters? I'll tell you. None. You do a lot of *thinking*, but no meditating.'

'You presume to know a lot about me.'

'I don't know very much about you, Lieutenant Peters, but I know that much.'

Dave was silent for a while. It irked him to think that she was probably right. If the spirit was like a muscle that needed exercising to reach its full potential, then Danny was several blocks ahead of him.

'OK,' Dave said quietly, after a while, 'you've explained why you're in love with Danny, and why I don't really understand. Now I'd like you to explain why you climb fences and sit on windowsills. You some kind of voyeur?'

This time his own observations hit home. 'How dare you? You think I get kicks watching people make love or something? That's disgusting.'

'Lady, peeping is just a harmless occupation where I come from. The disgusting things involve warped, participating adults with lots of instruments. Just *looking* is kindergarten stuff – you show me yours and I'll show you mine, that kind of thing.'

Her nostrils flared and her eyes narrowed. 'I wasn't on the windowsill, I was on the dividing wall, and I was looking in at my family.'

This opened his eyes a little. 'Family? You're married?'

'I mean my mother, father and brother.'

Something nasty trickled through Dave's brain, but he was quick to divert it. He had been wrong about this woman several times now and he did not want to make any more prejudgements.

'OK,' he said, 'you've told me this much. Why would you want to see your parents without letting them see you? Did your father throw you out, never to darken his door again? Or maybe it's your wicked stepmother, who wants the family rid of you?'

The sorrow evident in her eyes made him regret he was pushing her. 'No,' she said, 'neither of those. My family

137

believe I'm dead. It's necessary to let them continue in that belief, though I wish it weren't. I don't have to explain any more to you. There's nothing terribly wrong in what I'm doing. I mean, it is horrible that they think I'm dead, but I'm not allowing them to continue in that belief for selfish reasons. It really is impossible for me to tell them at the moment.'

Dave, who had met and sometimes arrested countless men and women who had gone 'missing, presumed dead' in his time, felt that further questioning of Petra would prove fruitless.

The situation wasn't that unusual. He had known young people, perhaps more girls than boys, who had run away from home but occasionally rang their mothers and fathers to hear their voices without wanting their parents to hear them, or know where they were. Families were controlling agencies, some far more extreme than others. Once you escaped the control of loved ones – even though they were *loved* ones – you wanted to remain outside the family's manipulations. Thus you might want to call them without speaking yourself, or peek in a window and see how they were all doing without you. That was human nature. To want the security of *having* a family, without wishing to be inside it, being told what to do.

'OK, I give in,' Dave said. 'Let's forget it.'

She smiled at his final understanding.

As they walked back to the hotel, Petra slipped something into Dave's hand. It was a pendant on a silver chain. 'If anything should happen to me,' she said, 'please give this to Danny.'

Dave stared at the piece of jewellery and shrugged. 'Sure,' he said, 'why not?'

Chapter Twenty

Later that evening Stan Gates reported that Danny had boarded flight VA765 for San Francisco, but told Dave, 'I don't know whether he'll call in when he gets there. He said something about a trip to Hawaii – said he'd had enough of the force and wanted out of it.'

This statement puzzled and irritated Dave. 'Hawaii?' he repeated. 'Why would he want to go to Hawaii?'

Gates shrugged. 'I dunno, but from the look on his face it could have been Mexico or Alaska. I've seen that look before. He wants to hide himself for a while. I think he's angry and upset.'

Dave grimaced. 'Well, if he wants to sulk, then let him. I don't think I had any choice but to send him back.'

Gates smiled. 'If my opinion is worth anything, I think you did the right thing – the *only* thing, in the circumstances. When a policeman's work is being affected by his emotions, then you have to part him from it until he recovers his senses. I've never believed in mixing private life with public service.'

'Thanks, Stan, my feelings exactly.' But even as he said it Dave felt guilty. He felt like a hypocrite, knowing that when he had been hunting the angel in '96, he had also been falling in love with Vanessa. *That was different*, he told himself. *That was entirely accidental and I didn't know I was going through it until it was over.* He added with some satisfaction and easing of his conscience that, as a divinity professor, Vanessa had been essential to solving the problem with the angel.

If he'd stopped to consider it honestly, he would have realized the two cases paralleled each other almost exactly. Danny had not gone into his affair with any prior knowledge, and Petra was essential as the mouthpiece of the archangel.

After seeing Gates, Dave went to his room. He sat on the

edge of his bed for a few moments, then undressed, showered and crawled between the sheets, noting they hadn't been changed. The plague of lice had probably thrown everything out of kilter. Even now the little pests were eating into him. He resisted scratching, but cracked a few between his nails, taking great satisfaction in the act.

Dave was woken by the phone. He looked at the digital clock set in the hotel radio: 3.30 a.m.

'Hello?' he croaked into the receiver.

'Dave? This is Lloyd. Could you come down to the Jasmine Suite right away? Something – something important has happened.'

Something in the sound of Lloyd's voice activated alarm bells in Dave's brain. He was instantly awake and reaching for his slacks.

He went to the window and stared out. The dome of light was still evident. The archangel was still there, so that was not what Lloyd wanted to talk to him about. Lloyd had called him *Dave*. It was the first time he'd used his Christian name. Was that significant? *Dave* sounded awkward, incongruous, coming from the mouth of Smith, who was usually correct, English, inclined towards formal address.

One of the hotel staff, an under-manager, was just leaving the suite as Dave entered. 'Coffee,' he murmured to them. 'I've just made it. It's on the table.'

'Thanks,' said Dave, wondering if he was going to need it.

What he needed in the end was a good quart of bourbon.

Lloyd was poker-faced, pacing the room when he entered. He gestured to some chairs.

'Sit down,' he said. 'I have some very grave news.'

The Archdeacon was pale and obviously agitated as he spoke. Dave's heart plummeted. What the hell was wrong? Was he being sent home, replaced, what?

'I'm dreadfully sorry, Dave . . .' again, that unusual use of his first name '. . . but flight VA765 went down in the Atlantic not an hour ago.'

At first this didn't register on Dave's brain. Then he

140

remembered. Stan Gates had said Danny caught flight VA765. *Danny!* Danny was on that plane. Danny had plunged into the ocean!

'Jesus Christ,' said Dave, his brain going numb.

'I'm very, very sorry,' said Lloyd again.

'No survivors?' asked Dave. 'Are they searching?'

'I'm afraid there's not even a trace of wreckage. They sent out a Mayday call when a port engine caught fire. The fire spread along the wing. The last call from the pilot was that they were going down.'

Dave buried his face in his hands. 'Oh, God,' he groaned. 'My fault. I ordered Danny home. I killed him.'

Lloyd's voice was firmer. 'That's a stupid thing to say, Lieutenant, and I'm surprised to hear it from a pragmatist like yourself. You know you can't possibly predict which aeroplanes are going to crash—'

Dave looked up, blinded by an inner fury. 'Why do you upper-class faggots always fancy-up words? *Aer-o-planes!* What's wrong with the right word? It's *airplanes*, damnit. *Airplanes.*'

Lloyd said calmly, 'In English it is *aeroplane*, for the whole of our nation. Only in American English is it *airplane*.'

They all realized that Dave's outburst was caused by his inability to handle the immediate impact of his grief, but there was a long embarrassed silence, before he finally choked out an apology. 'I'm sorry, Lloyd. I just wanted to hurt someone.'

'You weren't yourself, that's the whole point. I've been called worse in my time, and not always to my face. I think it's a peculiar word, don't you? *Faggot?* It's always bewildered me. I get this mental image of a piece of sixteenth-century firewood. How on earth it ever came to be slang for a homosexual is beyond me. If you ever find out, I should be interested to know.'

Dave nodded, still acutely embarrassed, caught up in a tangle of emotions ranging from sorrow to anger.

They drank lots of coffee, talked about the remote possibility of it being a mistake, of Danny having caught another flight altogether, of the flight number of the crashed plane being misreported, of survivors being picked up. They talked about these things, but they knew there was no hope, that Danny had been killed alongside five hundred others.

Eventually Dave went up to his room to call Vanessa. She was distressed as he knew she would be. He wished they were together, holding one another, stroking one another, so that they could offer each other physical comfort and support.

'I know a cop should expect to get it in the line of duty,' said Dave. 'I *know* that. But when something like this happens it hits you just as hard.'

'Of course it does,' said Vanessa.

'I just can't believe it. I don't know what to do – I feel helpless.'

She gave a little sob. 'There's nothing you *can* do, except go on and finish what you started. Danny would understand that.'

'I guess so,' said Dave, wearily, drained of emotion. 'I guess he would.'

Manovitch was standing on the top of a tall building, facing north. There was a man nearby, looking desolate. He had been, before Manovitch got hold of him, a gentle man, a *good* man, but he had debased himself for money. He felt sordid and depraved at having taken part in an act which would have made him angry and sick only the day before. Admittedly, it was a *lot* of money, but now that it was over he felt that he wanted to kill himself.

'Get out of my sight,' said Manovitch, 'before I kill you.'

The man walked to the edge of the building, gave Manovitch a pathetic look, and stepped over. He didn't even scream as he fell the seventeen storeys. Manovitch shrugged. His power had been replenished. That was all he cared about.

Manovitch stared over the capital. He had now discarded his demons, having no more use for them. They had gone back to their holes, back into hiding again. They had been of use to him in the short run, but he wanted to continue the task alone, unhampered by their vain stupidity.

142

It was true that he had not yet broken up the Meeting, but he knew before he undertook it that it would be no easy task. It was pointless killing one or two of them: that would merely strengthen the resolve of the others. What he had to do was make life in London unbearable, wear their resistance down, get them to leave in a dispirited frame of mind. In any case, several would die when he visited the last plague upon them: the deaths of all the firstborn.

Manovitch had not received any communication from Satan since he had been on earth, but he felt his foul lord would be pleased with the way things were going. Manovitch felt the plagues were an inspired touch that would be appreciated in hell. The passivity of the immobile archangel was heartening, too. It would not make its move until the mortals failed completely and by that time it might be too late. The destruction that would be caused by single combat between Manovitch and the archangel was worth the risk of being obliterated for ever – almost, but then Manovitch was not *that* selfless.

Manovitch had risen to power when Satan had begun using dead souls for his troops on the plains of Armageddon. The demons were continually being beaten back and though dead souls were traditionally neutral, the battle being between angels and fallen angels, Satan had thrust aside any qualms about further corrupting the souls of dead mortals. Manovitch had become one of his greatest generals, feared by angels, admired by demons.

Manovitch surveyed the scene around him.

After a moment, something crawled out of the corner of his mouth, between his lips. It was a fly. It buzzed away on the wind. He opened his mouth slightly and two more came out. He stretched wide his jaws. Three, four, a dozen, a hundred, until flies were pouring out of the open mouth in a steady black stream as thick as a man's arm. Manovitch spread his arms, a look of triumph in his eyes, as the flies poured forth from him in their thousands, their millions, trillions.

143

Chapter Twenty-one

Seven-year-old Tommy Jenkins woke his mother in the middle of the night, by shaking her shoulder vigorously.

'I think God's coming,' he said.

Sandra Jenkins lived in a top-floor flat in Bayswater. She was a bright, intelligent woman of thirty-three who had never seen the need to get married and had raised her child alone. She had had a steady boyfriend for several years, who was, she argued, a good male role model for her son, and there were those who said she made a better success of child-rearing than many couples. Her son had inherited her intelligence.

'What is it, darling?' she murmured, still half asleep.

'Listen!' insisted young Tommy. 'Isn't that God?'

Sandra sat up in bed and was finally awake enough to hear the distant drone. She had worked for voluntary overseas organizations for two years after leaving university and had been in an African country at war with another. She knew what a squadron of bombers sounded like, and this was similar. Her nerves began tingling with fear.

She leapt out of bed. 'Quick, under the kitchen table, Tommy, quickly, quickly.'

Tommy began to get frightened now, hearing the anxiety in his mother's tone, seeing how the sound had affected her.

'What's the matter, Mummy? What's wrong?'

Sandra, realizing her manner was affecting her son, fought to remain calm. The noise was getting louder outside and though her panic rose with it, she battled for composure.

'It's nothing dreadful, Tommy, but I think we'd better just sit under the kitchen table. Something might rock the building and the plaster will come down. We don't want to get covered in plaster, do we now?'

'No,' replied Tommy, doubtfully.

144

They went into the small kitchen and crouched under the little table, holding hands. Sandra wasn't sure that the table would bear the weight of the ceiling if it did come down, but it was all they had for protection. In Africa she'd gone under the staircase, just like her grandparents during the Second World War, but in the flat there was no staircase under which to hide.

The noise became louder and louder, until it sounded nothing like a squadron of bombers, being much too low in height, and much too high in pitch. Whatever it was, it was coming in at ground level. What on earth could it be? Some kind of machine entering the city? Many machines?

Cautiously, with her heart pounding, Sandra crawled out from under the table, still clutching her son's hand. They went to the window together and looked out over the darkness of early-morning London. At first there was nothing to be seen, but when Sandra looked up at the pale moon, a black cloud suddenly obscured it. In the distance, street-lights and building lights were going out, rapidly. A darkness seemed to be rushing in towards the Bayswater flats.

'What is it?' she said, less frightened now that she could see no heavy machines of death in the skies.

The darkness and the noise kept pace with one another, until finally they reached and engulfed the flats. Every window on the south side rattled with the impact of the black cloud as it struck with the force of a tidal wave from the ocean. The building juddered on its foundations. She could see then, in the light from her own windows, that the cloud was made up of a mass of dots, millions upon millions of them, and was not as she first thought, of smoky density. It was as if the dots that made up its blackness were soft hailstones: not strong enough to shatter the glass, but numerous enough to cause the building to shudder.

The noise outside was appalling.

'What is it, Mummy?' shrieked Tommy, losing his former composure.

'Nothing to be afraid of,' she said, stroking his head, not believing her own words.

The dots began entering the flat then, forcing themselves through ventilators and tiny gaps between window and sill.

Then she saw what they were as they buzzed around her living room, bedroom, bathroom and kitchen.

Flies!

Had she been an entomologist, Sandra would have seen that the bulk of the flies was made up of a species known as St Mark's fly, but this creature had many squadrons of others accompanying it on its raid of London.

Some were enormous bluebottles, but among the buzzing multitude were black flies, warble flies, bot flies, gall flies, robber flies, window flies, soldier flies, huge horse flies, house flies, fruit flies and stilt-legged flies. There were also gnats, midges, black flies, moth flies and crane flies.

'Oh, God,' she said, disgusted.

She went immediately to the cupboard under the kitchen sink, to get the fly spray, but something told her the enormity of the problem was not going to be solved by a single can of SWAT. Instead, she sensibly grabbed some rags, soaked them, ran back to the windows and began blocking the air vents and gaps, until the flies stopped coming inside. Then she sealed up around the front door, for they would be using the main entrance soon enough, she was sure.

Tommy had armed himself with a rolled-up newspaper and was setting about destroying the army of intruders.

'Got another one, Mum,' he yelled, swiping the wall dangerously near to an expensive vase. Blotches of bright red with a black centre were beginning to decorate the white kitchen wall.

Sandra armed herself with a wet dishcloth and followed in Tommy's wake, alternately wiping the marks from the wall and swatting with the rag, which proved an effective weapon. She did not want to use the can of SWAT now because with no ventilation the fumes would soon fill the air of the flat.

Between them these two stalwart Goliaths managed to keep at bay the hordes of Davids that were threatening to over-whelm them. Others in the city were not so lucky. Other women, and men, had no vigilant Tommy to wake and warn them of the invasion. They were caught in their beds, swallowing flies, choking on clouds of black insects which crawled in their ears, up their noses, down their throats. Some of the flies inflicted nasty bites while others were merely a nuisance, but they were there in their billions, dropping their little black droppings on everything, rendering dirty all exposed plates and crockery, feasting on any food that was not under sealed cover. They mated and died in their own filth, and, like the frogs, began to clog everything from clocks to trains.

Although the plague did not extend as far as Heathrow and Gatwick, any aircraft over London that night had to seek height quickly to avoid their engines sucking in masses of insects and bringing them down among the buildings.

It was the ugliest plague yet.

Dave had still not recovered from the shock of Danny's death when the flies struck London. He decided to escape them for a couple of days and drove out of London into the Suffolk countryside. It was like another world. Peaceful, quiet, getting on with its business. There were flies out there, but in normal numbers. He shuddered as he drove along, thinking of the filth the insects would bring with them. There would be more disease. Life would become unbearable for a while, once more, like with the frogs and lice.

When they had arrived, Dave had luckily been in the hotel, behind glass. The staff were quick to seal it off. In the streets outside, people were dying. Through the double-glazing Dave watched as one old man disappeared in a cloud that swept through the streets and fell choking to death, his throat clogged, his eyes blinded and running, his ears and nose stuffed with black flies. He got back to his feet and tried to run, but fell again, for the last time, three or four paces later. Once he had been asphyxiated by wads of their dead comrades, the living flies began to feed on the corpse's juices, which leaked from its orifices.

The flies went swarming through the streets, flying almost as a single body, and the volume of their buzzing was earsplitting. It was like having squadrons of aircraft flying between

147

the tall buildings. They were a black mass of winged filth, which brought people to their knees within seconds if a handkerchief or scarf was not forthcoming quickly to block the entrance to the mouth and throat. Later people would begin to wear gas masks, but initially none was prepared for such a density of insects. Citizens died in their dozens, swallowing flies in gobbets, unwillingly filling their stomachs with thick plugs of the insects as if they were gobbling caviar by the handful.

Dave had managed to procure a gas mask and took the A12 out of the metropolis. On the way he saw the city corporation garbage men, similarly masked, collecting bodies and throwing them into the back of garbage trucks. There was no time for niceties. Dave saw people with running sores caused by the plague of lice, the wounds black with flies feeding on pus. He saw corpses moving as if they were still alive, shivering with a complete blanket of insects swarming over them. It was an ugly journey.

His vision impaired, it took a long while for Dave to get out of the city and although in that time his car filled with flies, once in the open countryside, he was able to open all the doors and get most of them out.

Since he was late in deciding to leave, all the hotels and boarding houses immediately around London were full, so he went further out, heading for a small fishing village called Walberswick.

There were seagulls and terns in the air, above the restless waves of the green North Sea. He could see a huge structure to the south, no doubt a power station, and the west was flanked by sand dunes. Marshy pools lay exposed after the retreat of the tide, and he almost trod on some bird's eggs just lying in a shallow basin of sand and pebbles. When he looked up, there were other such clutches, all along the beach.

'Watch out, bird's eggs,' he said to himself.

A strong breeze was blowing, whipping up the waves, and he sensed the excitement of late spring in the air. Wading birds searched for crustaceans and molluscs where the ocean met the land. Sea cabbage plants dotted the upper reaches of the strand and spume-washed driftwood, dried seaweed and beetle-shaped egg pouches lay in a neat, wavy line along the high tide mark, following the wiggly coastline south.

What a dump, thought Dave. Who could live here? No real waves, to speak of – they're puny when you compare them to Pacific rollers. The only birds I can recognize are the good old gulls.

He sighed again, thinking of Danny.

Me, miss that little jerk? He was a pain in the ass most of the time. I mean, he was a good cop, but he had these habits, you know? Like licking the powder from around the lip of his plastic coffee cup. Used to drive me crazy. And all that stuff with the whores and the priests afterwards. The guy was a mass of complexities.

Sure I miss him, he admitted to himself, or I will, when I can get to believe he's gone. The little shit.

Dave's eyes filled with tears in the biting wind from the North Sea and he wiped them away with the back of his hand.

Chapter Twenty-two

The flies were not so numerous now. Nevertheless, they were a great nuisance, clouds of them hovering over certain areas while in others they remained individual pests.

The ceiling of the Princess Louise was decorated with fly papers, black with their dead. In the corners of the bar, dozens were attracted to a caged blue light which frizzled them to nothing. An old-fashioned method of jam floating on water in a jam-jar was drowning a few on the bar itself.

Stan Gates was drinking in the Princess Louise when he got into an argument with a group of out-of-towners from Tilbury, come up to Wembley for a football match between Scotland and England. Tilbury supporters considered themselves a tough bunch and accepted no criticism of themselves or their team. Stan, who was part Scottish, might have been torn in his loyalties whenever the two neighbouring countries played each other, except that he had no liking for soccer whatsoever.

'So who do you support, then?' shouted a lout from among the group.

Stan waved his hand automatically over his beer glass to chase away the flies and glared at the caller sourly. He had watched the rowdy group getting drunker and drunker on real ale and whisky chasers, and as their drunkenness increased, so did his annoyance. He had come to the Princess for a few quiet bevvies, not to be intimidated by a bunch of hooligans still wet behind the ears.

'Well?' yelled another. 'Someone's talking to you, mate.'

'Someone's talking to me, but I'm not listening,' replied Stan, without even turning round. He could see them in the bar mirror. There were five of them. They were big men – probably dock workers, if they were employed.

150

'It's about time you listened to *someone*, cloth ears,' said one, with a blue chin. 'You might get into trouble, not listenin' when people talk to you.'

Stan looked at the man in the mirror, not really wanting any problems to solve.

'Listen, shitface, I'm a police officer. I don't want trouble with you, but if you insist I'll bloody well oblige understand?'

There was silence from the table for a few moments, then someone muttered, 'Fuckin' dick, ain't he?'

Stan knew that men from Tilbury, a dark and sinister area, would have little respect for authority – *any* authority – but they might just feel insecure enough in the big city to let matters alone. However, after a while, the heckling began again.

'Hey, copper, you support Mongolia in the World Cup, or what?'

He turned to face them then and leaned back on the bar with his elbows, flies buzzing round his face.

'I don't like football. It's a game for tossers, watched by tossers. I don't like toads from Tilbury either – they're all paedophiles and wife killers. Putting the two together, you can understand why I want to puke every time I look in your direction, which is why I'm going to turn back to the bar and ignore your stupid bloody remarks for the rest of the evening.'

He returned to his drink.

Blue Chin started to rise out of his chair, but two of the others grabbed him and urged him to sit back down.

''E's not worth it, Den, forget it.'

Den didn't forget it, but he sat down again, muttering something like, 'I'll 'ave that bastard. I'll 'it 'im so 'ard 'e'll be wipin' his nose at the back of his head.'

Eventually the gang got up and staggered outside. Stan heaved a sigh of relief. He'd been feeling a bit peculiar lately for some reason, and didn't want to get into any rough-housing with a gang of yobs anyway. It was nothing too serious, he thought. Just short lapses of memory. He'd suddenly find himself somewhere and not know how he got there or what he'd been doing for the last few hours. The doctor had told him it was quite common, or at least not rare. Still, a punch or two in the head would do him no good, that was certain.

At half past ten he finished his last pint, and, shouting goodbye to the barman, stepped out into the street.

High Holborn, a mainly business area, was virtually deserted. A tramp was lurking in the doorway of My Old Dutch restaurant across the street. He was covered in crawling flies, a living halo of them hovering over his head. He made no attempt to chase them away, letting them enter his mouth and nostrils at will.

Stan shuddered, and waved a few away from the vicinity of his own head. He started to walk down towards Shaftesbury Avenue, thinking to pick up a coffee at a Greek restaurant. As he passed Drury Lane, three men stepped out and he found his way barred.

'What d'you want?' said Stan.

'You!' said Den, grinning.

Stan stepped back and whipped out his mobile phone, intending to dial the two digits necessary to get help. A foot lashed out and sent it spinning away into the road.

'You'll regret that,' Stan growled. 'That's police property.'

'When I'm through with you, you won't be worryin' about little things like that no more.'

He was a big man now that he was on his two feet. He stood about six foot three in this thick boots. The other two were smaller, but both were heavy set. Stan guessed they were some kind of local Tilbury Mafia, who did a bit of protection here and there, lifted a few crates of this and that, and stole a few cars to ship over to the continent. There were groups like them in every town. He had arrested one in Billingsgate a few months ago, after they had broken into a shop, smashed in the skulls of two Dobermann guard dogs with two-pound hammers, and had broken the owner's arms over a counter for non-payment of protection money. Stan had to let them go in the end, because the shop owner refused to identify them. They'd threatened to meet the man's grandchildren out of school if he pressed charges, and he gave in and refused to co-operate with the police. Stan couldn't blame him. The police couldn't protect the man's family for ever. The only way society got rid of little Mafias like this one, was when a mild-mannered citizen was pushed over the edge, bought himself a shotgun, and blew the lot of them away.

'You don't want to do this,' said Stan firmly. 'You could be in big trouble.'

He stepped out into the road and retrieved his phone. He could see it was broken. It went into his pocket.

'You won't be worried about it,' Den was saying, ''cause you'll be in hospital.'

Stan threw a punch at the man's jaw, but Blue Chin had obviously done some boxing in his time and neatly side-stepped the blow. A heavy fist landed on Stan's temple and pain shot through his skull and awakened something deep inside him. As he shook his head to clear it, he had one of those blackouts he'd recently been experiencing.

Den, satisfied with his punch, smiled as he saw Stan totter backwards under the blow.

'Ain't fuckin' laughing now, are you, copper?' he crowed.

Then he saw Stan straighten and noticed that the police-man's eyes had changed. His stance was hunched now, in a crab-like pose. And he had a very peculiar smile on his face.

'Not laughing?' said Stan. 'I'm *killing* myself.'

'Do 'im,' snapped one of the others, rushing forward, anxious to prove his manhood.

Stan's hand shot out. Two of his fingers sank into the man's eye-sockets up to the knuckles, through the eyeballs and into the brain. The man screamed as blood poured down his face. Permanently blinded, he tottered and fell over sideways on to the pavement. Stan's boot lashed out and dislocated his spine, separating the head and torso. The man was dead before his skull struck the concrete with a crack like a coconut falling to the street from a great height.

'You still want to play?' he asked the other two.

They stared down at their comrade, horrified and astounded.

Den let out a yell of anguish. 'My mate! You've killed the poor bastard.'

153

The dead man's brains were leaking out of his eye-sockets on to the pavement.

Stan stepped forward and took Den's head in the heels of his hands. He pressed inwards with his palms in a quick pumping action. Blue Chin's skull imploded and became a mass of bone shards and fragments of teeth. He fell to the ground twitching and jerking spasmodically, as if trying to jump up on to his feet. Within seconds he was still.

The third member of the trio wisely decided it was time to go. He was the shortest of the three, but fast on his feet. The speed and horror of the other two deaths had sent his mind spinning somewhere out in space. He was so terrified he had lost all reason and was just screaming incoherently, his feet pounding the pavement unrhythmically.

Stan reached into his pocket and pulled out his gun. It was the special weapon he'd been given with which to destroy fiends and demons: the incendiary gun.

He aimed at the running man's back, very carefully, and squeezed the trigger. The fleeing man burst into flame. He continued running, his body burning like wax. His legs were running so fast, on a fuel of terror, that they refused to acknowledge his death. For a few moments after his skin had been burned from his flesh, and his flesh was being burned from his bone, he continued in his retreat. Stan could hear the flare of the flames, fanned by the rushing wind that a running man creates for himself, and the crackle of roasting pork. The stench of charred tissue wafted back to him on the breeze.

He sniffed deeply and replaced his gun in its holster. Then, without looking down at the bodies again, he strode up High Holborn, back past the Princess Louise, and to the hotel. No one had seen what he had done. He wouldn't even have to account for his actions.

Walking along Southampton Row, he suddenly came to his full senses. 'Wha—' he cried, catching himself in half-stride. 'What happened?'

He felt as if he had been doing physical exercises, but had no idea if it were true or not. He had no recollection of the

154

previous half-hour. All he could remember was leaving the pub and heading towards his favourite Greek restaurant. Nothing else.

He turned yet again and retraced his steps. When he got to Drury Lane two ambulances and four police cars were parked on the corners. Stan was curious. He went over to them.

He flipped his i-d at one of the officers. 'What's this, an accident?'

'An *accident?*' snorted the officer, who looked a sickly green. 'No, it ain't that, Sarge. Looks like a gangland killing. These two have been battered to death and there's one down the street who looks like a lump of charcoal.'

'Any witnesses?'

'We got some old geezer – tramp –– who says he saw a bloke do all three of them. Must have been a professional, if it was only one man. Must have been, to take on three at one go and come out tops, mustn't he? Bloody flies,' said the constable, waving his hand in front of his face. 'Makes you bloody sick, don't it?'

'Well, best of luck – you got a description?'

'Trying to get one out of the old goat now, but his brain's atrophied. I think he's been drinkin' paraffin.'

Stan looked over the constable's shoulder to see the tramp he had noticed earlier in the evening, sitting in a police car with two other cops who were trying to keep him awake now that he was in a warm place. One of them was plying him with coffee, while the other looked exasperated.

'Doesn't look as if they're getting very far,' said Stan, who was thinking, *I might have seen what happened here, but I can't remember.*

'Nah,' replied the constable. 'That old soak wouldn't recognize his own grandmother . . .'

Stan left the scene and passed another little group around the blackened body of the third victim. It was all very curious. If Manovitch had still been around, he told himself, this might have been *his* doing. But he was convinced that the fiend had been destroyed, despite the coming of the flies. Stan had

155

been the one who had burned Manovitch and he was proud of his success. Archdeacon Smith had brought two hot-shot cops from the States to get this fiend, and it had been Sergeant Gates who had made the challenge and had wiped him out. That was what stuck in their craws: the fact that after spending all that money it had been a home-grown copper who'd got the bastard in the end. Peters understood that, so why couldn't Smith?

'They don't bloody appreciate me,' said Stan to himself, as he walked along, 'that's their bloody trouble.'

He nodded. 'I'm a good copper, one of the best. I do my job and I do it well. And that's that. Manovitch has gone and it was me who took him out. They'll have to get used to that and give me my dues. Manovitch is back in hell for ever.'

A siren in the distance seemed to belie his words.

Chapter Twenty-three

Danny was just able to touch the floor of the star-shaped chamber with the tips of his toes.

A miserable grey light shone down from an arrow-loop close to the high vaulted ceiling. It was a light unworthy of any day: the kind of light that creeps into neglected buildings. It uncovered only cold stone of a similar colour to itself. Even the green-grey toad, tucked in the crevice of the arrow-loop, was not impressed by this contemptible light, too drab to illuminate the dust motes in its shaft, too heavy and damp to do anything but fall leadenly upon the slabs beneath.

There were rusty chains passing through holes in Danny's hands and these were attached to two large iron hoops, fitted high above his head, fixed to the stone wall. Furthermore, Danny was hanging facing the wall, flat against the stonework which was wet and covered in algae and fungi. He had been investigated by spiders and a rat had nipped at his testicles, making them bleed on to the stone. The pain from the wounds in his hands had at first been excruciating, but was now merely a long, endless dull ache.

He was naked and shivering with the cold that seemed locked inside the stone. He had not eaten for endless, unknown hours. To quench his thirst he had to lick the foul water that ran down the wall. There had been a savage attempt at rape, but Danny had passed out during the attack and it had not been carried to its conclusion, possibly because Manovitch wanted Danny wide awake when he administered humiliation and pain.

Danny realized he was in terrible trouble. No key had been used on the chains that held him. Instead, Manovitch had bent two of the links with his immensely strong fingers, so that it would take cutting tools to free him.

'Stan Gates,' Danny murmured to himself. 'Stan Gates is Manovitch. *Shit, fuck, damn.* Oh, Christ,' he wept in frustration and fear, 'Lord, I need help. Please help me, Lord,' he prayed. 'Don't let me die like this, please.' He was half delirious from lack of food, from the cold, and from the shock of his ordeal. He tried to remember what had happened. It came back to him in misty patches of grey and black, like a very old *film noir* playing in his head.

Stan Gates had driven him to the airport – to Heathrow – except that they never got there. He had stopped the car, saying, 'I think we've got a puncture,' then, as Danny opened the passenger door to get out to have a look, something struck him on the back of the neck and he blacked out.

He regained semi-consciousness when he was in some cold, clammy water. Danny at first thought it was the moat of some dreadful old place like the House of Usher, because of the vertical stone banks. Then in his groggy state he realized there were lights, both on the river and on the banks, which moved swimmingly around his vision.

Someone – Stan Gates? – was swimming with him in the water, which he came to realize was the river Thames, because of the buildings. Danny remembered seeing the lights of Tower Bridge, as they moved towards it, snaking through the currents. Snub-nosed barges went by, but the creature who held him paid no attention to the river traffic, and presumably they could not see him in the darkness. He was like some foul amphibious monster, emerging from the depths, sliding along the surface, seeking prey.

Danny tried to fight at one point, but found himself tightly bound with cord, and he ceased struggling in case his captor just let him go, leaving him to drown.

After a long, cold time in the water, the swimmer made for the bank. When they touched stone they slipped alongside a vertical wall, like river lizards following the flow, until there was a gap in the brickwork. Inside a deep slimy arch was an iron gate or grid, which Stan gripped and wrenched open with one hand, snapping the rusted padlock. Danny had felt the beards of weeds sliding over him like dead green tongues.

Then they entered a passage of darkness and Danny slipped into complete unconsciousness again.

When he woke, it was dawn. He was on his back, naked, on a cold stone-flagged floor. Stan was sitting astride his chest, looking down on him. His face was a twisted thing in which was buried a goblin's eyes that glinted with triumph.

'At last,' said Manovitch's voice, 'I have one of you.'

With his knees across Danny's elbows, Manovitch took each hand in turn and punctured it with one of his own fingers, the nails of which were spikes. Danny screamed as his palms were pierced and Manovitch laughed.

'Stigmata,' cried the fiend. 'You should be pleased, you miserable slob, to be able to share the same fate as the One you follow.'

Danny almost fainted in fear and agony at that point, but had remained on the edge of consciousness as Manovitch's voice had continued to gibe and taunt him. Then the attempt at rape had come and Danny had fallen down a deep dark shaft of terror, at the bottom of which was blissful nothingness. When he came round he found that the chains had been passed through the holes in his hands and he had been hung facing the wall.

'Mother of God, help me,' he screamed. He stared up at the arrow-loop he could see high above his head. 'Is there anyone out there? Someone help me!'

No one came. He could hear in the distance the faint sounds of traffic, of the bustle of a large city. Where the hell was he? In some forgotten ruin? Surely there was nowhere in London which was not visited by people? Someone would be bound to come and free him soon. He listened hard for sounds in the cell and heard only scratchings, which he suspected were rats or mice.

The stones in front of his face were crumbling with age and wet rot. Mortar like paste came away on his tongue when he tried to lick the water which ran down the walls. His arms ached continually from being above his head, and his legs were in agony since he could only just touch the floor. Had he been left dangling, however, he suspected he would not have lasted, but would have died fairly quickly. He wanted to die now.

While he hung there sobbing, his cheekbone and nose pressed hard against the stones, he heard a door creaking behind him.

'Hello,' said the malicious voice. 'Still here?'

It was Stan – or rather, Manovitch – back again. A quiver of terror went through Danny. Would Manovitch try to rape him again? Manovitch took hold of his ankles and put some weight to bear on them, making Danny scream out in pain.

'I'd like to break your legs below the knee,' muttered Manovitch, 'but it would probably kill you. I want you alive when I bring your partner down here to see your miserable remains, this heap of bones and hair. I want to hear Peters gasp, knowing when he sees you that I'm going to do the same to him, only prolong it more, drag it out, while you, you poor slob, witness his degradation.'

'Dave will burn you alive,' screamed Danny, in a rash fit of bravado.

Manovitch laughed. 'You stupid creature. Don't you see? I have you both now. You walked into my hands. Peters has disappeared somewhere into the country, but I'll have you both in a little while. You want to know what I'm going to do to him?' He patiently described the sexual tortures he was going to perpetrate upon the body and mind of Dave Peters.

'Christ will punish you for this,' cried Danny. 'Christ will see you in hell.'

Manovitch shrieked with laughter. 'I've *been* in hell, Danny boy, and I rose above it. I'm invincible. I'm Satan's blue-eyed boy. As for your Christ, he's afraid of me. He's been hitting me with all he has and getting nowhere.'

'Wrong,' cried Danny, twisting on his chains sending a ripple of pain through himself, to get himself mad. 'Wrong, wrong, wrong. You've been battling against the angels, maybe archangels, but when Christ wants you destroyed he'll snuff you out like a wick. You're nothing to him, *nothing*. You're lower than the dirt on his sandals. You're an insignificant insect next to the Lord, a sick, whining wretch with a soul that's rotting away to nothing – to *nothing*.'

Manovitch screamed and whipped a claw down Danny's back, opening the flesh to the bone. Danny screamed, too, higher and shriller than Manovitch.

The fiend laughed then. 'I can see your lungs through that hole. I can see them pumping against your ribcage. You'll regret tormenting me, Danny boy, when that wound begins to fester.'

Danny's head swam with sickness. He wished Manovitch would kill him outright now. His body was in tatters.

'How long can I last like this?' he cried to himself, rather than to Manovitch.

'Oh, you'll last a *long* time,' said Manovitch. 'I'll make sure of that. You'll be close to death, but you won't die. You think I want you going to join those shining slobs on the plains of Armageddon? You'll get there, soon enough, and even then you won't escape me. I'll seek you out up there, and destroy your soul. I'll send your soul into oblivion for eternity. How does that sound?

'You see, even this is not the end! You'll see me again, at the head of my troops, and you'll suffer pain there like you've never suffered before. Spiritual pain? Oh, it's a million times worse than mere physical or mental pain. I'll make sure you're obliterated, that's a certainty. You and your kind. Peters with you. You'll all be less than dust under *my* sandals. Ain't that quaint?'

Danny listened to this tirade with a sick heart. That he should suffer here and now was unavoidable, but as a believer he had hoped, if he reached heaven, to spend the rest of eternity in peace. Perhaps this *was* purgatory, here in this place, and he was being purified by suffering, before going on to heaven. That would make sense. Maybe Manovitch was some terrible instrument of the Lord, who had been sent to cleanse the soul of Danny Spitz, before it ascended.

'Oh, please, yes,' murmured Danny. 'Maybe I died in a car crash on the way to the airport. Or even on the plane.'

Manovitch laughed. 'Die? You didn't die. But you will,

don't worry about that, when I've given you enough pain.'

This taunting, too, could be part of the purging. Danny began to feel hope in his breast. He was being tortured to prepare him for the way of the Lord. All those sins of the flesh he had committed on earth, the dirty magazines he had read, the women he had corrupted by taking what they had to offer and giving them money to debase themselves: all these terrible deeds were coming home to him now.

Demons would come, to make his stay in purgatory a ghastly experience, an experience which would seal his soul for ever in a casket of Good. They would choose their words carefully: words that would wound like the talons of Manovitch had wounded his back. He must welcome the pain they inflicted, bear it with dignity like a saint. But he must not consider himself a saint. He was a foul sinner, undergoing the fires of hell, and he must remain humble.

'Hurt me some more,' he mumbled. 'Hurt me.'

Manovitch obliged him and soon Danny was shrieking for mercy once again.

When Manovitch stopped, Danny wept. 'I know who you are,' sobbed Danny. 'I know who you are and I shall come through it, pure and beautiful. I don't care about this old body. I shall have a new form soon, shining and immaculate.'

'For a very short while, perhaps,' muttered Manovitch, 'until I find you again.'

After a while Danny heard the door creaking closed again and he went limp and continued weeping for a very long while. But there was something bright in his head now, of which he did not intend to let go readily – an ember of hope.

'Those demons,' said Danny, 'they think they can fool me, but they can't. I know I'm dead. These are the dungeons, the pits of hell. This is where they try to break you, destroy your faith in the Lord. They'll *never* get me to deny my faith. There must be others here, undergoing similar tortures. I can *feel* I'm dead. I don't know how I died, but I died, and I'm going to come through it into a new world soon . . .'

162

Chapter Twenty-four

Lloyd Smith had met a nice woman at the British Museum, who seemed to like his company, and he was feeling a lot better about himself and with the world at large. His keen analytical brain, unhampered now by personal worries, once again applied itself to the problem of the archangel. It seemed that Manovitch was still at large. Petra had told him that the archangel could still sense the presence of the fiend in the city. Lloyd thus deduced that the possessor of his nephew's body and mind had not been Manovitch, but possibly some demon who had lost control of himself. Normally demons did not make waves, since they were fugitive creatures, deserters hiding from the wrath of Satan as well as from the justice of angels.

Walking along the north bank of the Thames with Petra, Lloyd was considering their next move. 'Clearly the loss of Danny Spitz has affected Lieutenant Peters quite deeply, Petra. He's due back in London today, isn't he? I wonder if we should now dispense with his services? His presence here has not drawn Manovitch out of the woodwork and I feel we're using him needlessly.'

Petra shook her head at this proposal. 'I think we should hold on to him. I have the feeling something's bubbling just below the surface. Something's not quite as it seems.'

Lloyd stopped and looked at her. 'Can you be more specific?'

Petra shook her head. 'I don't think Danny is dead. I don't have any proof, but I've sent for the passenger list for flight VA765. I used your name, I hope you don't mind. They don't give out lists unless there's some authority behind the request.'

Lloyd said, 'Let's sit on this bench. I like Whitehall

Gardens, don't you? They always arrange the flower-beds so artistically . . . Now, you were saying, you think Spitz is still alive, that he wasn't on the flight? But Sergeant Gates said he put him on the plane.'

'That's just a figure of speech, isn't it? I mean, he wouldn't have gone all the way to the aircraft with Danny. He'd leave him at passport control. Somewhere between there and boarding the plane, Danny has been spirited away.'

'Are you sure an outside agency is involved? Couldn't he have just walked off of his own accord, peeved by the lieutenant's orders to return to the USA? This is assuming you're correct about him not being on that flight.'

Petra looked down at her feet. If Danny had been able to, he would have contacted me ages ago. He hasn't. Therefore I can only guess that he's being held somewhere against his will. I'm certain he's not dead. The archangel doesn't number him among the recent souls in . . . in heaven.'

'Well, I'll take your word for it that he hasn't gone anywhere else.'

Petra suddenly stood up, her faced creased with anxiety. Lloyd's heart almost stopped. He read from her expression that something was about to happen, something terrible. Ought they to run?

'What is it?' he cried, jumping up. 'What's happening?'

Petra looked around her quickly, as if she were sniffing the air, then she said, 'Get away from here, Lloyd, we both have to get away. Everybody,' she shrieked at passers-by, 'Get away! *Get away!*'

Lloyd grabbed her arm and pulled her with him, not knowing which way to run. Finally, he chose to go to the river. There was a set of steps not far away, which led down to a quay where tourists boarded boats for Kew Gardens. Petra was screaming at people to get away from a huge Whitehall building, people who had stopped to look about them, wondering what this incomprehensible woman was yelling at them for. Some decided to run, having been through blood, lice, frogs and flies: they believed it was something to do with the next plague. Lloyd hurried her down the quay steps, so that they could shelter behind the wall, before the building exploded, or whatever.

'I don't *know* what's going to happen,' said Petra. 'I just know something is wrong – with that place.'

Just as Petra spoke those words, London stopped. That is to say, all the vehicles going past Whitehall Gardens at that moment, gradually slid to a halt. A train, using Hungerford Bridge, clattered to a standstill. This was not isolated to the vehicles they could see. All the cars, taxis, lorries, buses, trains – every vehicle in London – had lost its power and slid to a halt.

People on foot were looking around them in amazement. Drivers began climbing out of their vehicles, scratching their heads, gesturing to one another, bewildered. The city was eerily silent, and, for once, all that mighty heart was indeed lying still. Lloyd, a Londoner, had never felt so strange.

'It's started,' he said, as he hurried over the road.

'Yes,' Petra replied.

He turned to look at her. 'You know what I'm talking about?'

'The fifth plague?'

'It has to be. The death of all the livestock in London would hardly be noticed, would it? In those days, of course, they depended on their domestic stock. What do we depend on? Our road transport – our vehicles. But what . . . ?'

At that moment there was a screaming sound from overhead and Lloyd saw Petra go pale. It was no human sound, that noise, which came from the heavens. It was too loud, too shrill, the pitch almost above the frequency range of the human ear. Gradually, the screaming turned to an ear-shattering roar. Lloyd stared about him frantically, his view blocked on one side by a bank of the Thames. Were they being attacked by a squadron of angels? Or demons, perhaps, flying out of the sky like Valkyries? Surely, he thought, as the volume of the noise increased, this must be the end of the world at last, the day of Salvation.

Yet there was no wind, no earthquake, no fire or flood, just a terrible noise.

165

He skipped up the flight of steps, desperate to see how the Lord was going to destroy the earth with his angels, as foretold by St John the Divine. Was the noise the trumpet blast of the seven angels? Was a third of the earth now going to be destroyed, a third of the waters poisoned by wormwood, a third of the population of the earth annihilated?

This he wanted to see, Gog and Magog, two hundred thousand horsemen with breastplates of fire, of jacinth and brimstone, with heads of lions and breath of fire. He wanted to see one of the avenging angels, clothed with a cloud, a rainbow about its head with a face that was the sun. Surely the seven seals had been broken?

Where was the great bottomless pit and the locusts with scorpion stings and faces of men and hair of women and teeth of lions? Where were the voices of the earth, the thunderings and lightnings? Where was the great beast with seven heads and ten horns, the sea of glass, the waters of blood, the rider on the white horse? He wanted to *see*. He wanted to bear witness.

He saw none of these things. What Lloyd saw was a star falling to earth, a great star from heaven, burning as if it were a lamp in the blazing sunlight, but its name was not Wormwood – its name was Jumbo.

Lloyd just managed to duck his head below the concrete bank as the giant aircraft struck the earth, ploughed through St James's Park, and came hurtling into the huge Whitehall building with a monstrous, thunderous din. The explosion was so loud that Lloyd thought his head would split apart. A great pillar of flame leapt up into the air, higher than the highest London building, and the ground shook as if it were indeed an earthquake. A wave of water and hot wind went down the river and boats rattled against the quay. Shining chunks of metal spun through the air above Lloyd's head, landing in the Thames with a sizzling sound. Debris rained around him, splashing on the surface of the water, some of it bits of bodies from either the passengers of the aircraft, or the occupants of the building, some of it bricks and mortar, park benches, waste-bins, and two hundred thousand other burning objects.

166

Flame belched above, overlapping the walls of the embankment, singeing Lloyd's hair. Petra, further down, was hunched against the bank, trying to avoid being struck by any of the falling junk, which whistled and sang as it flew through the air. Several cars had been blown over the parapet into the water and were sinking in the river. Lloyd could see the terrified faces of people behind glass, struggling to get out.

One of the giant engines sailed right over the river, like a bouncing bomb, and demolished a row of houses on the far side, crashing through them as if they were skittles, then spinning on to take out a gas tank in another huge explosion of flame and smoke.

The South Bank did not escape the catastrophe.

A piece of fuselage went skating up towards Temple, along the road, a runaway jagged-edged sledge. It sliced through people and lamp-posts and telephone poles, leaving the severed remains of animals and humans twitching on the pavements. It cut through vehicles as if they were soft fruit and a double decker bus was sliced in two, its lower deck left with the spurting bodies of decapitated passengers. Finally it came to rest buried in a bronze statue which bent quickly in the middle as if bowing politely to the author of the slaughter.

Sirens were going, and horns blasting, and a great cacophony of noise. People were screaming, some hurt, others merely shocked. The dead ones were silent.

Lloyd peeked cautiously over the parapet.

He could find no words to describe the holocaust before his eyes. It was a scene of utter devastation. Petra came up beside him. Just then two more explosions sounded, one behind the other. More aircraft had come down as they entered the airspace above the capital, where all engines had ceased to function. A helicopter went spinning down out of control above Tower Bridge, like a sycamore seed falling to earth. It crashed, tangled in some girders, little black shapes dropping from its cockpit into the water.

'Why don't they warn Heathrow and Gatwick?' cried Lloyd. 'Why don't they stop this?'

'They can't know yet – it takes time.'

'*You* knew,' he said accusingly.

She stared at him. 'I knew *something* was going to happen, but I didn't know what. I never thought of an aircraft, did you?'

Lloyd shook his head in frustration. 'I suppose so. Oh, why don't we see further than our noses? We're so stupid.'

The fire roared in front of them, minor explosions taking place in the heart of the flames. The conflagration scorched them and they had to back away towards Big Ben, where the heat was not quite as fierce.

Petra said, 'I didn't know it was going to be the engines, until it happened. The death of all the traffic in London . . .'

Lloyd sighed. 'Well, this is going to slow us all down a bit, isn't it? I don't know whether that's going to prove a good or a bad thing. I rather suspect this gives Manovitch an advantage – he's much swifter in the streets than we are.'

A driver climbed out of his vehicle and walked to the edge of the Thames, looking into the water as if the answer to the problem of his failed engine lay down there. His passenger remained where she was, no doubt hoping that at any moment whatever had gone wrong with the world would right itself.

Lloyd said, 'The archangel must work through you. You're its eyes and ears, aren't you?'

Petra's mouth was a firm line. 'I'm its eyes and ears, but the archangel isn't omniscient. It doesn't know what Manovitch is going to do from one minute to the next, any more than we do.'

Lloyd said. 'What about you? Have you lost all free will?'

'When I see something, the archangel sees it too. That's a matter of supernature.'

Lloyd considered this and decided there was nothing to be unduly alarmed about. At least if Petra was with them when they encountered Manovitch, there might be no need to burn the fiend themselves. Perhaps the archangel would do it remotely, from its static position in the City of London.

A wave of tenderness for Petra flowed through Lloyd. He was a man who fiercely guarded his own independence. He hated the thought of a mortal like himself being in thrall to a supernatural creature, even if that creature was on the side of Good. There was a love of money in his bones, which he knew was distasteful to many, but beyond that there was little about him which fair-minded people might criticize, and he was basically a kind, thoughtful person. He found himself reaching out and, without embarrassment on either side, spontaneously stroking her hair.

'My dear,' he said, 'will the archangel free you of your attachment to him when he returns to Armageddon?'

'I don't know,' said Petra. 'I really don't know.'

Behind them the fire was still burning, spurting flame and gas, crackling fiercely, though it was not the pyre that it had been a few minutes previously. The body of a taxi thrown along the street by the initial explosion, was now like a black-ened skull – the headbone of a Gog or Magog – with empty sockets and charred teeth.

Of the driver who had been trapped inside, they could see nothing.

'Typical. It looks as though the only thing still intact is the meter. I wonder if it's still running?' said Lloyd with an attempt at grisly humour.

Petra looked at him askance.

Lloyd shrugged. 'Yes, I know, a bit sick, but then the whole world's a bit sick, isn't it?'

Chapter Twenty-five

It being Saturday morning, Daphne was making a desultory effort at doing some housework around the flat. She wasn't a particularly house-proud person and tended to let things go until she couldn't stand to look at them any longer. There were far more important things to be doing, in her opinion, than creating temporary dust-free surfaces which, if she were to die tomorrow, would be just as dusty again before she was laid to rest. A Scottish aunt in her family had always been praised for the hard work she put into keeping her house clean. It appeared to be the lady's life's work, to be carved on her gravestone: SHE KEPT A SPOTLESS HOME. Wow! Daphne thought. What a legacy! Not for *me*.

However, everything had to be done by hand: anything with a motor just did not work. The fridge didn't work, the washing machine didn't work, the kitchen whisk and the vacuum cleaner did not work. Nothing was functioning. Consequently things were getting a little out of hand.

The only place in the flat where the dust really distressed her was on her books. There were books *everywhere*: on the shelves that lined most of the walls; in piles on the floors in the corners of rooms; on windowsills; stacked by the bed. Those by the bed were the books currently being read. Daphne always had about four or five on the go. They would vary from novels, to volumes of poetry, to works of reference.

Rajeb, who had not been a great reader before Daphne went to live with him, had caught the book habit. Since Daphne spent much of her time with her nose between the pages, Rajeb needed a distraction, too. Television was boring in large amounts, so he, too, began delving between the pages. It was true that in his case they contained mostly fantasy or action stories – he particularly liked American cop books – but reading was reading. Daphne was not one to sneer at anyone's taste in literature.

Rajeb had gone down to the market for the groceries. He'd had to walk because there had been no transport since the previous evening. When the doorbell rang, at eleven o'clock, she thought he'd forgotten his key and released the outer door's electronic lock without thinking. She heard some feet on the stairs and realized it was not Rajeb, but a stranger. She opened the door and looked down to see a man coming up.

'Hello, can I help you?'

The man paused and looked up. 'Yeah. I've come to speak to Rajeb Patel. Had to walk all the way over here and I'm pretty bushed.'

Daphne didn't want to let this man know that Rajeb was not at home, so she asked, 'Who wants to see him?'

'I do,' snapped the man.

'And who are you?' asked Daphne, beginning to feel a little uneasy.

'Stan Gates – Sergeant Stan Gates.'

Daphne heaved a sigh of relief at hearing the name Rajeb had used many times.

'Oh, you work with Raj, don't you?'

Gates gave her a lopsided smile. 'You could say that, or you could say I'm his boss.'

'Yes, that's what I meant. Well, Raj isn't here at the moment. Do you want to leave him a message? He's just gone out shopping.'

Gates didn't answer. He came on up the stairs, very slowly, until he reached the top. He was puffing a little.

'Have you ever thought,' he said, 'of getting a ground-floor flat?'

'We like it up here, away from the bustle and the noise of the traffic,' replied Daphne.

'Not much noise of traffic down there at the moment, but a good deal of bustle, I suppose. Can I come in for a minute? I could do with a cup of tea.'

Daphne looked at him quickly. Gates had used a tone of

voice which suggested he meant something other than a cup
of tea, but when she looked at him sharply, he was staring at
a picture on the wall and appeared completely innocent.

'All right,' she said at last. 'You can come and sit and wait
for Raj. He should be back in a few minutes.'

'Thanks.'

Gates walked through the door of the flat and stared around
him. 'Lot of books,' he said. 'You a bookworm, then?'

'I'm a teacher – yes, I do read a lot.'

'Don't get much time for reading,' he remarked, using the
age-old excuse for not doing something one felt one ought to
be doing.

Daphne became quickly irritated. So he didn't read much
– so what? Maybe he was a brilliant mathematician and spent
all his time doing magical things with figures. Maybe he was
a great sportsman and would one day compete in the Olymp-
ics. It was not essential to the survival of the race that every
single individual had to read mountains of books before they
died.

'Tea or coffee?' she asked.

'Tea, I think,' said Gates, 'but none of that fancy stuff –
your jasmine or Lapsang Souchong, whatever.'

'Why should I give you those?'

He smiled slyly. 'Well, you know, Raj's Indian, isn't he?
Probably drinks that perfumed muck all the time.'

Daphne stiffened. 'For a start, Raj is British, and you should
know that. Second, jasmine and Lapsang Souchong are
Chinese teas. Third, we only have breakfast tea anyway.'

'Oh, right,' smiled the thick-skinned visitor. 'Breakfast tea
– that's ordinary, is it?'

Daphne went into the tiny kitchenette. She was seething.
How could Raj work with a prick like this? And Raj had always
professed an admiration for Gates. Surely he wasn't that
bad a judge of character? She made the tea and carried it
back into the living room, to find Gates missing. Then she
heard a sound from behind her and saw that he was standing
in the doorway of the bedroom, where he'd obviously
been.

172

'So this is the bedroom, is it?' He sniffed, ostentatiously. 'I like bedroom smells, don't you?'

A chill went through her. She wanted Rajeb to come home now. She wanted him there with her. This Stan Gates was not the man Raj took him to be. There was a corruption in him. Daphne could sense it, just by his proximity.

'Come and sit down,' she said as lightly as she could. 'Here's your tea.'

'Not that thirsty now,' said Gates, 'but I'd like something else on the side.' He stared at her meaningfully.

There could be no mistaking him this time.

She said coldly, trying to hide her nervousness, 'I'm sorry, I'm a one-man woman. Raj—'

His face changed then and he stepped forward, spitting, 'Raj? Raj? What the fuck about him? I don't give a monkey's toss for Raj. All I know is I've got this,' he indicated the bulge in the front of his trousers, 'and I want to get rid of it. Now, how do you like it?'

Thoroughly terrified, Daphne dashed into the kitchenette and grabbed the carving-knife, holding it awkwardly like a dagger. She didn't know whether she could stab him or not – she had never had to consider such a thing before. It had been a reflex action, to grab the knife. But she knew she had to be aggressive, not submissive.

'You get away from me,' she screamed. 'You stay away. I'll cut your bloody balls off!'

He stopped and shrugged, smiling lopsidedly at her. 'Got a lot of spunk, ain't you? Well, you're going to get a bit more. Put that thing down or I'll ram it up your arse.'

Daphne felt faint, but she clung to the edge of the stove. She wished there was a boiling pan of water on top, so that she could throw it in his face. She wanted to scream with frustration, as well as fear, because of her helplessness. He looked a strong man and she knew she wasn't going to stand much of chance when he moved in close. She could try to stab him, but these things were not as simple as they looked in the movies. He had a thick jacket on for a start. Was she even going to be able to pierce his coat?

'Don't hurt me,' she shrieked. 'My neighbours will be up in a minute.'

'You can yell all you want, I saw them go out.'

'Oh, God—'

He jumped forward and instead of waiting to stab him, she threw the knife at his face. It bounced, blade-first, off his head, without penetrating. Daphne flung herself sideways, out of reach of his grip, then ran towards the door. Gates was on her before she got to the handle. He brought her down in a rugby tackle, even though she squirmed and tried to scratch at his eyes. He was, as she had guessed, immensely strong.

'Playing games, eh?' he hissed in her ear as he pulled her hair back painfully, so that her throat was exposed. 'I could bite through that nice white neck and kill you now.'

'Please,' she sobbed. 'Don't—'

Her arms were stretched out before her and her fingers sought something, anything, to use as a weapon. The Women's Survival Class tutor had told her: if you're in a life-threatening situation, use anything you have as a weapon, a hat pin, a sharp ring, even a dead match. Anything. Go for the eyes. If a man can't see you, he can't do much harm. Blind him, if possible. *In a life-threatening situation, it's either you or him, and you'd rather he was blind than you were dead, wouldn't you?* Terrified as she was, Daphne now knew what her teacher meant. There was no choice.

Don't be a compliant victim. Don't ask them what they want. Don't *ask* them any questions. Don't *answer* any questions. *Tell* them, abuse them, hurt them, if you can, especially in their most vulnerable place. Be unfeminine. Be hostile.

She spat as viciously as she could into his eyes.

He ripped open her blouse and took hold of one of her breasts, twisting it savagely. Her eyes watered, but she tried to knee him in the groin, failing, hitting his thigh instead. It clearly hadn't hurt him because he laughed.

'You get the fuck off me, you dirty bastard,' she yelled in his face. 'I'll kick your balls when I get up.'

174

She tried to bite his hand.

Her change of attitude made him hesitate and relax his hold. She reached out and grabbed a book. It just happened to be a good solid New English Bible. She rammed the corner in Gates's right eye, causing him to grunt and release his hold on her. She scrambled away from him, kicking out with her feet, catching him on the nose.

'Shit!' he said, angrily.

'What's the matter?' she shouted at him. 'Is this the only way you can get a woman? Impotent, are you? You fucking miserable excuse for a man—'

Blind fury came over him and he made a rush at her. She picked up a table lamp and tried to ram it in his face. He knocked this aside, got his hand inside the waistband of her slacks, and pulled, ripping the front.

At that moment a voice yelled, 'You touch her again and I'll blow your fucking head off, Gates.'

Daphne looked at the doorway. Rajeb was standing there with a gun in his hand, pointing it at Gates. The groceries he had been sent to buy were scattered all over the floor of the flat and hallway where he had dropped them. She hadn't heard him open the door or noticed the sound of the goods falling on the floor.

Gates straightened and dusted off his trousers. 'She was asking for it, Patel. I just came to tell you that Smith wants us in the Jasmine Suite. She offered and then changed her mind—'

'I did not,' choked Daphne, dismayed at the deviousness of the man. 'I didn't!'

Stan Gates laughed. 'Well, she would say that, wouldn't she?'

Rajeb stepped forward, still pointing the incendiary gun at Gates's head.

'I ought to burn you like a piece of trash,' said Rajeb, with emotional undertones. 'I ought to burn you now.'

'There's a problem there, my son,' said Gates, patronizingly. 'You'd burn down this block of flats, wouldn't you? Maybe your tart here with them.'

Rajeb struck him across the face with the gun, causing a welt to appear.

'Get the fuck out of here, Gates, before I take the chance,' he said. 'I'll sort you out later.'

'I never touched her,' said Gates, still staring at the muzzle of the gun. 'It was her.'

'*Out!*' shouted Rajeb.

Gates walked towards the doorway and disappeared down the stairs.

Daphne collapsed on the floor, sobbing. Rajeb picked her up and carried her tenderly to the bed, where he laid her down and began to undress her.

'What are you doing?' she cried, grabbing his wrist.

'Changing your clothes. These are all torn. Then I'm going to take you to the doctor's.'

She touched her breast. It was very sore. 'I'm just a little bruised, that's all. The doctor won't do anything for me.'

'I want him to *see* the bruises.'

She helped him change her clothes, then she said, 'No, I don't want to go. It won't do any good. You know how many rapes ever reach the court-room. You know how many convictions of rapists there are. I wasn't even raped.'

'Then we'll get him on assault. He attacked you, didn't he?'

'Yes, he attacked me, but you know what he'll say. He'll tell them I egged him on. He'll say I was a tease, then changed my mind half-way through. You know how it can be twisted. You're a policeman, for Christ's sake. You know how they can make it sound when everyone's calm and sedate in a court-room. He's a policeman, too. He knows how to manipulate. He knows how to show remorse, even when he doesn't feel it. We'd be lucky to get him reprimanded, let alone punished. You know that, Raj.'

Raj did know it. He showed by his face that he knew it. But also in his face was a promise that it would not be allowed to rest there. 'Then I'll sort him out,' said Raj. 'In my own good time.'

She nodded. They made some coffee with brandy in it,

176

then he sat on the sofa and just held her for a while, hugging some confidence back into her.

'Thank you, Raj,' she said, after a while.

'What for, darlin'?'

'For not questioning me for an instant. For believing me. For not listening to his lies. I love you, Raj. You didn't even stop to consider that he might have been telling the truth, did you? You trusted my word. I love you to bits for that, you lovely man.'

She was crying now, sobbing on his shoulder, and he chewed his lip, not saying anything, hoping she was right. It had been such a shock, such a turmoiled few minutes, that he couldn't remember how he had felt or what he had said. He was just glad she didn't doubt his loyalty. 'I love you too, babe,' he said, into her hair. 'I won't let anyone ever hurt you again . . .'

Chapter Twenty-six

As he was driving back into London, when vehicles were able to cross that magic line beyond which their engines had ceased to function, Dave was again struck by the beauty of the archangel's hemisphere of light. It occurred to him that beauty had come into conflict with money, the destruction having been wrought on the financial district, and that perhaps the archangel was making a point. Maybe it was saying, Here is a false god: use money as a means of easy exchange but don't begin to worship it for its own sake.

Money, beyond a certain amount, had always represented power as well as wealth. Those with it often assumed a certain arrogance, a superiority over those without it. To some it was not sufficient to have enough: they had to have more than enough – much more. It became, then, not a means of exchange, but a means of control.

These reflections of his, Dave realized, were truisms, of course, but it didn't do any harm to be reminded that ultimately money meant nothing at all, and that spiritual things, symbolized by the archangel, were far more powerful.

When Dave finally arrived back at the hotel he found Rajeb Patel and Stan Gates having a furious argument in the lobby. Dave went over to them.

'What's this all about?' he asked.

Gates looked at him as if he were about to tell him to mind his own business, but then his countenance underwent a change and he smiled. 'Nothing much, Dave. Since we've lost Danny, so to speak, I thought I'd start driving you around now, but my constable here is objecting. I can deal with it.'

Dave looked at Rajeb, who appeared to be smouldering. The young man's face was full of hatred. Dave's street instincts told him that more was going on here than just an argument over who was driving whom. Something pretty deep was running between these two men and it might jeopardize the operation. You needed to have men who trusted each other, who would back each other right to the hilt in a tight situation. By the look of him, Dave reckoned that Rajeb Patel would let his sergeant go to hell in a bucket and not lift a finger to help him.

'OK, you two,' said Dave, 'tell me what's really going on.'

'Nothing's going on,' snapped Gates. 'As sergeant in charge of this operation, I feel I'm entitled to say who drives you around. As for Patel here, hell, he says I made a pass at his girlfriend. I never went near his girlfriend – or his flat. He's trying to accuse me of something, I don't know what. He's bloody barmy, if you ask me.'

Rajeb blurted out, 'You shut your filthy mouth. This is between you and me.'

The young man was about to explode, possibly into violence, and Dave placed a restraining hand on his shoulder. 'Let's calm down, keep our voices low, and try to remain a little rational here. Now, what the hell is this about?'

'I really don't think it's any of your concern, Lieutenant,' said Gates, hard-faced.

'Anything that endangers the outcome of this operation is my concern,' replied Dave. 'You're forgetting something, Sergeant – I've been put in charge, not you. I get my orders from Smith and I pass them on to you, got it? So don't screw around with me, or you'll be back in the station house.'

Again, something passed over Gates's face like a dark storm, then cleared again.

'Yeah, I was forgetting. Sorry, Lieutenant. I apologize. Too used to giving orders, I expect. Anyway, I still think I should be doing the driving.'

Dave said, 'I'm quite satisfied with Patel here, and that's an end to it.'

Rajeb nodded and walked away, presumably to cool off.

Dave said, 'What's all this about – with Patel's girl?'

The other man shrugged. 'I told you, I don't know what he's talking about. Maybe his girlfriend has got me mixed up

179

with someone else – I don't remember ever meeting her. He just went nuts on me when I walked through the door this morning. I'm . . . I'm a bit confused.'

'It would be better if you didn't get confused again,' said Dave. 'Not until this is all over. Then you and Patel can punch it out in some back alley for all I care. Just keep your private affairs out of my nose.'

'I still think I ought to be driving you.'

Dave knew that if he allowed the swap it would be sending the wrong message to Rajeb.

'I like the way it is,' he said. 'I think I'm old enough to choose my own driver.'

The sergeant nodded grimly, and walked off in the opposite direction to Rajeb. Dave didn't want to get into a heated argument in the lobby, so he followed the bell-boy with his luggage towards the elevator.

Later, he met Lloyd Smith in the coffee shop, who looked a lot better than when Dave had last seen him. 'How are you, Lloyd? You look somewhat more chipper.'

'Yes, I am. Feeling good, as you people say.'

The waitress came up to the table with a smug look on her face. With her pencil poised over her order pad, she said to Dave, 'Would you like some Colombian coffee, sir?'

Dave looked at her. 'You have Colombian?'

'Ordered it in specially,' she said.

A warm glow went through him. 'Well, now,' he said, 'this is more civilized. Yes, I *would* like some coffee,' he looked at the name tag on her breast pocket, 'Sylvia, thank you. And I appreciate this a lot.'

'And you, sir?' she enquired of Lloyd.

'I'll try some Colombian, too, since it seems to be the life-blood of the lieutenant here.'

'Right.' She bounced away.

'How was your holiday?' Lloyd asked.

'Fine, if you could call it a holiday. It was more like a brief rest.'

'I've got something very important to tell you. I'm not *sure* it's good news, but it might well be. It concerns your partner.'

'Danny?' Dave's head shot up. A small candle flame of hope flared in his heart.

Lloyd said, 'We don't know whether he's alive or not, but when Petra sent for the passenger list of that aircraft that came down, Danny's name was nowhere to be seen. It's possible he used a false name, of course, but I can't see the point of that, can you?'

Dave frowned. 'Gates said something about Danny wanting to skip once he reached the States. It could be that he used a false name so that my department wouldn't be able to trace his movements afterwards. But it doesn't seem very likely. Have you broken the list down?'

Lloyd nodded. 'Four hundred passengers. Three hundred and thirty-seven were made up of opposite-sex couples or families. Thirty were same-sex couples, mostly young women. There was a sporting group of six males. There were only twenty-seven singles on the flight. Seven of those were women, one was a child of twelve going to visit his people in the USA, the rest were mostly businessmen. In fact, we can eliminate all but three names. Alexander Ross, Werner Heizmann and J. Randolph Baker.'

'If Danny was going to use a false name, the last sounds the most likely, he's always wanted an impressive first initial. Randolph? Doesn't sound like Danny. Are you checking on those last three, for age and description?'

'We're still in the process.'

The coffee arrived and Dave was able to give Sylvia a dazzling smile. A lot of weight had been lifted from his mind. There was a chance that Danny had come back from the dead. It was wonderful. The world was suddenly a much lighter place.

Sylvia responded in kind. 'Your Colombian coffee, sirs.'

'Sylvia,' said Dave, 'back home we would call you one hell of a gal.'

'You can do that here if you like,' she called, laughing as she left them.

'Colombian,' mused Lloyd as he sipped his coffee. 'Is there cocaine in this, or what?'

'Just pure, delicious coffee,' said Dave. 'Enjoy.'

'So,' said Lloyd, returning to the question in hand. 'Where does that leave us?'

'It leaves us with two possibilities. Either Danny caught another flight, to Mongolia or wherever, or he stayed here and is in hiding in London.'

'There is a third possibility,' said Lloyd.

'What's that?'

'Manovitch wasn't destroyed and has somehow got hold of Danny.'

Dave had already considered this. 'Doesn't make sense,' he said. 'It would have had to be an incredible coincidence for Manovitch to be at the airport right about the time Gates was taking Danny to his flight.'

Lloyd nodded. 'That's true, of course, but we'll appeal for any witnesses to any incident on that date. We'll check with the airport staff and put out a general request on television, for members of the public to come forward. You never know.'

'One thing. Gates said he was with Danny when he caught the flight.'

'He said he left him at the ticket desk.'

Petra arrived at the table. She sat down and gave Dave a smile that would have melted the Antarctic. 'The last of those passengers has been found. None of them could have been Danny.'

Dave slammed a fist into his palm. 'Terrific. Have some coffee, Petra. It's great.'

He left them at the table, took the elevator up to his room and immediately called Vanessa.

'Good news,' he said. 'Danny's alive.'

Her delighted voice came back. 'He survived the crash?'

'No one survived the crash. He wasn't even on the flight.'

'But Stan Gates . . .'

'Gates left him at the *ticket* desk. He didn't accompany him to the plane. You can't do that. Non-passengers can't go into the departure lounge, can they?'

'That's true. So Danny's still alive somewhere? Do we know where?'

'No, but that doesn't worry me at the moment. Friar Tuck can surface when he wants to, the old warrior-priest. I feel good, Vanessa, *very* good.'

'I can hear you feeling good,' she murmured.

'Well, I hope we can do something about that pretty soon.'

'I love you too, Dave – oh, so much. You'll never, never know . . .'

Chapter Twenty-seven

It was night.

The woman was driving home late from visiting her mother who lived in a village near High Wycombe. The roads out of Chalfont St Peter were unlit and dark. This kind of driving frightened her badly and she was glad to enter the brightness of London. However, her own home was down by the western canal in among some deserted old warehouses, and there, too, her night fears began to make her heart race a little. She parked the car at the end of the row of terraces and hurried directly to the second one along, opening her front door with her key.

She went straight to her kitchen to make herself a cup of strong tea, glad to be home. While she was filling the kettle at the sink, she heard a faint sound coming from the living room. Once again the terror rose like vomit to her throat, threatening to choke this time. Having escaped rape and murder on the highway, her second biggest fear was overcoming her: that of having a dangerous stranger in her home at night, when there was no one around to help her. Her husband, a dockland security man, had gone on shift at eight o'clock.

With her heart beating in terror she snatched a carving-knife from the block and stood there waiting and listening, wondering if she should scream. The clock in the hall chimed once, softly, and made her skin prickle. She wanted to start crying, but her fear wouldn't let her. Instead, she stayed frozen to the spot, the knife poised.

It remained quiet for a while. Then came a moaning sound – and someone stumbled into the hallway.

'Keep away from me,' she shrieked. 'I've got a knife.'

A moment later it staggered through the kitchen door

towards her. It was foul and ugly, like something out of a horror movie. Covered in protrusions, lumps and bumps all over its body, it was running with blood and pus. It was obviously blind, since its eyes were buried deep below the swellings on its face, and its mouth was a pinched hole which disappeared among the craters that seemed about to erupt in viscous matter all over its weeping chest.

'Oh, God!' she screamed, her knuckles white as she gripped the handle of the knife. 'Keep away!'

The alien creature did not seem inclined to take notice of her pleading. Several of its swellings were already bursting, splattering the kitchen floor. It gave out another muffled moan and reached out for her, trying to touch her. She screamed again and slashed at the disfigured arms, slicing at the gutted sores. Blood spurted down the creature's lumpy body, running over the blistering skin.

It made a sound like a rat being skewered and backed off towards the kitchen door. The woman picked up a bottle from the draining board and threw it hard at the retreating form. The bottle struck the doorframe and split open, showering the creature with concentrated bleach. The creature stopped, waved its swollen upper limbs, and came forward again, thrashing, letting out a piercing yell.

She stabbed it repeatedly among the lumps on its chest, hoping it had a heart. The knife was sharp and the blows swift and hard and soon the bubbling monster fell beneath the long blade, to convulse in a pool of its own repulsive fluids on the kitchen tiles at her feet. Even as it lay dying, the swellings grew on its skin, bulged and burst, and new grotesque lumps appeared where the old ones had left their craters.

Finally, she was able to run from the kitchen to the main doorway and call for assistance. A neighbour answered, coming from next door. To the woman's astonishment she, too, had several lumps and sores, though much of her skin area was clear. The woman dropped her knife and let out a wail of despair. As she looked down at herself, boils began to appear on her arms and legs: ugly swellings with nasty cores and weeping craters. The neighbour spoke to her in a soothing

185

voice, telling her it was all right, that there was nothing to be frightened of really.

'It's the boils. Everyone's got them – some worse than others. The plague of boils. Your Ken,' she said, 'he's very bad – couldn't possibly go to work. He's lying on the living-room sofa, waiting for you . . .'

Manovitch swam alongside the algae-bearded wall of the Thames towards Tower Bridge, the dirty water stinging the profusion of boils on Stan Gates's neck, face and shoulders. As a fiend, Manovitch was not subject to the plagues put out by the archangel, but his human body had to suffer. Gates had the boils and Manovitch had to tolerate their presence in times when he came forward and took over.

When Stan Gates had incinerated Holden Xavier, the instant before the projectile struck, Manovitch had transferred himself. It was an empty body that fell flaming from the roof of the building into the alley below. Moreover, Manovitch had learned his lesson: he had not immediately destroyed his victim's mind and taken over the shell. Instead, for the most part he stayed well back, just pulling a few strings here and there, not greatly interfering with Stan Gates's lifestyle, personality or character. From his remote position, Manovitch could observe all, yet remain hidden, even from the probings of the archangel and its agents. Gates was a brilliant hideout. And when he had to, Manovitch could take over the whole body, forcing Gates into some nether region of his own cerebrum.

Manovitch was not impatient with the slow way things were going, but he knew that the longer he held Spitz prisoner in the dungeon, the more likely it would be that things would go wrong and turn against him. He had almost revealed himself in that encounter in Patel's flat, when his lust got the better of his caution. And already Peters knew that Spitz was not dead. He had hoped to be driving Peters around by now, but that interfering fool Patel had got in the way of his plans.

Something had to be done about that, very soon.

If Patel were to die suddenly, there would be a lot of suspicion in the air. Manovitch couldn't afford that. He knew he was vulnerable in a human body. He would not be able to get out of Gates as fast as he had out of Xavier, because not owning the body completely meant that movements of his dead soul were more sluggish and harder to control. First he would have to destroy Stan Gates, *then* he could fly from the body into that of a nearby other.

Manovitch reached the archway that held the iron grid. He entered the temporarily abandoned Tower of London by climbing over St Thomas's Tower through which ran Traitor's Gate.

Manovitch had sifted through Gates's mind in order to know this place intimately. It was necessary for his safety and security that he was able to identify the buildings within the Tower's walls and understand the geography. Gates had taken visitors to the Tower on various occasions and knew its confines well: he had always thought that the complex ought to be called the Towers of London since there were over a dozen of them.

Manovitch had used Gates's knowledge to find the star-shaped stone chamber, the vaulted ceiling of which disappeared into darkness, where he was keeping his prisoner. Danny Spitz hung in chains from the dank walls below the chamber's cross-configured window.

Manovitch made his way to the cell. As he approached he could hear the low, repetitive sound of a human voice. Curiosity made him stop to listen.

It was the sound of chanting.

> '*Manovitch*
> *Is a son-of-a-bitch.*'

The words were croaked over and over, like a mantra, occasionally interrupted by the words,

> '*Danny Spitz*
> *Lives at the Ritz.*'

187

or

> *'Friar Tuck*
> *Needs a damn good fuck.'*

Manovitch smiled to himself. His victim was going crazy. Danny Spitz was losing his reason.

The dead soul walked into the chamber, to find a scrawny, filthy figure hanging from its chains. Friar Tuck had managed to twist himself round so that he was awkwardly facing the front, away from the wall, his chains crossing each other. His gaunt face, with its bulging eyes and chapped lips, stared at Manovitch. There were boils on his shoulders, down his back: even manacled prisoners wasting away in oubliettes were not immune from the plague, as if they did not have enough sores and open wounds with which to contend. Insects were doing things among the creases of his skin, in his ragged beard and hair, around his genitals. He seemed to have a permanent erection, which was more to do with starvation than sex.

As Manovitch approached him, Danny urinated, his bladder unfortunately too weak to reach his target.

'Nice try,' sneered Manovitch. 'What are you, a poet now, boy? I heard you chanting nursery rhymes.'

> *'Manovitch*
> *Is a son-of-a-bitch,'*

droned Danny, his hunger-bright eyes like twin mad candle flames.

'Very good, very good,' smiled Manovitch. 'Robert Frost look out. I've brought you some food.'

Manovitch produced some sodden crusts from his pocket, which he began feeding to his victim. Danny, full of hatred as he was, remained too sick to reject the food. He sucked it up and swallowed it, just as he snatched cockroaches with his teeth from his shoulders and crunched them with great relish, savouring the protein. When you're starving, you eat anything – dirt, lice, ancient mortar, beetles, flies, anything.

There was excrement on Danny's legs, over the wall, on the floor, all around him, testifying to dysentery. Danny was dying, very slowly, only keeping himself alive with his little mantras, hoping that at some time a person other than Stan Gates was going to wander in through the doorway to the cell.

When Danny had swallowed the last of the food, Manovitch gave him some water. It was in Manovitch's interests to keep him alive until his friend Peters could see how he had suffered. He was to be a role model for Peters, once the big cop was in Manovitch's hands.

Manovitch knew that Danny was still holding some hope in his breast and he determined to tweak it. While Danny was staring at him, Manovitch allowed Stan Gates to come forward.

Gates stared wildly about him, finding himself in a moonlit place of damp stone: a stinking tomb of some kind? He was wet through. He gagged on a terrible, sickening smell. Then a scream rose to his throat as he wondered if he had been thought dead and immured in stone, alive – one of his greatest and most secret fears. A stench of death hung about the slick walls and slimy floors.

Something stirred in front of him – a mere shuddering of the wind as if through a piece of linen – and Gates noticed a strange creature dangling on the wall. It was an emaciated form, a Christ-figure, with prominent ribs and stringy arms and legs. Fever-ridden eyes burned in the face. The blistered lips were moving, as the creature moaned softly.

'AAAAHHHHGGGH!' screamed Gates, backing away in terror, his hair bristling. There was a lump in his throat the size of an apple and he knew it was a ball of fear on which he would choke if he allowed his reason to flee. His breath was coming out in gasps as he fought to keep hold of his rational mind.

He found his voice and then cried, 'Where the fuck am I? Who the hell are you? What's going on here?'

Danny stared at Gates, aware that some kind of transformation had taken place. The voice, the gestures, his whole

189

demeanour was different. The madness in Gates had disappeared and the normal man had emerged.

'It's me,' croaked Danny. 'Danny Spitz.'

'Spitz?' cried Gates. 'Jesus Christ, what's happened to you?'

'Manovitch,' moaned Danny. 'He's holding me prisoner.'

Gates stepped forward, nervously examining the chains that held Danny. He found the links that had been broken and bent together. After a few minutes of trying to part them with his bare hands, he gave up, and looked around for an instrument with which to prise them open.

'I still don't understand where we are,' he said. 'How come I'm here? I just had one of my headaches.'

'Manovitch,' moaned Danny. 'He's inside you.'

The mind of Stan Gates was barely hinged. He grabbed at these words and considered them. Manovitch was *inside* him? He could feel nothing. There was no one inside him. This had to be some kind of dope dream. Someone had slipped him LSD, or cocaine, or something. He was not here. He was somewhere like the Princess Louise, and there was a crowd round him, as he struggled with his black subconscious fears, on the floor of the pub. That was it.

'You're not real, Danny,' he said.

'I don't feel real,' moaned Danny. 'I feel dead.'

Something twitched in Gates's brain. 'Dead? Yes, that's it. They said you didn't come down in the crash, but you did, didn't you? Somehow you were on board that plane.'

'Then what the fuck are you doing here?' growled Danny, in a moment of lucidity.

'Me? I'm – asleep.'

'You fuckin' might as well be, you're not doing me any good, you asshole,' groaned Danny.

Gates didn't know what to do next. If he carried on searching for some kind of iron bar or tool with which to open Danny's links, then he would be pandering to the dark forces of insanity that had overtaken him recently. Yet he couldn't just stand there, doing nothing, waiting for the dream to go away. He could actually *smell* things in this dream. You weren't supposed to be able to do that, not without there

190

being some external reason. Had he shit himself while in some kind of fit, surrounded by strangers? God, that would be embarrassing beyond belief. He would die of shame.

Manovitch had had enough of this indecision.

He came forward again, pushing Gates back into the far-off reaches of the far side of the brain, burying him there.

'Well, you had your chance, dickhead,' he said to Danny. 'You blew it.'

Danny gathered a globule of spit and projected it towards his antagonist. It fell short. Manovitch laughed.

'Is that the best you can do?'

The boils on Danny's back were scraping against the wall with every movement he made on the chains, so he stopped trying to do something to Manovitch and began chanting his mantras again, over and over, until Manovitch was sick of them and left by Traitor's Gate, slipping into the cold waters of the Thames and floating down to the next landing point.

Once out of the water he trudged back to Holborn, walking all the way. He made his way to the Princess Louise and walked in. A few stares greeted him. He ignored the open mouths of the bar staff and ordered a pint of beer. When it was safely in his hand he let Stan Gates out.

Stan gave a jolt of alarm as he found himself at the bar.

'Jesus Christ,' he said, his face a picture for the onlookers. He stared down at himself in dismay.

He was soaking wet and dripping on to the brass rail below.

'I'm sorry,' he said to the witnesses. 'I had a blackout or something. I *knew* it was a dream.'

'You all right now?' asked a bystander.

'Yeah, yeah, fine,' said Stan, not feeling fine at all. 'I just – I think I've got that – what's it – schizophrenia or something. I keep doing things without knowing what I'm doing.'

'You've been having a bath with your clothes on, that's what,' said an old woman at the end of the bar.

Stan laughed nervously. 'Looks like it, don't it?'

'You'd better go home and dry out,' said the barman.

'Yes, I'd better. Sorry about this.'

'Don't worry about it,' said a youth, then he added, contradicting himself, 'You need to see a doctor.'

'Yes – a doctor.'

Stan left the pub and got into his car. Thankfully all London transport was now back to normal. The plague of dead cars was over. The machines had come to life again. There were just these ugly boils to contend with. Everyone had them, mostly on the neck and face. There was a great deal of ugliness about, one way and another.

Stan started the car and drove home quickly, took a bath and changed his clothes. He sat in his living room with a whisky in his hands, prepared to get drunk. Something was very wrong with him, but he didn't want to report sick until this assignment was over. He hated neglecting his duty. It was an important case and though he seemed to have aroused the antipathy of both Rajeb Patel and Lieutenant Peters, he wanted to see it through to the finish.

He drank his whisky, hoping the fever would leave him.

Chapter Twenty-eight

A slight rift had appeared between Daphne and Rajeb since the attempted rape. It was not a serious problem in their relationship, but it was something they were going to have to deal with sooner or later. Daphne had wisely decided to undergo counselling after the incident and Rajeb was upset and confused as to why she was going to a stranger to talk things over when he was there to comfort her. They were sitting drinking tea in their living room in the early evening, discussing the issue.

'You don't understand—' said Daphne.

'Too right, I don't,' Rajeb replied. 'That's why I'm asking you *why*.'

'Look, I'm going to this woman *because* she's a stranger, a stranger skilled in helping people cope with a traumatic experience. If I were to ask you to counsel me, the whole thing becomes confused. You're too emotionally involved.'

'*I* didn't try to rape you.'

Daphne sighed. 'No, of course you didn't – I'm not implying that all men are alike or anything like that. But you and I love each – I *hope* we love each other – and in a case like this we might feed each other the wrong medicine. I *need* to talk to someone, Rajeb. Don't make this difficult for me.'

He rocked back and forth in his chair. She could see he was desperately unhappy. In his family culture, you kept private things private, and didn't go spilling them out to some stranger. 'We deal with our own,' he was fond of saying. If Rajeb's family had a skeleton, they locked it up in a cupboard immediately, and the only people allowed to know it was there were close family members.

Though Rajeb was normally a rational, sensible person, when it came to solving problems, Daphne was having to battle against this deeply ingrained family tradition. He squirmed every time counselling was mentioned.

'I just don't understand.' He sighed.

'In that case, we're going to have to leave it to stand, because I've explained as best as I can. These people are like doctors, Raj. They have a code of ethics, they keep confidentiality, and it's a fifty-million to one chance that you'll run into her at a party, in the street or at a supermarket, so you needn't give me that argument. My mental health is more important than your embarrassment, in any case. This is going to remain a secret between four people, instead of three, that's all.'

'Four?'

'I imagine Stan Gates hasn't forgotten it. And I say *four* because I'm assuming he isn't shooting his mouth off about it in the pub.'

Rajeb's eyes opened wide. The idea that Gates might blab about the incident was so monstrous to him it probably hadn't occurred to him before. 'If he so much as mentions a word, I'll fucking *kill* the bastard, I swear it.'

'You will not, Raj. Look, you told me he's already hinted at it to Lieutenant Peters. Let's just calm down. This is what I mean about being emotionally involved. I *can't* talk to you about it rationally. I have to talk to someone else and the best person is a trained counsellor. Now, let's just have a nice evening together and not mention it again.'

Raj nodded, reluctant to let the issue drop, but sensible enough to see they were getting nowhere.

'There's a western on TV,' he said. 'You want to watch it?'

Daphne did not want to watch a western. 'In fact,' she said, 'I have to go to the library. It's open till eight tonight.'

'You want me to come with you?'

'No, I'll manage. You'll only get bored helping me search for what I want. You stay and watch the film. I won't be too long, I promise.'

'OK. How about bringing a Chinese home with you?'

'What would you like? Apart from spare ribs, which you *always* have.'

'I don't always have spare ribs – but yeah, I would like them tonight, and Malaysian-style king prawn fried rice. It's spicier than the other.'

'All right.'

Daphne put on her light coat and left him switching on the television. It hurt him, she knew, that she did not share his enthusiasm for westerns, but there was a point where she drew the line at togetherness. If the film seemed one which dealt with real issues, sensitively, then she didn't mind, but tonight's was just the usual shit about two men in mortal single combat. One would kill the other whether it was necessary or not, and Rajeb would be glued to the screen while the bullets flew.

Daphne took the car and drove to their local library. She parked in the multi-storey car park, having to go to the seventh level because a lot of shoppers were out taking advantage of a nearby street market. The lift wasn't working, so she had to walk down the stairs to ground level. The library was only a hundred yards from the car park.

For the next hour she was absorbed in her research on the educational problems suffered by gypsy children, which she hoped one day to turn into an MA. She was gradually building up a list of works which would be turned into a review of literature and incorporated into a thesis. Rajeb had given her some help in locating gypsy families in sites around the East End and she had found them fascinating to talk to. They had their own particular slant on life. One old man, a 'settled' gypsy, when asked why at the end of his life he had finally accepted a council flat, had answered, 'I got dizzy,' referring to the circular travelling life he had led.

When she felt she had stayed away from the flat long enough, Daphne gathered together those books she was taking home with her and checked them out at the desk.

Outside, the market traders were taking their stalls apart, unbolting the frames that held the canvas tent in place. Daphne bought some fruit from a woman who was loading the back of her van, getting it a little cheaper than usual because the woman was in a hurry and it was the end of the

195

day. The sun was going down and shone low between two high-rise buildings. Daphne carried a heavy bag in each hand, towards the car park.

The lift still wasn't working, so she began to climb the stairs wearily. Once, she thought she heard the echo of footsteps behind her, but when she stopped to listen, the vertical concrete tunnel remained silent. She continued to the seventh level, pushing open the heavy metal door and staggering out into the depressing concrete void covered in seedy graffiti. Underfoot were empty drink cans and other rubbish. She hated the sordid gloom of places like this. There were now only two other cars on the platform besides hers: an old battered Ford and a Mini, hand-painted purple.

The dying sunlight was cutting through the open edge of the car park and illuminating her own vehicle. From the other direction, east, came the light from the archangel's dome. In the middle was a dismal wasteland. She crossed the desolate area and unlocked her car, put the greengroceries and books on the back seat, rather than open the boot.

As she straightened to put the front seat back into position, she was grabbed from behind.

'What—?'

At first, when the arms went around her ribcage, hurting her breasts, she had the wild thought that it was Rajeb, playing some kind of game. But this idea was instantly dispelled by the thickness of the arms and the clothing, neither of which belonged to Rajeb.

'Stop it,' she cried, 'you're hurting me.'

Whoever it was made no comment but instead carried her to the parapet and lifted her up.

Daphne's shoe fell off as she panicked and kicked out at the concrete wall, pushing herself away from the gap beyond which was a narrow drop of seven storeys between two buildings. She managed to ram her head under the chin of her assailant, but apart from a grunt this did nothing to improve her position. The man – she could smell the stale sweat of his underarms – heaved her effortlessly up again to the top.

Daphne kicked out once more and screamed as her tights

196

ripped on the rough-cast concrete. She grazed her calf but felt nothing. The terror surging through her numbed her to all pain. She gripped the top of the wall with her hands and skewed herself sideways. Her purse dropped from her pocket and went spinning down to the deserted gap between the buildings below, to burst open and scatter coins in the passage.

'Leave me alone!' she shrieked. 'Leave me alone!'

Her hands were ripped away from the wall.

'Hey,' yelled a voice. 'What're you doin' to that lady?'

Daphne, with a sideways view of the car park, could see a large black woman standing by the purple Mini.

'Mind your own business,' growled the man, speaking for the first time. 'Unless you want some of the same.'

It was Gates.

'Help me!' cried Daphne. 'Please help me! This man's trying to kill me!'

The black woman hurriedly got into her Mini and started the engine, which echoed in the near empty car park. She slid back her window, yelling, 'I'm goin' to get the police – you better leave that lady alone, man.'

Daphne said, 'Please, I'll give you what you want. You can have it here, in the back of the car if you like.'

'Too late,' rasped Gates's voice, and with one decisive movement he lifted her higher and threw her out into space. 'Try shagging concrete instead.'

She fell seven storeys to earth.

Daphne's legs and arms were still flailing as she struck the flagstones, face first, below.

Manovitch then turned his attention to the woman in the Mini, whose eyes had gone huge and white. She tried to gun the engine and smash the car into gear at the same time, which resulted in the engine stalling. Manovitch ran to the small car and turned it on its back like a turtle. The woman slid down the seat on her head and was collected in an awkward heap, jammed between the dashboard and the floor pedals.

Manovitch reached inside and took her by the throat,

197

throttling her swiftly with one hand. When she had stopped gagging and struggling, he righted the Mini, pulled the body out, and took the keys from the ignition. He locked the car, put the keys in the woman's handbag and carried her over to the parapet. He threw out the body, handbag and all, which hurtled to the ground to smash down next to Daphne's corpse.

'That'll give them a mystery to sort out.' Manovitch laughed softly to himself. 'Two women jumping from a multi-storey car park together.'

Manovitch then left the scene, walking back to Stan Gates's part of London. There he let Stan out, who went to a restaurant and had a meal. After eating, Stan Gates went straight home to bed.

Lloyd Smith seemed to be in a funny mood.

'Hello, what's up?' Stan Gates asked, cheerfully.

Lloyd Smith said, 'Constable Patel. His girlfriend died yesterday.'

Stan, who, as far as he knew, had never met Rajeb Patel's girlfriend, was shocked.

'Christ, what happened?'

'She jumped – or was pushed – from a multi-storey car park. Seven storeys. The fall fractured her skull . . .' Lloyd Smith sighed, '. . . or rather, smashed it to pulp. Patel, as you can imagine, is devastated. He's with her parents at the moment. Terrible thing . . .'

'Why do you say "jumped or pushed"? Doesn't anybody know?'

'Well, she was in a pretty depressed state, according to Patel, though he refuses to say why, but there's a few things which don't add up. I don't know. It'll be investigated, I've no doubt. The strangest part of it is, another woman was lying beside her, who suffered a similar fate. Both their cars were on the same level – the seventh – but the other woman appeared to have suffered throat injuries before the fall.'

Stan nodded thoughtfully. 'You mean she was probably strangled. Sounds like either Rajeb's girl or this other woman was being attacked when the second party happened on the

198

scene, so the killer or killers did for both of them to get rid of witnesses.'

'You're the policeman,' said Lloyd.

'Nothing stolen?'

'Not a bean.'

'You want my opinion, it sounds like Manovitch. Anyway, what happens now?'

Lloyd shuffled some papers into his briefcase.

'Well, it looks as if you'll have to replace Patel as the lieutenant's driver, for now at least. Patel won't be up to working for a while yet. Lieutenant Peters is anxious to try to trace the movements of Sergeant Spitz after you left him at the airport.'

'OK,' said Stan, 'fair enough. Where's the lieutenant now?'

'Up in his room.'

'I'll go and see him.'

'No, I'll do that,' said Lloyd. 'You wait here.'

Chapter Twenty-nine

'Thank God those horrible boils have gone,' said Petra, running her hand around the base of her neck. They had disappeared as they had come, in a single night. She had hated the things: great volcanic lumps full of pus. 'I hope I never have anything like them again.' She was sitting in the lounge, drinking the first cup of coffee of the day.

The headlines of the newspaper were also exclaiming relief over the disappearance of the last plague, but it also warned of the next plague to come. People were asked to stay indoors or, at least, if they had to go out to stay within immediate reach of shelter. The next expected plague was hail.

'It says here,' Petra remarked, as Dave stared out through the lobby window, 'that in Ancient Egypt the plague of hail killed all the slaves left out in the open. My ancestors were slaves so perhaps I should stay in.'

It was a joke, but Dave was never good at picking up on jokes directed at him, especially when he was absorbed in his own thoughts as he was this morning.

'Slave – who's a slave?'

'Never mind,' sighed Petra.

Dave said, 'What are you going to do today?'

'If the hail comes and goes early, to the Tower of London. The archangel has asked me to look there.'

Dave frowned. 'What for?'

'I'm never told what for,' replied Petra.

'I thought the Tower was closed for repairs?'

'It is. It's closed because of wet rot or something, but Lloyd got us a pass to go inside and a man to show us around. He is an archdeacon, after all.'

'You sure it's safe?'

'What do you mean?'

'I mean, it isn't going to fall down on your head while you're sightseeing?'

Petra laughed. 'I don't think it's *that* bad. The plaster and brickwork are crumbling, but I don't think they're going to let it fall down yet.'

'Well, you watch it.'

'No, Lieutenant Peters,' she said, seriously, '*you* watch it. Manovitch is still out there. He's probably waiting for you to pick up on Danny's trail, so he can get the two of you together.'

Lloyd Smith joined them at the table, settling down into his chair. His thin hands were visibly shaking.

'What's the matter?' asked Petra, alarmed.

'Manovitch has killed Constable Patel's girlfriend,' he said, quietly. 'The poor boy is absolutely devastated.'

'Oh, Lord,' cried Petra.

'He's with her relations now. They're all trying to comfort one another, but you know this grief thing goes around in circles. When I left them they were all crying.' A wetness came to Lloyd's eyes, but he wiped it away quickly with a handkerchief.

'How did it happen?' asked Dave. 'Are you sure it was Manovitch?'

'Not absolutely sure, of course, but there was no evident motive – no theft, nothing like that. Another woman died, too. They were both found in the narrow space between two high-rise blocks. It appears they were thrown off a multi-storey car park. There were signs of a struggle from Daphne, and the other victim had been strangled first. She was probably dead before being hurled from the building – a very large lady – it would have to be an extremely strong man to lift a dead weight of a hundred and ninety-eight pounds and heave it over a four-foot-high wall.'

'Anything else?' asked Dave. 'Any other signs?'

'The second victim, a Mrs Lydia Storkey, owned a Mini car. There were signs that the vehicle had been rolled on to its roof and back again.'

'You mean someone drove it, skidded, and the thing turned over?'

'I don't know,' said Lloyd, helplessly. 'I'm just giving you the facts.'

Dave stared out of the window. London traffic was light this morning. The plagues were taken seriously now, and the seventh one was imminent. The most important item on Dave's agenda, however, was to find Danny. Once that was done, they could tackle Manovitch together. The fiend was getting closer, that much was certain. Daphne had been on the periphery of the group, an innocent connection, but if Manovitch knew of that connection then he was close to getting to Friar Tuck and Mother Teresa. Dave was also concerned about Petra.

'Should you go to the Tower today?'

'Why, just because it's getting dangerous? You've got to be joking, Dave Peters. When are you going to stop protecting women and let them take part?' said Petra.

'I'm protecting the public. You're not a policewoman.'

'I can take care of myself, thank you.'

He sighed, seeing he was fighting a lost battle. Turning to Lloyd instead, he asked, 'What happens now?'

'Stan Gates will be your driver.'

'I don't want him,' said Dave. 'I don't altogether trust him.'

'You could drive yourself, but you need back-up, Lieutenant. London is not a place to be out on your own, now Manovitch seems to be closing in.'

Petra said, 'Lloyd's right. You need Gates.'

'OK,' grumbled Dave. 'Where is he now?'

'Outside in the car, waiting for you.'

'Then I'm on my way.'

Dave left Petra to calm Lloyd, who seemed genuinely distressed at the death of Patel's girlfriend. Dave guessed that Lloyd was still suffering the effects of his own encounter with Manovitch. You didn't go through a terrible experience like rape and get away without mental suffering. Every time Manovitch's name was mentioned, Lloyd began to tremble.

Dave didn't blame the older man for that. The big cop squirmed internally when he thought about what Lloyd had gone through. It must have been absolute hell. Dave had a lot of admiration for Lloyd, who was made of stronger stuff than he looked. Most men would have given up the assignment after such an experience.

It also reminded him that Vanessa, too, had been raped many times, as a child, by her own father. What a godawful world, thought Dave. How the hell do these people manage to stay sane?

When Dave reached the lobby, Stan Gates was waiting for him.

'Looks like you got what you wanted, after all,' said Dave.

Stan looked puzzled. 'What do you mean?'

'You get to drive me around London. I could probably do without you if this city wasn't riddled with one-way streets. I guess I'll have to have you.'

Stan appeared affronted. 'Look, I don't mind driving you around, Lieutenant, but it's not my idea of a favourite pastime. What makes you think I want this job so badly?'

'You told me you did.'

Stan shook his head. 'I don't remember that. Anyway,' he asked, 'where do you want to go today?'

'Heathrow Airport.'

The first few sprays of hail came as they walked towards the car. They were obviously only warning shots, telling people to get under cover. Dave stared towards the archangel's hemisphere of light, wondering what was going through the creature's mind – if it had a mind. Maybe it doesn't have a brain, or even the equivalent, he thought. Maybe it's fashioned out of some completely different materials from us ordinary mortals.

Stan and Dave ignored the initial bursts of hail and pulled out into the road. They headed south-west, for the airport. Then, when the *real* hail came down, hammering like rocks on the roof of the car, Stan had to pull into the kerb. Other cars were doing the same. They had stopped in the middle of a bridge and stayed there, while the roof became dented and great chunks of ice bounced from the wings.

The noise was tremendous and the two men had to shout at the tops of their lungs to communicate with one another. They saw a driver foolishly get out of his torn and shattered convertible, where he had at least partial protection. He staggered a few paces, only to be beaten down savagely by the white storm. Helpless to assist him, they watched as he sank to his knees. His face had a blank look to it, mouth hanging open, eyes staring. The hail bruised the skin, then began to strip it from the man's cheekbones, until finally he fell flat on the ground, as the hail bounced from his limp body. He had been effectively stoned to death in front of their eyes.

Vision was down to zero and it appeared to the occupants of each car that they were isolated, encased, as it were, in ice.

Icy white walls surrounded them, but after half an hour the strength and density of the storm began to ease off, and Dave could see the car in front. The paint had been stripped from the entire vehicle, leaving only shiny metal exposed to the air. What he could see of their own car was in a similar condition.

Broken windows from the cars lay all around them and over the road. Fortunately their own vehicle had reinforced bullet-proof glass, which had stood up to the storm, but others were not so lucky and were knee deep in hailstones in their cars. Humps of whiteness, bodies under the chips of ice, were not moving. People who had not been lucky enough to get out of the storm in time lay on the pavements, battered to death by the hail. Others, staggering around, were a mass of bruises, cuts and weals. It was an ugly sight.

'Jesus, would you look at that,' he said.

Stan did not feel inclined to comment.

The hail continued to fall, though less densely, for over an hour, during which time the street filled with chunks of ice the size of old-fashioned moth-balls. Finally, the blizzard slimmed down and then trickled away to nothing. Eventually, the traffic began to move, and they went with it.

The city looked as if it had been packed in polystyrene chips, ready to send off somewhere by post.

The roads were hazardous, cars skidding all over the place. However, the hailstones were melting swiftly, causing minor floods in the gutters and over the road surface. Ambulances were taking away the dead and injured. It was slow progress through the streets.

'It's supposed to be locusts next,' said Dave, more to himself than Stan Gates. 'We sure as hell won't get locusts.'

'Grasshoppers, maybe?' offered Stan.

'Nah. Pests like locusts and grasshoppers are associated with the country. They're woods and fields things – they attack crops. How much farmland do you have in the middle of London? A few parks maybe, but who would care if they were stripped? This will be something like when the car engines stopped – you'll see.'

'Flying metal-eaters to strip the cars down to their chassis?' queried Stan, with an uncommon touch of humour.

'Who knows?' Dave said. 'Then, 'Hey, where the hell are we going? We're heading towards the archangel.'

Stan shook his head. 'I thought we'd take the route over Tower Bridge and south from there.'

Dave tried to recall the maps he'd studied. It seemed to him they were going in completely the wrong direction. They had to cross the river sometime, but wasn't this a little early? 'You sure you know what you're doing?' he said.

Stan Gates glanced at him. 'I've lived in London all my life, Lieutenant. I know *exactly* what I'm doing.'

'Well, I don't know . . .' Dave still wasn't happy.

'OK,' snapped Stan Gates, 'you want to drive? Fine. Here, take the wheel.'

He pulled the car into the kerb.

Dave said, 'No need to get uptight . . .'

Gates had turned in his seat to face Dave while he was speaking. His fist flashed out and suddenly struck Dave a blow on the temple. Dave couldn't think what he had said to make the sergeant so mad. Gates had hit him for no reason. Dave slumped forward, hitting his chin on the dashboard, stunned but not entirely out. He lifted a hand in protest, bewildered by what was happening. Had Gates gone crazy? What the hell was going on?

A second heavy, vicious blow took him into complete unconsciousness.

Chapter Thirty

Dave came to semi-consciousness as he was being carried through a stone passageway. He could see what he thought were grey stone walls slipping by him like a river and it was a minute or two before he realized that what he was seeing was the floor. He was tied, hand and foot, and slung over the shoulder of a man whom he rightly guessed was Gates.

Dave realized also that he was soaking wet, as was Gates.

'Where am I?' he moaned.

'The Tower of London – ain't that a gas? You're going to die here. Feel privileged, cop. Lords and ladies have been wasted in this place. Kings and queens, even. My close friend Stan Gates knows all about this joint. Heads have rolled here. Princes have been suffocated here. Royalty has spilled its guts on the grass outside. I bet you feel good about that, eh? Noble, even. Your red American blood will be staining the same stones as the blue blood of British aristocrats – makes you think, don't it? A common jerk like you, mixing with the gentry. Your mother would've been proud.'

'What the hell's going on?' mumbled Dave.

'What's going on?' said his captor, gleefully. 'It's your old pal, Manny here. You remember me, don't you? I'll tell you what's going on, Peters. First I'm going to rape you like I raped your chum Lloyd, so I can humiliate you, degrade you, make your stinking spirit shrink in your body. Then you're going to die, very slowly and as painfully as I can make it. Then, just when you think you've seen the last of me, we'll meet again on the plains of Armageddon, where I'll obliterate your soul. How's that? Sound good, eh?'

'You sick bastard,' Dave spat out.

Manovitch laughed. 'Sick? What the hell's *sick* got to do with it? I'm *dead*. Oh, and by the way, your buddy and mine

207

Danny Spitz is hanging on the wall in here. Shit, you ought to be proud of him, he's a hard one to kill. I've starved him, hung him in chains by his hands, and tortured him – yet still the little bastard hangs on . . .' Manovitch chuckled. 'Makes you think, doesn't it, a dumb little bastard like that? Let's hope you got the same amount of guts.'

'Oh, God, poor Danny,' groaned Dave.

'Yeah . . .' Manovitch sneered, as they entered a chamber at the end of the passageway.

Manovitch stopped in his tracks in the doorway. Dave was aware that something was wrong. He was dropped to the filthy floor and landed heavily on his shoulder. He gasped for breath as Manovitch ran to the far side of the cell. Rolling over he saw Manovitch, running his hands all over the wall.

The fiend cried out in anguish, 'Where's he gone? Where's the little shit gone?'

Dave found himself laughing hysterically. 'He's escaped, hasn't he, you dumb cluck. Danny's got away.'

'He couldn't get away,' screamed Manovitch. 'I chained him through holes in his hands. I crucified the bastard. He was wasted, gangrened – there was nothing left of him. A piece of loose skin hanging on to some bones. He was all but dead.'

Dave winced at this description of Danny's condition, but he wasn't going to show Manovitch. 'You can't kill people like Danny. His faith is too strong. He's been saved by his own convictions. It's what's defeated evil bastards like you throughout the centuries.'

Manovitch raged, 'I tell you he was done for. I broke him. I destroyed him, utterly.'

'You're a damned liar and you know it. You couldn't break Danny in a million years. I bet he sang, didn't he?'

Danny always hummed or sang to himself when he was under stress, and Dave guessed that at some time in this place, he would have resorted to singing to comfort himself.

'He was begging for mercy,' shrieked Manovitch, staring wildly around the cell.

'*Liar!*' yelled Dave.

208

Manovitch came over and kicked him hard in the kidneys. 'Shut your mouth!' He grabbed Dave by the collar and began to drag him, choking, along the passageway. 'I'll find somewhere else for you,' snarled Manovitch. 'Then I'll look for the other one. Maybe the rats have got him.'

Dave was dragged painfully along the passageway, the stones bruising his body. But there was a glimmer of hope in him now. Danny had escaped. But how? And was he really in no fit state to help?

Dave was pulled through a short tunnel, out on to Tower Green, where many had lost their heads, and then towards the river. When they were almost at Traitor's Gate there was a shout from somewhere behind them. Dave managed to turn his head. It was Petra and a man he didn't recognize.

Manovitch let go of his collar and swore loudly. Then the fiend took off, into the air, flying towards the wall. Dave saw Petra crouching and aiming an incendiary gun. There was a report and something struck the brickwork of the wall, two yards away from Manovitch, and exploded into flame. The brickwork burned, but Manovitch was over the wall, unharmed.

Petra came running over to Dave, her face pale, and dropped her weapon to untie him.

'Are you hurt?' she cried.

She couldn't undo the knots, they were so tight, but between them she and the Tower guide managed to set him free. The guide went off to phone Smith, while Petra fussed over Dave.

'You didn't get him,' said Dave in despair.

'I missed,' admitted Petra. 'I tried . . .'

Dave was puzzled by something. 'Manovitch has two guns – Stan Gates's and mine. Why didn't he use either of them?'

'He probably doesn't know *how* to use them. Gates does, but then Manovitch can't force him to kill his friends.'

Dave stood up, rubbing his wrists. 'He took over Stan's body, huh?'

Petra nodded. 'Just as I took over Petra's.'

209

Dave stared at the dark woman, wondering what she meant. 'What's going on? Where's Danny?'

'I don't know.' Petra stared at the wall over which Manovitch had escaped. 'We should have got him this time – I wish we had got him. My time's running out fast.'

Dave said bitterly, 'We're back where we started.'

'Not exactly,' replied Petra. 'You see, Manovitch didn't destroy Stan when he entered Stan's body. When he entered Xavier's he rended and ate the soul of the occupant, obliterating it for ever. But Manovitch needed to keep Stan's soul at the front end, to hide deep down inside when I was around. I couldn't sense Manovitch's presence while he was enveloped by Stan's soul. Also, he had to use Stan, who knew the district. He needed Stan's knowledge.

'However, he's become enmeshed with the spirit of Stan Gates, and can't free himself now. He's a dead soul entangled with a live soul. Manovitch is the controlling entity, but he can't escape from Stan Gates – can't leave his body, like he did Xavier's, and transfer to another – he's trapped. Once we find Stan Gates we can be sure we've found Manovitch, and we can destroy him . . .'

'But to destroy him, we have to kill Stan Gates,' said Dave.

Petra turned to him and said, 'Gates was doomed the moment Manovitch entered him, body and soul. If Stan's eternal spirit is strong, he won't be corrupted by the fiend that possesses him. But certainly, his earthly life is at an end. Even if we never catch Manovitch, when the fiend leaves his body, Stan will die.'

Dave slammed his right fist into his left palm. 'Now we've got someone to hunt! Now we've got a description to circulate. We'll run the bastard to ground, or send him back to hell where he belongs.'

'We – that is, the archangel doesn't want Manovitch back in hell. It wants him here where he can be destroyed,' said Petra.

'The archangel can want anything it likes,' said Dave, with narrowed eyes. 'So far as I'm concerned, if we get rid of Manovitch, we get rid of the archangel. This isn't Armaged-

210

don, this is the land of living down here. You can fight your battles in your own time and place.'

'You will be involved, one day.'

'Until then, I don't give a damn,' Dave replied.

The guide came running back across the green. 'Jesus Christ,' he was saying breathlessly as he ran, 'you've got to come! I've found someone. He's in a wretched state. You wouldn't believe. He was hiding in a corner.'

'Danny,' said Dave. 'Come on.'

He followed the distressed guide, who was saying, 'I've called an ambulance, but I don't know . . .'

They found a creature lighter in weight than a young child, a dirty, naked human being, crouched in a filthy corner of another cell, where he had presumably crawled. The guide's description of 'a wretched state' was hopelessly understated. The man was close to death. He was emaciated and diseased, in a terrible condition.

Dave looked down and saw a victim of the holocaust. He saw a man who had gone over the edge into a world that could not be entered by the sane. He saw a brittle, thin creature, covered in sores, sharp bones almost piercing the translucent skin, his wildly staring eyes protruding from his skull-like head, his features ravaged by open wounds from rats and skin disease. The creature on the floor stank of something horrible, like rotting flesh, as well as filth. It was a fetid bag full of fear and death. Dave fought to prevent himself from gagging, but was unsuccessful.

It couldn't be Danny.

'That's not Danny,' Dave said, in a high voice. 'That ain't Danny, I tell you.'

Petra said to Dave, 'Could you wait outside?'

'It's no good,' Dave said, 'I don't believe that's Danny – Danny's not—'

The creature on the floor croaked, 'Dave? Dave, is that you? Oh, God – I'm *blind*, Dave, I'm blind.'

A chill went through Dave and he shuddered with fear. 'Is it really him?' he whispered.

How could this be Danny Spitz – jolly Friar Tuck? How

could that be? There was nothing but a skinful of bones and hair on the floor, waiting to be collected and thrown in a grave. Dave still couldn't believe it.

The cracked voice came again. 'I fooled him, Dave, I got away. I ate through my hands.'

Danny showed them his palms, like a small boy revealing something he has taken without consent. Danny had gnawed through them like a wild beast caught in a gin-trap. He had chewed through the flesh to a point where he could rip his hands free from the chains that had been threaded through them. Then he had crawled away somewhere to die in peace.

Dave felt faint and ill. What sort of spirit kept a man alive in that condition? Dave's mind spun with the horror of what he had heard, what he was witnessing here and now.

A short while later Lloyd Smith arrived, along with the police and an ambulance. Danny was taken away to hospital. Lloyd gave Dave the bad news.

'They can't save him,' he said. 'It's gone too far. Renal failure will probably take him, if his heart lasts out the night. I'm sorry, Dave.' He placed a hand on Dave's shoulder.

'He'll be going somewhere good . . .' Petra said.

Dave's head jerked up and he snapped, 'I don't want him to go somewhere *good*. I want him to stay down here. He's young. He has a lot of life to look forward to.'

'He's always been unhappy,' she said, softly.

'I'd rather he was miserable and alive, than dead and happy,' said Dave, selfishly. 'I *need* him.'

Petra shrugged and left him alone, saying, 'We'll do everything we can. *Everything* – to keep him here. You'll see.'

Dave didn't know what she meant, but it was the most hopeful thing he had heard from anyone yet.

'What?' he asked. 'What can we do?'

Chapter Thirty-one

Lloyd Smith was feeling more satisfied with the world, more positive in his outlook.

For the first time in his life he had felt an attraction for a woman his own age, and it seemed to be the right thing. His other cause for joy was to do with his position as an arch-deacon: he had been reliably informed that the world's religious leaders were close to success. Then Dave Peters came into the Jasmine Suite, looking harrowed. Lloyd's heart sank immediately.

'I need your help,' said Dave. His face had a worn, pasty look brought on by lack of sleep. 'I need your authority to help Danny.'

Lloyd's mind ran over the possibilities swiftly. What was required? The best doctors in the world? A mercy flight to the USA where, perhaps, Peters believed the doctors to be more skilled? A miracle? For once he decided to go against his political training, and give an open promise, without reservations.

'Anything I can do,' he said, 'I will do.'

'I want you to get us into the archangel's territory,' replied Dave, firmly. 'I need to get past the barriers.'

Lloyd straightened. 'The Prime Minister himself has ordered—'

'I know what the damn Prime Minister has ordered,' shouted Dave. 'I want *you* to talk to someone, get them to open doors for me. What is the archangel? Some kind of national secret? A potential weapon to be used against the forces of evil? What do they think they can do – harness its power?'

Lloyd nodded. 'Something like that. You know what these people are like. We're not all the same, but there are those who see the archangel as something which might be exploited – the military in particular.'

'God damn their eyes,' cried Dave. 'I hope they rot. *I know* where the evil is in this world. Can you do it? Can you at least *try*? I want to take Danny in there. It's his only chance. I want to put him in the archangel's lap and say, "This is your doing, now put it right."'

'No one's ever come out of there, Dave.'

Dave nodded. 'I know. I'm going in with Petra. She'll get me out again. She's part of it.'

This sounded quite feasible to Lloyd, but he knew how hard-headed some of the army generals were. When the military was intent on something, it was difficult to dissuade them. Danny was less than expendable to them. What they were interested in was the source of power and whether it could be employed as some kind of a weapon. They had said, 'A weapon of a *deterrent* nature,' but they meant 'destructive'.

'I'll make some phone calls, Dave, but I can't promise anything.'

'You just did. You promised me you would do *anything*.'

'Maybe I did, but I can't work miracles.'

Lloyd made several phone calls in the next two hours, during which time he knew that Danny would be sinking fast. He was pushed from pillar to post. He tried to go right to the top, but the PM was not available. When he did find sympathetic ears they did not belong to people with any clout. In the end, he had to admit defeat.

'Right,' said Dave, 'that's it. I notice you have a Road Rover. That's a pretty tough vehicle, isn't it? Crash bar on the front?'

'Yes, it is – but—'

'Loan it to me. I can't promise to get it back in one piece, but it'll be dripping with holy dew. You can sell it to some archbishop afterwards.'

'You're going to smash through the barrier,' Lloyd said. It was not a question.

'Too damn right I am.'

Lloyd wondered if his career as a Churchman was on the line and found he didn't much care. He sighed. He had always been more interested in the money market in any case. Perhaps it would do him good to get back to multi-million-pound deals again. One knew where one was with money.

'Meet me out front,' said Lloyd. 'You'll have your vehicle. You're right – it's got a crash bar across the front. You should get through the barrier, but I can't guarantee it.'

'I'll try to keep it in one piece,' said Dave.

'Don't worry about it,' replied Lloyd.

Lloyd's Road Rover, purchased when his silver Lamborghini went up in smoke on the descent of the archangel, was fetched from the hotel car park. Dave jumped behind the wheel. Lloyd gave him a quick run-down on the controls and stepped out to let Petra into the passenger seat.

'Thanks a lot,' Dave said. 'See you.'

He pulled out into the traffic, with Petra murmuring, 'Left, keep left.'

'I know, I know,' he said. 'I've been here long enough to know that,' but he had to admit to himself that he was drifting towards the centre of the road.

Petra had an *A–Z* London guide and directed him towards the hospital where Danny was being treated.

He parked directly outside the main doors and went striding up the hospital steps and into the main corridor. He took the lift to the second floor, found Danny's room and went inside. A nurse was in attendance.

'Excuse me,' said Dave, and proceeded to remove the tubes and lines connected to Danny's body.

'Hey!' yelled the nurse. 'You can't do that.'

He grabbed Dave's wrist, and seemed a fairly strong man, but Dave pulled out his gun.

'Back off, fellah,' he said. 'I don't want to hurt you, but I will if you force me to.'

He reached down and gathered Danny into his arms, sheet and blanket as well.

He ran from the room. His partner was lighter than a child and his eyes were closed: he was in a coma now, and Dave knew that time was of the utmost importance. He could hear the nurse yelling behind him, and bleepers and alarms were going, but hospitals are not geared for body-snatchers – it doesn't happen that often. Dave knew there would be confusion all around him.

A woman tried to stop him as he ran towards the main doorway, but Dave yelled at her, 'I'll drop him on his head, and it'll be your responsibility.'

She stepped aside at the last minute.

Dave rushed down the steps and laid Danny carefully in the back seat of the vehicle. Petra was at the wheel. Dave closed the back door of the Road Rover. Someone grabbed his jacket, but Dave shrugged them off with a quick push in the chest. He jumped in beside Petra.

'Are you driving?' he said.

'Yes.'

'Well, hit the gas, then!'

They shot out of the hospital driveway in a shower of gravel, out on to the main road, and towards the great dome of light. Dave had brought the dark glasses given to him by Lloyd. These had been used at the testing of nuclear weapons and were the most suitable equipment available. Dave hoped that once they were in the hemisphere, the glasses would allow him to see adequately enough to get Danny to his destination. He had a pair to put on Danny, too, but Petra said she didn't need any artificial means to protect her eyes from the brilliance.

They reached the deserted area between the perimeter of the light and occupied habitation. Dave put the dark glasses on Danny and himself, and strapped Danny in with seat belts to prevent him rolling forward. Petra stopped the Road Rover about a hundred yards away from the barrier, manned by both civil police and the army. She gunned the engine.

'Ready?' she asked.

'Ready,' confirmed Dave, gripping the dashboard.

'Let's go, then.'

Petra cruised the vehicle slowly towards the barrier, as if she was unsure where she was going. A policeman stared at her and then started to walk forward, no doubt to tell them they were not permitted to go any further. When the barrier was thirty yards away Petra slammed her foot down hard. The Road Rover hurtled forward. The policeman's eyes opened wide and he went to draw a revolver. An army corporal unslung his automatic weapon. But both had been caught by surprise and were too slow.

The Road Rover hit the red and white metal pole, and ripped it from its catch. It flew open, bent in the middle by the force of the blow, and catapulted sideways, destroying a small hut. The Road Rover then hit some concrete blocks laid across the road, but managed to crash over them without any serious damage. There were shouts behind them now and one or two shots were fired. A plunking sound on the back of the vehicle told Dave they had been hit. Then they were in a bright, dazzling place, hidden from view by the light.

'Slow down now,' he urged. 'We don't want to hit anything else.'

The brilliance of the light gave the place an otherworldly atmosphere, a surreal appearance. It was like driving through shining mist or fog, the path ahead obscured by refulgence. No dark shapes emerged, no silhouettes, as in a place of gloom, but instead fuzzy-edged blocks of light came out of the inner, intense lustre. One might be a building, another an abandoned truck, a third a slim street-light, or the ruins of any of these, but it was like solid light within light, a place that flowed with iridescence. It was as if a lost antiquated city had suddenly risen from shining waters: the ruins of an ancient world wrapped in bands of light.

The further in the vehicle went, the more awed Dave became. He did not feel he was on earth any more, but on some alien world, a star that had lost its heat but retained its luminosity, if such a thing were possible. The magnitude of the light increased as Petra took them closer to its core, wherein was placed the creature responsible for its rays.

Petra drove slowly and carefully, so as not to jolt Danny too much. Finally, they reached where the archangel sat, waiting for the mundane world to destroy its enemy. The creature was on some kind of altar, though the precise position in which it sat was not evident. All Dave could see was the

217

vague shape of the altar block and on top, in the centre of this, a blurred, humanoid, incandescent shape, edged with what Dave could only describe as 'holy light', having no other words to fit the scene before him.

Petra brought the vehicle to a halt, climbed out, and went up the steps. Somewhere between the bottom and the top, she seemed to merge with the brilliant figure, becoming lost to Dave's sight.

As Dave got out of the Road Rover he felt weighty and lethargic: a cumbersome form in this world of light. Around him danced shimmering weightless ribbons, as if he were the creator of these monochrome rainbows, and when he moved and disturbed them, the manipulator too. He unsettled them as one might rustle silver foil hanging from ceiling decorations when someone opens a door to let in a draught. They were wraiths, and he was mortal, blundering around in their fragile, delicate environment.

It was impossible not to feel a deep sense of timelessness coupled with infinite patience while moving slowly through that sea of light. Dave was completely overpowered by his insignificance beside the creature that produced the aura. He was made to be aware that he was a mortal within the influence of a preternatural being, and he felt his mortality as one might feel a terrible burden, not just upon his back, but within and through him. His soul had mass and poundage, his spirit was a dead albatross, centring him to the earth with its plumb-bob load. He felt an incredible sluggishness, ponderous and unwieldy in movement and thought.

Slowly he lifted Danny's frail body from the back seat of the vehicle, then placed him reverently on the ground. The poor violated form of his friend, ravaged beyond recognition, was like the brown husk of some dehydrated effigy found among the dead leaves of autumn: a scarecrow. Beneath the covering sheet the shallow chest rose and fell, slowly, rhythmically. Danny, full of holes, eaten by disease, shrunken by lack of moisture and sustenance, was just barely alive, a shadow of a shadow, clinging tenaciously to the edge of here and now.

218

Dave ripped out the back-seat cushions and laid them on the ground, then placed Danny carefully on them, draping his loose form over them like an offering to a deity.

Dave lifted his face to the effulgence, and cried, 'I'm not asking you to bring him to life – he's got that already and he'll hold on to that himself, as long as he's allowed to – I'm just telling you to make him whole again. You better not let me down, or I'll join Manovitch when I die and hunt you down, so help me, if it means eternal damnation, I will.'

Whether it was wise to threaten, rather than to plead, was debatable, but Dave Peters was not a man to beg. Not when he was after simple justice. He had begged once before, for the return of his wife to the living, but his entreaties had been ignored. Now he wanted what he felt he deserved: the life of his friend, not yet taken from him, therefore easier to give.

He climbed back into the vehicle and waited.

After some time, Petra emerged from the light, externally radiant at least.

She got in beside Dave and drove the Road Rover westward, towards the real world.

Chapter Thirty-two

While the eyes of London were on the skies, watching for the locusts to come with the same intent that Londoners watched for aircraft in the first half of the fourth decade, the eighth plague surprised them by coming from a completely different direction.

It came out of the drains, the skirting boards, the cracks in the walls, the light fittings, and a multitude of other sources. It brought with it a sense of disgust even greater than when the flies were abroad, sticking to dinner plates, getting into the bread and cakes, laying their blow-fly maggot eggs on the meat. It brought with it – revulsion.

The Plague of Cockroaches had arrived.

The hotel kitchen staff were in hysterics, men and women, managers and staff. There were cockroaches everywhere, especially in the sweet things. Cockroaches had died in the honeys and jams, their black-and-brown crisp bodies drowning in the sweet swamps. They swam in the soups. They appeared, white and ghostly, in the flour used for cakes and bread: the flour bins heaved and boiled with them. They crawled all over the savouries, leaving filthy track-marks. They brought the muck from the sewers on their legs and deposited it on the cream slices and strawberries. They gorged on the food, and vomited on the food. They left their own excrement where they walked, on pies and among french fries, in the sauces, in the salad dressing: black flecks that might have been grains of pepper or bits of *herbes de Provence*.

A moving layer of cockroaches covered the kitchens, the dining rooms, the floors and ceilings. They crackled and ticked, their lacquer-hard shells rubbing against each other, catching each other's wings. Those in the air could find no empty landing space.

They were large cockroaches, of the Far Eastern variety, with bodies over an inch long. They flew. They scuttled. They crept. Their carapaces had an oily sheen and when they were occasionally caught on a hard surface, crunched underfoot and shattered, their yellowy pus-like innards oozed out, discharging a particularly obnoxious odour. They were able to squeeze into cracks a fraction their own size, as if they were made of sponge rubber. It was once said that the one creature which would survive a nuclear holocaust would be the cockroach, being almost indestructible.

The head chef threw up her hands in despair.

'What am I to do?' she cried. 'They're everywhere. If anyone is to eat, they must eat cockroaches, or cockroach filth. There is nothing else for it.'

'We've got to open cans,' said the manager. 'We'll have to have canned food.'

'But they get into it before it's on the tables,' wailed the chef.

The manager was an astute woman of fifty years and knew a crisis had to be handled as a crisis.

'Then we'll open the cans *at* the tables. They can eat it cold. The plagues never last more than a couple of days. Guests can survive on cold canned food for that long. They won't find it any different anywhere else. The whole of London is covered in the vile creatures.'

'They were in me bed,' sobbed the kitchen boy. 'They were in me pyjamas this morning, crawlin' all over me pillow, tryin' to get in me mouf . . .'

Even as he spoke he brushed inquisitive cockroaches from his legs.

'Everyone's having the same experience, Albert. You're not special,' she rebuked, but gave him a hug none the less.

'My hair!' shrieked one of the waitresses. 'They're in my hair!'

'Don't make a fuss,' said the manager. 'If you'd have put your cap on straight they wouldn't have got underneath.'

It was worse than the lice and flies. The fleas and flies had been small, disgusting but small. You could kill a bunch of them with one blow. Whereas you could attack a whole pool of cockroaches, their antennae waving, their shiny carapaces clustered together, and not get a single one. You could swing a broom down among them and they would scatter into the far corners of the room within a split second. You might pick one out, like a hunting cheetah picks out a sick calf and stays with it until the death, no matter what the distractions, and still come away empty-handed, since it appeared that cockroaches could scuttle almost at the speed of light, veering this way and that, frustrating every attempt to land them a blow.

It seemed the only way you killed them was by accident: you hit one while aiming at another.

There were, of course, various traps and powders which claimed success at killing them, the Cheops trap being the most popular. This consisted of a cardboard fold-out hollow pyramid, with a sticky base, into which the cockroach would be lured by the scent of something to eat – though cockroaches will eat *anything* from horse shit to building bricks – and there they would stick like flies to flypaper. A measure of success was to be had from the Cheops trap, but in the numbers that abounded within the vicinity of London, no traps or powders were very effective.

It was the worst plague yet, surpassing even the boils, and Londoners were repulsed by it. If there had been any captive nation to release, they would have petitioned their pharaoh and told him, 'Let those people go!' But there were no Hebrew slaves to whom one could open the gates.

Danny had been inside the dome, at the feet of the archangel, for twelve hours now, and had not yet walked out of the light. Petra told Dave that they could not expect anything immediately: that the archangel would deliberate the wisdom of allowing a dying man to take up his bed and walk. Miracles are not the normal province of a warrior archangel sent to Earth to oversee the destruction of a terrible fiend. The archangel had other priorities, but if the life of one miserable cop was of use to it or, at least, was not a hindrance to the archangel's overall strategy, then perhaps Danny would indeed be told to get up and go.

Dave had to be patient.

Lloyd was saying, 'I'm told by Petra that it isn't possible to save Sergeant Gates – that he is, in effect, already dead. If we don't catch Manovitch, then the fiend will eventually kill Gates's body, in order to escape from it and return to hell or Armageddon. So, believe me, people, we *will* find him. We have every available member of the police force combing London. We have a tight security ring around London. There's nowhere for him to hide, nowhere to run to. We've got him this time.'

He went to take a sip from his cup and then noticed something floating around in the coffee. It was a large, fat cockroach: its legs were still moving. He shuddered and gently pushed the cup and saucer aside.

Rajeb Patel looked at Lloyd with a hard face. 'There's a couple of things I still don't understand. If we do catch him, there's no use in burning down a house, say, in order to burn him?'

Lloyd said, 'Petra tells us he has to be destroyed with holy fire.'

Rajeb said, 'But Petra also says that demons can be destroyed with ordinary fire, that holy fire is quicker and better but any fire will do.'

Petra explained, 'Look, when a mortal dies he sometimes dies in a fire. A mortal's soul isn't destroyed in that fire, otherwise fire victims would not go to heaven or hell but would be obliterated. That wouldn't be right, because it's often innocent people who are burned to death. However, once a soul has been sent to hell, it *can* be destroyed by *holy fire*. It becomes a dead soul and vulnerable to supernatural forces, either on the battlefields of Armageddon, or down here on earth—'

'But demons—' interrupted Rajeb.

'I'm coming to that,' said Petra. 'Demons can be destroyed by *any* kind of fire, down here, because they're different beings altogether. A demon is a fallen angel, a supernatural creature from its first creation, and on descent to earth its spirit turns to flesh. A demon is a demon, nothing more or less. You burn the flesh, you burn the whole demon, spirit and all. On the other hand, a dead soul – or fiend, if you will – possesses the body of another. It is still spirit. That evil spirit has to be destroyed by holy fire.'

Rajeb nodded grimly. 'Our incendiary weapons will do it, because they've been blessed by an archbishop?'

'We think so,' said Lloyd, looking a little uncomfortable, 'but of course we can't be *absolutely* sure.'

Dave said, 'Shit! You *think* so.'

'It seems reasonable, doesn't it, that the Church can produce holy fire as it produces holy water, by a blessing?'

Dave looked across the table at Petra, who shrugged. 'I'm not omniscient – neither is the archangel. We make certain guesses too.'

Dave successfully cracked and squashed a cockroach with a spoon. 'Let's calm down a little here, and look at our choices. We obviously can't go carrying holy candles about, hoping to set fire to Manovitch's clothes. The Church itself doesn't produce weapons. If it did, it would be a safer bet. But though monks or nuns might manufacture certain items, armaments are not among them. There are no crusaders' swords or lances which would be effective here. We have to take a secular weapon and try to turn it into a hallowed one. We won't know if we've been successful at that until we try it.'

Rajeb, his face ravaged by grief and bitterness, leaned back in his chair. 'That's not good enough for me. We've got to be sure this bastard really goes up in smoke. We've got to be certain he'll be destroyed. I need him obliterated.'

Lloyd, sensitive to the young man's feelings, said, 'That's all very well, Rajeb, but what do you suggest?'

Rajeb took a deep breath. 'Look, Manovitch thinks he's already got rid of Danny Spitz. That leaves Dave, right? He's the bait.'

'Bait for what?' asked Lloyd, patiently, aware that all other eyes were on the young policeman.

'The trap. There's a new building gone up on the site of the old Battersea Power Station. You know what it is? A crematorium. It's got the biggest crematorium furnace in the whole of Britain. They've got this massive gas-fired furnace.'

Dave said, 'I think we can all see where Rajeb's going. We've got to be sure Manovitch's soul is destroyed. The guns *might* do it, but the cremation furnace definitely will. It's got a direct connection with religion. Holy words have been said, sacred deeds have been done. Raj has a good point.'

'So,' Lloyd said, taking up the thread, 'it seems that what is being suggested, is this. We put Dave in the crematorium and we herd Manovitch in his direction. Once we have Manovitch inside the crematorium . . .' he turned to Rajeb '. . . what then?'

Rajeb shrugged. 'They say he's very strong.'

Petra leaned on the table and said, 'He's *immensely* strong. You'd need twenty men to overpower him and they'd get in each other's way while they were doing it. He has other powers, too – powers you can only imagine.' Cockroaches ran over the backs of her hands to get to the sugar bowl.

Dave said, 'Let's just get him there. Once he's in our sights, we can burn him to a crisp or blast him to pieces then put him on the fire. You can call in the air force, for all I care. This bastard has got to be destroyed. Have people standing by with flame-throwers, rocket-launchers, even heavy artillery if you want, but let's *do it*.'

'Too fucking right,' cried Rajeb, slamming his fist on the table.

Chapter Thirty-three

Rajeb Patel placed some white flowers on a grave beneath which lay Daphne's ashes, contained in a cedarwood casket. Rajeb was not a Christian, neither did he follow any specific religion, but he acknowledged the presence of a supreme being of some kind. In his view the universe was far too complex for ordinary mortals and since he believed that nothing that existed was beyond *all* understanding, some being, some entity had to be there to comprehend its complexities. He had no idea what form this entity took, but he was willing to stand up and be counted with those who thought there was some meaning to life.

'I'll get him,' whispered Rajeb. 'I'll make sure he pays for what he's done to you, darling.'

Cockroaches were crawling all over the graves and Rajeb was glad that Daphne had been cremated. He would have been upset to think that they might have been feeding on her remains.

It was a windy, grey day, with the clouds moving like fleeing refugees across the sky and the treetops lashing and whipping. A sheet of black-and-white paper blew across the graveyard, finally sticking against the iron railings of the fence. Rajeb's long raven hair blew around his neck and flicked at the collar of his shirt. It was the kind of day that made saying goodbye that much more melancholy. A dark moodiness had descended from some region without a sun and now hung above the earth making the atmosphere dull, heavy and as dirty as smoke from a steam train.

Rajeb was not above indulging in wild thoughts of revenge. His ancestors had belonged to a savage tribe, who counted blood feuds as honourable and right. They would have been willing to kill a man for stepping on their shadows or staring

too long at their women. The fierce nature of Rajeb's grand-
fathers had not been completely filtered from his blood by a
mere two generations. Even as a boy in a London school
playground, Rajeb's temper had earned him respect, and
taught the bullies and racists to walk well clear of him.

The flowers he had placed on the grave were white roses,
for purity and innocence. Rajeb was bitter that she had been
caught up in a web created by his work. If she had not been
the girlfriend of Rajeb Patel, she would not have died. He
saw through Manovitch's plan now, to get him out of the way
by immobilizing him with grief. Well, it had worked, to a
certain extent, but now the time for weeping had passed and
the time for action had arrived. Rajeb wanted the Gates-
Manovitch creature destroyed and he wanted to be personally
involved.

Rajeb looked up, sensing a movement on the other side of
the cemetery. A sombre figure was standing there. It was
someone he knew. The figure came towards him, weaving
between the gravestones, careful not to step on the mounds.

Rajeb said, 'Archdeacon?'

'I just came to pay my respects,' said Lloyd, solemnly. He
was quiet for a moment, staring down at the newly turned
earth. 'Funny, the expressions we use. *Respects*. I hardly
knew her, of course, so why should I respect her in death?
Perhaps . . .' he looked at Rajeb, 'perhaps it's because I
respect you that I believe she was a person in whom integrity
and honour would be strong characteristics. I see those traits
in you, Rajeb, and thus assume they must have been in
Daphne. Am I right?'

Rajeb continued to stare at Daphne's grave. 'I don't know.'

'I think I'm right,' said Lloyd. 'They're good things in a
man, especially a policeman. It's easy to become corrupted
in your profession – and mine. Not necessarily corrupted by
financial greed, but by the nature of the work. Policemen
deal with the sordid side of life so much they can easily be
fooled into thinking the whole world is like that – that there
are no decent people around, and that it is better to get any
conviction than none at all, even if it means someone else has

227

to pay for another's crimes. Habitual contact with bad people can be responsible for the idea that if everyone is bad, then it doesn't matter who's punished for a crime. That, in my opinion, is wrong thinking.'

'What are you trying to tell me, Mr Smith?'

Lloyd sighed. 'I suppose I see in you a good policeman, a good detective. That goodness needs to be preserved. Don't let this incident twist you with bitterness. You're too young to be tainted by the rottenness of creatures like Manovitch.'

Rajeb hunched inside his coat. 'I have to see him destroyed, Mr Smith. I'd like to see him suffer, too, but I don't suppose that'll happen. Just the same, I want to see him burn.'

'That's natural enough, but leave it there. Once he's gone, walk away from it. Don't continue to seek him out in other people.'

The young policeman nodded. 'I'll try not to.'

Lloyd smiled and placed a hand on Rajeb's shoulder. 'Come on, we've got work to do. We can't let the Yanks gather all the glory. We have to play our part, too.'

'I intend to,' said Rajeb, crushing a cockroach with his foot. 'I've got another idea.'

Lloyd glanced at him. 'Idea?'

'For getting Manovitch.'

Lloyd nodded. 'Well, it's a bit late in the day, but let's hear it then.'

They walked together, across the windy cemetery, towards the wrought iron gates.

Dave Peters stood at the barrier to the hemisphere of light, under the eyes of cautious guards. He hadn't been forgiven for busting through the barrier yet and many military men would have been glad to have seen him booted out of Britain. It was only the influence of Lloyd Smith that had prevented such a thing from happening. Dave had trespassed on ground that had been designated military, he was a foreigner, and the combination of these two was enough for the generals to splutter promises and threats into their gin and tonics at the Whitehall pubs.

228

Dave was spending his last few moments behind his dark glasses, hoping that Danny would come out before he left for the crematorium. Dave wanted to see his friend alive and well, in case something should happen and he were never to see him again.

A policeman called from the vehicle, not far away. 'Lieutenant,' he said, 'Constable Patel and Archdeacon Smith have left the cemetery. They've had two sightings of Manovitch already.'

Dave adjusted his dark glasses, took one long last look into the light, turned and walked to the car. 'He's been seen?'

'South of the river,' confirmed the policeman. 'He's on foot, but he's heading towards Battersea. They've been broadcasting through the streets that you're ready to meet Manovitch in the crematorium.'

'Right,' Dave said, jumping into the car.

The young policeman took him down to the river and Chelsea Bridge.

All along the Thames, on both sides, and the river itself, was quiet. The whole area had been evacuated. River traffic had been halted downstream and upstream, so that no craft would be travelling past Battersea. Road traffic barriers were up between Albert and Vauxhall Bridge. Grosvenor Bridge was closed off to the trains that normally used it and only an old barge remained beneath it, flanked by two police launches.

Army personnel were stationed at regular intervals along the stretch, and the police waited by stationary vehicles. The only thing that was moving on the landscape was the car carrying Dave. Expectancy settled on the scene. Men and women were watchful. Eyes were occasionally turned in the direction of the archangel.

Those with ringside seats felt both fortunate and apprehensive.

As they crossed slowly over the bridge, Dave looked up at the fretful skies, wondering about the British weather. Yesterday had been warm and fine, with not a cloud in the heavens. This morning they had awoken to rain. Now it was blustery, with a chill in the air. Crazy weather, he thought. It changes by the minute. 'The water looks funny today,' he said, looking down on the Thames. The surface of the river was much calmer than he had ever seen it before.

'It's because of the boats,' said the driver. 'There's none going up and down to disturb the water.'

'Yeah,' Dave said, 'that must be it.'

When they were half-way across the bridge, another car came the other way, from the south side of the river. It was Lloyd Smith's Road Rover. The two vehicles met half-way and stopped, facing each other. Lloyd got out, flanked by four burly policemen.

Dave climbed out to meet him. 'What's wrong?' he asked.

'There's been a change of plan,' said Lloyd, briskly.

'You should have consulted me.' Dave felt frustrated and annoyed. 'What is it?'

Lloyd put an arm around Dave's shoulder and led him to the edge of the bridge.

'We're going to put you on a barge in the middle of the river. This other plan, to incinerate Manovitch in one of the crematorium ovens, it just wouldn't work, you know. It's fraught with danger and it's too intricate, too chancy. The new plan is much safer.'

'Give it to me.'

'Well, as I say, you go on to a barge in the middle of the river. When Manovitch tries to reach you, we'll have him in the open and we'll net him.'

'Net him?'

'Yes, we've got a helicopter standing by – two, in fact – and we'll swoop down and catch him. Then we can do what we like with him. We'll make a pyre and drop him into it. Or hand him over to the archangel. It doesn't matter – we'll have him.'

Dave wasn't sure this would work. It sounded just as elaborate as trying to get Manovitch into one of the furnaces.

'What happens if he breaks the net?'

'He won't,' said Lloyd. 'It's steel, with an extremely high tensile strength. He'll never break it.'

Dave shook his head slowly and looked down at the river. A flat-topped barge was being towed out to the middle of the flow, where it would presumably be moored. 'I've heard that – or variations of it – a dozen times before. It always proves to be wrong. What happens if I refuse and want to stick to the original plan?'

Lloyd said, 'I'm afraid you have no choice. You're our bait and I'm prepared to use force if it's necessary. I hope it isn't necessary. I'd rather you were a willing participant.'

Dave looked at the four policemen and decided he could take out two of them, but would eventually be overpowered.

'OK.' He sighed. 'You got me.'

'Very wise, Dave. I'm glad you're co-operating. There's very little that can go wrong, you know.'

'I've heard that one before, too.'

Dave and Lloyd got into Lloyd's vehicle and Dave was taken to a floating jetty. A police launch picked them up and took them out to the barge, which was now anchored in the middle of the Thames. There Dave was deposited.

Lloyd said to him, 'Have you got your weapon?'

'Yeah, but tell me I won't need it.'

'You won't need it. We'll pick him up before he reaches you. Don't worry. See that straw over there?'

Dave noticed that straw had been strewn over a large area of the centre of the barge. It looked natural enough, with bits of sacking and bailing string also lying loose, as if the barge had been carrying livestock. His eyes narrowed in thought. 'Yeah.'

Lloyd said, 'You have to get Manovitch on to that area, without going there yourself. Don't go there yourself. Lure him across it. There are man traps underneath.'

'OK.'

'It should be easy,' said Lloyd.

Dave said grimly, 'Why does that sound a little hollow to me?'

Lloyd shrugged. 'Good luck.'

'Yeah.'

The launch engines gave out a throaty roar and the vessel

231

sped away, leaving Dave, a lonely figure, standing on the flat-topped barge waiting for his enemy to strike. Around him the day swirled in greyness. In the buildings around the Thames, media cameras were aimed, zoom lenses ready to capture the final conflict. To the east, the light burned steadily, its occupant waiting. At its feet, a man lay, ready for resurrection.

Further downriver, standing on Albert Bridge, was another lonely figure: that of Rajeb Patel. He, too, was waiting with vengeance in his heart.

Chapter Thirty-four

Heavy rains had come during the morning, which had washed away the cockroaches down the drains. Manovitch had been sorry for that. The cockroaches had kept people busy, kept their minds occupied with things other than chasing fiends. Now the black-brown crispy beetles had gone, back where they had come from, back to the filth in the sewers.

Manovitch knew they were herding him down towards the river. At any time he could have turned on the beaters who were trying to flush him out into the open like a leopard, but his instincts were to go where they were pressing him to go, because he knew Peters would be waiting for him. He was going to tear his body to pieces.

The pitiful fragment that remained of the original Stan Gates navigated Manovitch over the rooftops towards Battersea crematorium. On the way, Manovitch noticed that the streets down below were deserted. Now and again, he spied a man or woman watching him from what they believed to be a safe distance. Overhead a helicopter buzzed, presumably also keeping him under observation. Single cars cruised the area.

Manovitch smiled at these silly antics, knowing that at any time he could kill the body of Gates and flee from Earth. All he had to do was throw himself from a rooftop. They were obviously hoping to burn him, but they had to catch him first. They could try to destroy him, of course, trap his soul inside the body with those fire weapons, but Manovitch wasn't so sure those weapons would obliterate his spirit.

In the grounds of the Tower of London, the woman had fired at him. They had missed but the flames had scorched his arm. The pain had been ordinary mortal pain, not that which holy fire would have caused: a searing of the spirit.

Manovitch believed *he* was safe from the weapons, if not his body.

He stopped in the shelter of a rooftop shack that stored window-cleaning equipment. The way ahead seemed clear enough. He would have to go down to street level soon, and that concerned him a little, but there was a huge gap between the buildings he was using and the roof of the crematorium. A gap far too wide to leap, even for a remarkable athlete. Instead, he flew across, like a bat.

The helicopter veered off, heading towards the far side of the river. Manovitch landed. A policewoman watching from below gave out a startled cry as he sped down the side of the building like a crab down a vertical rock. He leapt on her from fifty feet up, using her body to break his own fall. Her neck snapped with the impact. The radio into which she was yelling spun away from her grasp and went rattling along the gutter.

Tossing the body aside, Manovitch muttered, 'That should teach them to keep their distance.'

Darting up the steps he threw himself through a window, shattering the glass, causing himself multiple lacerations. When he landed on his feet in the crematorium chapel someone fired at him from the shadows. The missile hit the wall behind him and flames erupted from the plaster. This time he was burned down his back. It was only physical pain. He had been right.

He picked up a brass plate from a nearby table and skimmed it at the point from which the muzzle-flash had come. A man grunted and fell out of the shadows, the offering plate buried quarter-way in his right shoulder. He hit the floor awkwardly and the brass plate was dislodged and went clattering down the altar steps, to wobble like a spun coin.

Manovitch knew there would be others in the building, waiting for him to show himself. He crept into the main area, wondering where his quarry might be. It was to locate Peters he had come into this place, not to kill these other mortals. There was an open ceiling with hardwood rafters. Manovitch

234

climbed the wall and crouched among the rafters, moving about like a spider. His enemies were still watching for him at ground level, unaware that he was now above, staring down on them.

After investigating the wandering thoughts of Stan Gates, Manovitch had guessed they were trying to get him to the crematorium's furnace. A crematorium was for burning the dead. Why else would they get him to a crematorium if it wasn't to burn him? Peters must be near the ovens.

'Ashes to ashes,' Manovitch murmured.

Silently he observed the nooks and crannies of the building, searching the dark with his keen eyes. Darkness was his forte. He loved darkness. He could sense shapes in it, see them with his mind's eye, like a rat in a sewer, a snake down a hole, a demon in a pit.

There *were* men in here, but not the man he was seeking.

Something was wrong. He should have been challenged by now, drawn towards the ovens. Peters should have revealed himself, offered himself up as bait. Manovitch was supposed to rush in blindly and attack Peters, get himself trapped in a furnace which they would fire remotely.

But no Peters.

He stood there, dripping blood from his cuts, wondering what to do next. From his vantage point he could see through one of the windows down on to the river. A man was there, on a kind of raft, or barge. Manovitch saw that it was Peters.

There he is, Manovitch thought with satisfaction. They're trying to draw me out into the open.

Peters was standing upright at one end of a barge, studying the crematorium.

He knows where I am, thought the fiend. That's interesting.

He began to apply his mind to the problem of reaching Peters without being injured on the way. Once he was there it would be finished. He could kill Peters and take his soul with him, back to the vast plains of Armageddon, there to annihilate it completely. It was simply a matter of getting to the spot where his enemy awaited him, without being hounded and shot at. He wasn't worried too much for himself but for the body he was using, which could be damaged.

The task of reaching Peters seemed difficult.

It was at this moment Manovitch visited the ninth plague on his enemies.

And the Lord said unto Moses, stretch out thine hand toward heaven, that there may be darkness over the land of Egypt, even darkness which may be felt. And Moses stretched forth his hand toward heaven; and there was a thick darkness in all the land of Egypt . . .

Dave had been talking to Lloyd on his portable phone when it happened.

Suddenly, London was plunged into insanity: a thick, gooey darkness that felt like clammy oil on Dave's skin. He panicked, thinking he would not be able to breathe, wanting to escape from the barge on which he was standing. His mind raced away almost into the regions of madness before he remembered the ninth plague.

'Damn it to hell,' he growled.

Dave stood stock still, not daring to move. He didn't know exactly what was under the straw, but he could guess. It wouldn't do him much good to go stumbling around the barge in the dark. What he had to do was try to stay cool, which, under the circumstances, wasn't easy.

'Mother Teresa,' he said, 'they nicknamed me after you. You always were a calm lady. I need your help bad.'

Through the thick darkness came noise of some activity on the banks of the Thames. Muffled shouts reached Dave's ears. Lights began to go on. Police launches on either side of the river switched on their powerful searchlights, and trained them on the barge. Other searchlights, probably borrowed from the Royal Festival Hall where they would normally be used to illuminate the edifice, came into play. Street-lights came on across the bridges, along the streets. Lights in the adjacent occupied buildings came on, weak and dim.

Normally the searchlights trained on the river would be

very bright. As it was, the darkness was so dense they barely penetrated it. It was almost viscous in its consistency. Pale yellow beams shone on the water with the effect of moons hidden behind thunderclouds. The archangel's light was a dim glow, like a grounded dying sun, which shed no light upon the scene on the river.

Dave tried his portable phone again. 'Lloyd, are you there?'

A wet crackling was Dave's only answer. The stew around him was obviously blanketing radio waves. The last he had heard from Lloyd was that Manovitch was inside the crematorium. The fiend had killed one person and severely wounded another, then they lost him somewhere inside the building. The suggestion was that he had taken to the rooftops again, but no one could be sure.

Dave flipped his phone shut in disgust and rammed it into his jacket pocket. Well, if he's anywhere now, he's on his way here, he thought.

A helicopter, dim lights glowing, came cruising down the river from the west, just a few yards above the water. It was moving slowly, perhaps cautiously. Dave comforted himself with the thought that the helos they were using had good radar and it wouldn't have mattered if the darkness was absolute, they would be able to find their way around objects. They were like mechanical bats in this sea of darkness. Lloyd's men would undoubtedly be setting up other equipment too, infrared night glasses, that sort of thing, thought Dave, hopefully.

He tried to imagine what Manovitch would do.

He would use the darkness, obviously, but how? Would he use his powers to fly to the raft? That would expose his vulnerable earthly body to weapons. No. Dave thought he would probably swim to the barge, underwater all the way, while the police were searching the skies for him.

Dave strained his ears for the sound of someone moving through the water. It was agony waiting, while he tried to peer through the murk to see if he could notice any ripples on the surface of the Thames. It was like being at the bottom of the ocean in a bathysphere, staring into a gloom lit only

237

by phosphorescence. Nothing. He could neither see nor hear anything. He concentrated harder.

'DAVE, ARE YOU THERE?'

Dave almost leapt overboard in fright. Lloyd was using a megaphone on one of the police launches.

'DAVE, USE YOUR PHONE.'

Dave took it out and realized he hadn't pressed the line disconnect button after the last call. Lloyd had probably been trying to ring him. He pressed it now. The phone rang immediately. It was answered. 'Lloyd?'

'Yes, here. We're boosting the signal to get through this. This is a business, isn't it? I suppose we should have foreseen a blackout. Are you all right?'

'At the moment, yeah,' said Dave, looking around nervously, 'but our friend must be on his way. Have you thought he might swim underwater to the raft?'

'Listen,' said Lloyd. 'Stay in contact. Be ready.'

'Be ready to do what? What's going on, Lloyd?'

There was a moment's silence at the other end, then Lloyd replied, 'It'd make you too nervous, Lieutenant, believe me. This requires split-second timing and I don't want you losing it through panic. It's a good plan. Don't worry.'

'If you'd tell me what's going on,' cried Dave, 'I'd know what the hell to do, wouldn't I? How can this work, damn it? The whole place has been plunged into darkness.'

'The helicopters can still see.'

'Oh, I'm supposed to be relieved about that, am I?'

Lloyd sighed audibly into the phone at the other end. 'We'll look after you, man, don't worry.'

'Is that an official's promise, or a private citizen's promise?'

'That's the promise of a friend,' replied Lloyd.

'OK, I'll trust you. I've got to trust you. Wait, listen, I hear something . . .'

Chapter Thirty-five

There was a soft splashing sound from around the bows of the barge. Since Dave was standing at the front end of the craft he realized he was in immediate danger. He wondered whether he could jump over the straw-strewn patch in the middle of the barge, then decided against it. Instead, he hopped up on to the gunwales where he balanced precariously. He began to walk towards the stern, teetering every few steps on the worn strip of wood. He had nearly made it past the straw patch, when he slipped, his feet going from under him.

As he fell he grabbed a greasy stanchion, managing to cling to it despite its slippery surface. His body was skewed awkwardly over the edge of the barge. He hung there for a moment, his left foot trailing in the water, then he hooked his right leg back up over the gunwales. As he did this, half upside down, his gun fell out of its holster and down into the water with a goodbye *plop*. His phone might have gone too, except that it was hooked inside his jacket pocket.

'Shit,' Dave muttered.

He hauled himself along the side of the barge until he reached the stern of the craft. There, he pulled himself back up on to the deck. He spoke into his phone again.

'Lloyd, I've just moved down to the other end of the barge. I'm now at the stern end, got it?'

He stared out anxiously into the darkness. The unnatural night felt tropical, thoroughly humid and dank. He could barely make out the lights of the buildings on either side. It was as if they were shining through a thick, black fog. He could hear the muffled clatter of a helo's rotor blades to the south, moving adjacent to the river's course. The archangel's light, now that he was almost facing it, was a dim and ghostly bowl to the east.

'I'm glad you told me that,' came back the soft voice of the Archdeacon. 'I would hate to get the wrong one in my net. Is he on board yet?'

Even as Lloyd was speaking, a dripping figure was climbing over the bows and on to the deck. The sturdy body of Stan Gates, now occupied by Manovitch, stood confronting Dave from ten yards away. There was a grim expression on the creature's face, a determination evident in his demeanour, that sent a chill through Dave.

Dave instinctively reached for his gun, only to find his empty holster.

Manovitch watched these antics with apparent delight. 'You seem to be a bit naked, Peters. Is this what you're looking for?'

Manovitch opened his mouth and flames leapt out, crossing the barge, to singe Dave's hair.

'Jesus Christ,' cried Dave.

'He won't help you,' laughed Manovitch. 'He's busy.'

Dave said, 'You're determined to kill me, aren't you?'

'Eventually, then visit the final plague on these stupid people to break up that group of holy men.'

Dave stalled for time. 'You think that will do it? They're close to an agreement now. You may be too late.'

'The deaths of all the firstborn in London will shatter them apart – I know it, you know it.'

Dave did know it – and he also knew that if Manovitch wished to, he could leap the whole length of the craft from a standing jump. Dave would not stand a chance in hand-to-hand combat, were he the reincarnation of Bruce Lee. It was not even worth laying odds on such a contest. The best he could hope for was to get the fiend into position, then perhaps jump into the Thames at the last moment and try to swim for it.

Manovitch began to walk slowly forwards, warily, suspecting some kind of attack. 'Where's it going to come from, eh?' he growled. 'You tell me, Peters. What're they using?

Rockets? Missiles? Flame-throwers? That Mixmaster from Jesus has got something to do with it, hasn't it?' he added.

'The helo? Yeah, it's a gunship. It'll blast you to pieces,' snarled Dave, with as much bravado as he could muster.

'As soon as they kill this body,' cried Manovitch, 'I'll be inside *you*. Have you thought of that? I'll take possession of that small, tidy mind, that tight, neat body, and destroy them both, slowly and painfully. I'll suck your guts up inside your skull until you've got shit for brains. I'll destroy your character – I'll make you into a child killer, a fornicator with old women, a thief and rapist. I'll find Vanessa and screw her until she screams for mercy. I'll fuck her damned eyes out – how'd you like them apples, shitface? I'll screw her until blood runs from every orifice in her body. The rest of the world will think she's having a great orgasm, Peters, and they'll laugh and say, "Listen to those two, celebrating the destruction of Manovitch." And all the while she'll be dying, violently, painfully, of too much *me*. Pretty funny, eh? You like that? So get your gunships down here, shoot Stan Gates to pieces, and then I'll be free to inhabit that clean, upright, tight-assed body of yours . . .'

Dave was not provoked into any retaliatory remarks; he was not going to give the fiend the satisfaction of knowing that he had not thought about being possessed himself. He had not considered beyond the idea that Manovitch wanted him dead. He had imagined torture, for a short period, and then, goodbye, world. Of course, if they were to kill the body Manovitch now possessed, he would be free of his spiritual entanglements, and perhaps able to make the leap between bodies.

It was a ghastly, terrifying thought, that Manovitch could jump inside him and begin using him like a puppet.

There was a strong smell in the air now, of some kind of fuel. Around Dave, the day-darkness swirled with unseen activity.

When Manovitch reached the straw he did not look down, possibly not suspecting that the attack would come from below, rather than from above or from the flanks.

There was a loud *clack* followed by the duller sound of metal jaws smacking into flesh and bone.

Manovitch grunted with the pain that shot through Gates's body. His foot had sprung a steel man-trap whose sharp metal teeth had buried themselves in his right leg. The calf muscles were torn, the bone shattered. Manovitch reached down and prised open the trap with his hands. Blood sprayed over the straw from the sliced artery.

'It's not over yet, Peters,' snarled Manovitch.

The fiend ran his hands down his calf and the bone knitted, the wound sealing itself.

The sound of a helicopter was getting closer now, as it flew down the river, its lights glowing yellow.

'Nothing will stop me now!' cried Manovitch. 'Nothing!' He was now only three yards away, determined to reach Dave, who was standing right on the edge of the boat's stern.

The noise of the helicopter's clatter was upon them, as the aircraft came swooping out of the darkness, a large trawl net on a flexible frame hanging from its undercarriage. Dave tried to step aside but he was swept off his feet, falling back into the net, and the chopper rose up above Manovitch.

'Not me!' cried Dave. 'Wrong one!'

Manovitch stepped forward, reached for the net as it passed above him, trying to grab at the framework, anxious not to let his quarry fly away. A man-trap slammed shut on his other leg. He caught the trawl net with his fingers, held on, was lifted up a short way, then the frame snapped when the anchoring chain of the man-trap tightened.

Manovitch crashed back on to the barge again. He was mangled by yet a third man-trap. Now his left arm was in the tenacious grip of a metal shark.

Below the helicopter, where Dave was doubled-up like a fish in the meshes, the net closed like an envelope, flapping loosely in the created wind, flopping from side to side as the helicopter veered away from the barge. His face squashed against the web, Dave saw a flaming torch fly like a spark from the parapet of Albert Bridge, and drop into the Thames.

In an instant the Thames below the bridge was alight. A

great wall of searing flame swept down river, twelve to fourteen feet high, rushing up from Albert Bridge towards Chelsea Bridge. The rampant fire seemed to gather strength on its journey, contained as it was by the banks of the river, as it roared along the watercourse. In those few brief seconds while the inferno rushed in a flood of flame along its natural channel, Manovitch managed to force his fist into the mouth of the man-trap that held his leg and, again, prised apart the jaws. Then, treading on it, he tore his fist free, leaving two fingers behind.

The helicopter reached the bank just as the flames roared past, singeing Dave's hair and eyebrows.

In the light from the fire, Dave saw Manovitch climb awkwardly to his feet, standing ineptly on his smashed legs. The fiend screamed in great fury, before he was engulfed by the onrush of the firestorm. He seemed to breathe in the fire, his screams mingling with the roaring flames, swallowing that which would swallow him. He burned brightly, with a high gaseous-green flame for a few minutes, and then his charred, blackened form fell back into the barge, which was now blazing furiously.

He rose to his feet yet again, as if refusing to be consumed.

The firewall travelled on, under further bridges, before it finally petered out near Tower Bridge, having run out of the fuel that had been pumped on to the river's surface.

The blazing barge snapped away from its moorings when the ropes burned through, and floated slowly down a dark Thames, casting an eerie light on the water. Standing again on the deck, the fiery figure of Stan Gates, containing the trapped dead soul of Manovitch, was being cremated: a soul evident as hissing flames, which flared through the mouth, nostrils and eye-sockets, and between the ribs on the ribcage.

Manovitch was at last being devoured by fire.

The blackened corpse of the fiend fell backwards into the sea of flame and disappeared beneath it.

By the time the burning raft had reached Tower Bridge, the darkness had lifted.

Dave climbed from the entanglements of the net that had

saved him, and thanked the helicopter's crew. He found his hand being shaken by a grim-faced Rajeb Patel.

'Well done,' Rajeb said.

Dave asked, 'Did you have anything to do with this?'

'I threw the flaming brand on to the river,' confirmed Rajeb. 'Holy fire – taken from the candles of a nearby church.'

'Ah.' Dave smiled. 'So that's how it was done?'

'It was split-second timing,' Rajeb said. 'We couldn't even start pumping the fuel on to the Thames until Manovitch was out of the water and on board the barge, or he might have guessed.'

Lloyd Smith arrived next and, again, Dave's hand was shaken with great vigour. 'Well done, man, well done. We got him. We got that rotten bastard. The archangel hasn't departed yet, but I'm sure it will very soon.'

Dave smiled. 'You'll be an archbishop before you know it.'

'Pah,' said Lloyd, without conviction. 'They can keep it.'

Chapter Thirty-six

While the group were standing around congratulating themselves a figure crawled unseen over the parapet of the Thames
and began stumbling towards them. It was slick with oil,
dripping water, and flaking ash. The shape was ugly in its
aspect: a blackened corpse charred beyond recognition. Pits
were where its eyes had once been, a hole in place of the
nose, the lips gone and the teeth set in a hideous grimace.
It was like some volcanic beast, risen from a dark grave of
lava, its contours badly copied from the human shape.

It moved by instinct only towards its victim. Its motivating
energy must have been pure revenge: a fierce intense hatred
that had a force and power of its own. There was no living
breathing life in the creature – nothing could have survived
that inferno on the Thames – just a core of enmity that burned
so hotly the body would not fall down, would not allow itself
to drop to the earth where it belonged.

Its prey was Dave Peters: the black fingers like crusted
claws were already curled in anticipation, its arms reaching
out for the San Francisco detective, ready to clutch his throat.

'Look out!' cried Rajeb Patel, seeing the figure for the first
time.

They all turned and stared in horror.

Lloyd staggered back, terrified, a sickly look on his face.

A policeman nearby had the sense to open fire with his
weapon, an ordinary revolver, but the bullets passed through
the encrusted creature, having no effect whatsoever.

A thin scream of triumph came from Manovitch's mouth as
he closed with Dave, knowing that nothing could save his
enemy now, that he would be taking him to hell with him.

Suddenly, out of the shadows, another figure ran forward,
swiftly. This figure reached Manovitch and wrapped its arms

around him in a tight embrace. Manovitch screamed, trying to break the hold, but the person was too strong for him. It had him bound to itself as closely as flesh to bone.

'Petra!' cried Dave.

Petra remained embracing the fiend as if she were its lover and it was going away on a long journey. Her cheek was next to the charred cheek, her hands laced and locked behind the fiend's back, her legs wrapped around its thick lower limbs.

'Get away, Dave,' she shrieked. 'Get back.'

Dave was undecided what to do. How could he leave her there to be crushed by Manovitch? Surely the dead soul was going to tear her to pieces with its enormous strength? Yet what could *he* do, a mere mortal? Petra seemed to have a certain power herself: she was managing to restrain the fiend.

'Go!' she shrieked at him again.

Dave saw something in Petra's eyes. Something which made him want to be a hundred miles away. He stepped back, once, twice, then turned and ran. Others were running, too – Lloyd, Rajeb – getting as far away as possible. Two dead souls were enmeshed in a terrible struggle and it seemed that neither was going to walk away unharmed from the conflict.

When Dave was a hundred yards down the road he heard the soft explosion, felt the heat on his back.

He turned to see the pillar of fire blazing where the two figures were locked together. It reached up to the cloudbase above, a spectacular tower of wan flame, blinding in its brilliance. The flames twisted and curled about each other to form thick cables: spliced together to create a dense column of white molten iron. The heat seared a telephone booth not far from the conflagration, the paint peeling, the glass shattering, metal dribbling away in the gutter as it melted. There were other, minor fires, within a few yards of the holy white weapon of the angels of the Lord.

The front of Dave's clothes was singed – he could smell the burning – and it was only because he was wet from the river that he did not catch fire himself. The other people around him had run for the alleys and buildings, and had managed to get under cover. He was the only one exposed to the fierce inferno that was Petra and Manovitch.

'Petra!' he yelled.

It was futile. Petra could no longer hear him, no longer hear *anyone*. She had sacrificed herself to rid heaven and the world of a terrible fiend. Petra had willingly gone to the void, had perished in her own white fire, in order that mankind and the angels should triumph. Her name was no longer Petra: her name was oblivion.

And when she died away, there was nothing left but coarse black ash mingled with fine white powder, and the wind came and blew them away, until there was nothing.

Once the dust and ashes had gone, there was an ascension from the City of London. The archangel rose and hovered over the Thames, shedding its light further and wider than it had ever done before. The streets and buildings basked in the bright rays which normally formed part of the lowest illumination of the light around God. Yet no mortal could look at that brilliance, which outshone the sun, not with the naked eye.

Then the archangel seemed to rise rapidly, accelerating all the time, until it was an arc across the sky. Those who saw it said it was like a star returning to the heavens. A sense of wonder was lodged within their hearts.

Holy Mick had returned to the battlefields of Armageddon, his mission complete.

To Londoners, who had got used to seeing the dome of light over the City, it appeared that something was missing from the landscape. There was an emptiness to the skyline, and a feeling of emptiness inside them. They had possessed an archangel, all of their own, for a brief time. Now it had gone, leaving behind it the devastating effects of its arrival.

Chapter Thirty-seven

The drive through the once famous 'Square Mile' known as the City of London was both eerie and strange.

The streets were as silent as a forest of sitka spruce: a forest that had been burned to its stumps by fire. Gone were the Kentish ragstone buildings that surrounded Bank; gone were the coffee and tea houses of Lombard Street; gone were the Bank of England, the insurance companies, the modern banks, the tall office blocks; gone, too, the chapels and churches, St Paul's Cathedral, the medieval churches of St Bartholomew the Great and All-Hallows, Barking; gone the Royal Exchange and Mansion House. It was as if the original Londinium had been bombed and fired to precise objectives. Ruins of once beautiful buildings lay on all sides. There was rubble in the streets, blocking roads, covering drains. The driver had great difficulty in navigating through this debris. Sewers overflowed, gas mains were exposed, electricity cables curled like black snakes in and out of crumbling walls. It was Beirut, it was Sarajevo, it was Mogadiscio, it was Kabul all rolled into one.

'Look at this,' Lloyd said in despair. 'It's going to cost a fortune to put right.'

'It's only money,' Rajeb replied.

'It's not just the money,' complained Lloyd, 'it's *history* too. The loss of the beautiful architecture alone . . .'

Rajeb said, 'I expect they said that after the Great Fire, yet the legacy of that was one of London's most beautiful buildings, St Paul's.'

'Which is now *ashes*,' moaned Lloyd.

'There was a St Paul's Cathedral before the Great Fire, but they built another more beautiful. Now's your chance to surpass even Wren's great feat. Perhaps St Paul's is *meant* to be rebuilt every few hundred years.'

Dave was surveying the ruins with a keen eye. 'At least,' he said, 'we managed to stop Manovitch from using the final plague. All the firstborn. I wonder how he would have managed that? All *whose* firstborn?'

'Everyone in London, I should imagine,' said Lloyd. 'I'm rather glad we did manage to stop him. I'm an only child.'

'And I'm the eldest of my lot,' reflected Rajeb. 'Though now Daphne's gone, I'm not sure I want to stay . . .'

'That's enough of that talk,' Lloyd said to the young policeman. 'Daphne wouldn't want you talking like that. She saw you both as two strong, independent people, didn't she?'

'Yeah,' sighed Rajeb. 'I guess so.'

The talk was beginning to frustrate Dave, who wanted to find his partner and friend. His eyes scanned the levelled City, hoping for a sign, a glimpse of a man walking from the ruins. Suddenly he saw something moving below a concrete arch. He strained his eyes for a clearer view.

'Look – look over there!' he cried.

The others all turned to stare.

Lloyd said then, 'Let's investigate.'

The car was driven over to a pile of rubble on which sat three people: a poorly dressed man, a woman with two plastic bags of clothes at her feet, and a young, scruffy-looking youth. They were staring about them in a kind of rapture, their eyes glistening. Lloyd called to them, 'What are you doing here?'

'Mind your own business,' snapped the woman, the tranquillity leaving her eyes for an instant.

'How did you get through the barriers?' insisted Lloyd.

It was the youth who answered. 'We never come through no barriers. We was 'ere before 'e came. We was 'ere when 'e landed, right 'ere, on this spot. Them who come through the barriers 'ave gone back to the Embankment.'

'What do you mean, *he*? The archangel?'

The youth nodded. 'Yeah, we was sleepin' in the shop doorway, the free of us. 'E said we could stay 'ere if we wanted.

'E didn't mind. Said we was to cover our eyes, though, to stop from bein' blind.'

'And you've been here all this time?' asked Lloyd, incredulously. 'What did you have to eat and drink?'

'All *what* time?' asked the youth. 'It was only last night, wunnit?'

'Tell you what, though,' said the man, speaking for the first time, 'it was the best night's sleep I've had for a long time.' He hawked and spat, to emphasize the truth of the statement.

'Drive on,' said Lloyd to the corporal at the wheel, but Dave said, 'Wait a minute.'

Then to the group outside, he said. 'Have you seen anyone else around these parts?'

'Nah.' The youth shook his head. 'Only us.'

They drove on, with Dave trying to guide them to the place where he and Petra had taken Danny. When they reached the area where Dave had left Danny on the steps, it was empty.

'Well, there's nothing more we can do here,' said Lloyd. 'I suggest we go back to the hotel.'

Dave was hoping Danny would be waiting for them when they returned, but Friar Tuck was nowhere to be seen.

At twelve o'clock, noon, that same day, the world's religious leaders emerged from their bunker. There was a smile on every face. They walked their separate ways, together.

Chapter Thirty-eight

Ten p.m., St Michael and All Angels Day, 2002 A.D., San Francisco.

Dave was sitting in Mario's, drinking a cup of Colombian coffee and biting into a focaccia, when Danny walked in through the doorway and said, 'I'll have what he's having.'

Dave nearly fell off his seat. 'Jesus Christ! Where the hell you been? I searched London for two months. We thought you were dead.'

Friar Tuck came and sat down at the table, grinning at Mother Teresa. He looked good – better than ever before, he had lost weight – and he was wearing a fashionable suit.

Danny frowned. 'Where have I been? I've been getting better, that's where I've been. I've been . . .' He looked a little bewildered then and added, 'Truth is, I don't know where I've been. I just found myself walking along Fisherman's Wharf at three o'clock this morning. I don't even know what date it is. I think Petra took me somewhere, before she—'

'You know about that?'

'Yeah.' Danny frowned. 'Don't ask me how – I just do. I've been having these dreams. I've got all these fuzzy pictures in my head. She sacrificed herself, right? She went up in a pillar of flame – a bright flame. She destroyed herself in a tower of holy fire.'

'She took Manovitch out.'

'Yeah,' said Danny. 'He lost again, the dumb cluck. That's because he got sidetracked into chasing us. Revenge may be sweet, but it's a hell of a distraction. If he'd have stuck to getting rid of the Meeting, he might have made it. Instead, he went a-hunting, and got caught in a trap. What a stupid guy he was, even when he was dead.'

'It took another dead soul to finish him, though.'

Danny nodded solemnly. 'Seems every time I find a woman, she gets taken away from me.'

'Hell, stop feeling sorry for yourself,' said Dave. 'What do you want – violins and roses? You think I haven't lost people, too? I lost my wife. I thought I'd lost you, too, you dumb shit, but I find I was being too optimistic.'

'You're a hard bastard,' growled Danny.

'I have to be with pathetic creatures like you around,' said his pal. 'We'd be up to our knees in tears otherwise.' Dave reached into his pocket and pulled out the pendant that Petra had given him. 'She told me to give you this.'

Danny snatched the pendant and studied it closely. It was a quarter of a coin attached to a silver chain.

Dave put an arm around his smaller friend. 'I'm sorry,' he said. 'I guess I am a jealous s.o.b. – she went for you, not me.'

They stared at each other for a few moments, then Dave laughed and kissed Danny on the cheek which, in a San Francisco coffee bar, raised only the eyebrows of a single tourist.

'Shit, you look good, Friar Tuck. Hey, did we burn that son-of-a-bitch Manovitch, or what? Did we show that archangel how the guys from San Francisco do it, or didn't we? Hell, are we the good guys, or are we the good guys?'

Danny smiled. 'Mother Teresa, my man, we're the goodest guys since Jimmy Stewart.'

On the same day, almost at the same moment though on a different clock time, Lloyd Smith was driving through the country lanes of Buckinghamshire, England, when he felt sharp pains in his abdomen. He blinked and pulled the car into the side of the road, using the gap formed by a farm gate, and there he sat, staring at the thorn hedgerow. The pangs came again, attacking him savagely. He sat and groaned and sweated.

Dark rolling clouds began moving over the rings of trees left by farmers on the crests of hills around the valley through which he had been driving. Lloyd began to feel hot and ill, seeing in those clouds some kind of ominous portent. He had been to see *Macbeth* the previous evening, at Stratford-upon-Avon, and he was still under its depressing influence.

A pain seared across his abdomen.

Ugly thoughts began to trickle through his brain as the sweat soaked his shirt. Dark, terrible thoughts. They were thoughts of death, and rape, and, indeed, birth. With waxing horror he began wondering what was the gestation period for a fiend. Was he now going to give unnatural life to some horrible creature, here, in his car? Should he prepare himself? Should he get the jack handle from the boot of the car and be ready to smash its brains in?

Fire. Would he need holy fire to destroy the creature? Would he even – oh, perish the thought – would he, not being able to help himself, would he even *love* the thing as his own offspring? Would he be unable to prevent himself from cherishing what was partly his own?

Thunder smacked the belly of the sky and made him jump in fright.

There was a tapping on the window.

Lloyd wound it down to see a woman in a waxed jacket and deerstalker hat staring at him. There was a golden retriever at the heels of her green wellington boots.

'You all right?' she said, almost severely. 'You look a bit off colour.'

'No, no, I'm not,' gasped Lloyd. 'I feel awful.'

She stared at him. 'What have you been eating?' she asked. 'You've got that grey pallor my husband gets whenever he eats a rotten curry.'

Lloyd suddenly thought, *Oysters*. He'd had oysters at three a.m. on Simon's houseboat. Relief washed through him. He wasn't giving birth to a fiend, after all. He was having a bout of food poisoning.

'Yes, I think you're right, I have eaten something.'

'I should chuck it up, if I were you,' advised the woman briskly. 'Get rid of the muck now.'

'Thank you, I shall, but if you don't mind, I prefer to do it in private.'

253

'Up to you,' she said stiffly, pulling the retriever by the leash. 'In the ditch is my advice.'

She left the unhappy Archdeacon, and hurried off along the darkening lane, to be swallowed up by the green hedgerows and folded fields studded with oaks and beeches. Lloyd remained sitting there, the pains running across his abdomen with irregular frequency. He didn't want to move for a while.

A few seconds later the skies opened and the rain came hissing down on the car roof. Thunder cracked again, rattling the foundations of the distant Cotswolds. A bright fork of light followed, piercing the copse on the nearest hill, and the world was instantly illuminated.